The Haunting of Sigma

To Eric -
Keep Believing!
[signature]

FRANK HOLES, JR.

THE HAUNTING OF SIGMA
A DOGMAN LEGEND

2008

The Haunting of Sigma

ACKNOWLEDGEMENTS

Once again, so many great people have added their voice to the growing legend of Michigan's Dogman. My deepest thanks go out to the following professionals who have aided the success of this novel: Craig Tollenaar, cover artist extraordinaire, who has designed the most impressive book covers in America; Daniel A. Van Beek, my editor, who spent countless hours digging through the text and providing us with fabulous feedback; Eli Holes, my grandfather, who, as always, continues to read, re-read, proofread, and comment upon my work even on short notice; John Rieck and the crew over at BookSurge who continue to impress me with their professionalism and true caring for the small time author.

The research crew: Eric Bottorff, Department of Natural Resources, who provided many of the technical aspects of the life of a conservation officer in Northern Michigan and was very patient with my many questions that probably seemed rather unusual; Sergeant Todd Woods, Mackinaw City Police Department, for his help once again with the technical details regarding law enforcement; and special thanks go to Steve Cook, creator of the song, "Dogman II—The Sigma Story," which was the inspiration for this novel. When Steve and I first envisioned the full legend of the Sigma village haunting, we knew the ending already. It was a matter of putting the 'meat on the bones' and of course the fun, down to earth, nitty-gritty details of real life in the backwoods of Northern Michigan. I do thank him so much for his great ideas and comments.

The novel that follows is a work of fiction. Although you can really visit Sigma, the village as it exists in the novel is a made up place. Residents will of course see the many geographical changes that have been made to properly tell the story. I've had a lot of fun stomping around Kalkaska County and getting the feel of the place, and I do hope no one there will take offense to using their community for our legend. Of course, any resemblance between the folks who live in the fictional Sigma and people who live in the real world is coincidental and unintended.

The Dogman, however, is very real to those who have seen or encountered the beast. Take a long walk outside in the north woods in the depths of the night if you don't believe me.

Official *Haunting of Sigma* information and merchandise can be found at our website:

http://www.dogman07.com

ALSO BY FRANK HOLES, JR.

Year of the Dogman

The Longquist Adventures: Western Odyssey

http://www.mythmichigan.com

To My Grandfather, Eli
To Steve Cook, The Father Of "The Legend"
And To Every Cryptozoology Fan

The Dogman Is Real.

Keep Believing...

Sunday

Sigma (I)

The town's name was Sigma. It sat right smack dab in the middle of Kalkaska County, about twenty-five miles from nowhere. It was a tiny dot on some Michigan maps, a nearly invisible spot in the green expanse of northern Michigan forest. But not all maps included the town. On some of the more recent ones, such ghost towns don't even exist.

Sigma was just a crossing of two roads in the deep Michigan woods, and from the middle of town only the northern one was paved. Viewed from high above, the two roads, which crossed each other directly at ninety-degree angles, formed the crosshairs of a gun sight. From its terminus a mile south of town, County Road 571 extended north for another seven miles before crossing M-72, the main thoroughfare between Grayling and Kalkaska. Lodi Road, the second of the pair, curved north and then east as an unpaved extension from M-66. At the town's crossing, it became basically a two-track as it headed east through the Dredge and on toward what is now the Camp Grayling Armed Forces Base.

In fact, even before the town had a name (and well before County Road 571 was paved, and that was in '49), this meeting of the roads was called Sigma Corners. Not much to look at; no, not much at all. Even calling Sigma a town was inaccurate. It wasn't even a village, technically. Though it appeared on maps, no incorporated settlement had ever occurred. Only a few small buildings housed the village's only businesses, and there were a couple of little homes and trailers for the occupants. No post office existed; the residents' addresses simply said "Sigma Township."

The town, though never heavily populated—here in 1987, a grand total of 329 folks were recorded on the Sigma Township clerk's register—was actually an important stop for a number of lumber transports on their way south. Originally developed as a logging camp, Sigma lay in the dense wilderness between Grand Traverse Bay and the Au Sable River. The Au Sable was much more important for logging for a few reasons. First, it flowed from its headwaters in the middle of the peninsula all the way to its mouth at Oscoda on Lake Huron just north of Saginaw Bay and the many mills and furniture companies residing in the Saginaw Valley area. Second, the great volume of its rushing water made for quick, easy, and effortless transport of the vast number of logs.

In the late 1800s, when the Sigma Logging Camp was established, Kalkaska County, as well as the surrounding counties of Crawford, Missaukee, Roscommon, Wexford, and Antrim, were vast expanses of virgin timber forests. Gigantic white pines dominated the sandy soils near Lake Michigan, while firs of various types spread through the lowlands and swampy areas inland. The softwoods were the first to be harvested in great number, but soon the demand from the Midwest's iron-smelting cities required the widespread cutting of hardwoods. By the late 1890s, the outpouring of logs of all types made Michigan the nation's number one lumber producer. In fact, there was more money made by the lumber from Michigan than from all the gold mined in California during this same period.

Very few humans had populated the area, and only a few small villages and logging camps existed. The local Native Americans, mostly living near Grand Traverse Bay, generally kept to themselves, only dealing with the whites who pestered them into trading furs for the generally useless junk white folk found a daily necessity. Since the loggers were of a single-minded purpose—working six days a week every day of the year—they were of little interest to the Indians.

Lying like a barren, sleepy prairie you'd expect to see someplace farther west like Iowa or South Dakota, the Dredge was a huge open area on the eastern side of town, bordered by the thin row of hardwoods that ran north and south along County Road 571 and the vast (and very dense) Au Sable Forest a mile to the east. The Dredge extended from Mecum Road south of town for several miles north until it was swallowed by the copse of trees just before Carroll Road, half a mile before M-72. Some of the Dredge was just empty land; only the occasional small tree or shrub broke up the wide open space. In other sections of the Dredge, a few local farmers had fenced off sections for corn, hay, or other small crops.

The Dredge made a great spot for hunting birds and game of all sizes. Each year a number of does, and even a few good-sized bucks, were bagged someplace along the Dredge. And of course, the local kids (never more than a handful lived in Sigma in any year) loved to explore its nooks and crannies; the land rippled in unusual fashion from its years serving the lumber camps.

Very few living in Sigma now had any exact idea why it was called the Dredge. Even old Doc Custer, who'd lived in the town for over fifty years, had only a vague notion of the name's lineage. Back when Sigma was a logging camp, the Dredge was home to a vast stand of gigantic white pines. Thus, it had been the first section cleared in the logging boom. The acres that now-a-days comprised the Dredge became the staging area for huge stacks of the monstrous logs that were pulled out of the forests for the surrounding counties. Thus the land was dredged—cleared out—for such a use. It was as good an explanation as any.

In winter, the easiest season in which to move lumber, great sledges and wagons pulled the massive logs to the Sigma staging area before they were then shipped down the Au Sable River to lower Michigan. Transporting logs in the summer was nearly impracticable until the mid-1880s when the first of the "Big Wheels" appeared, capable of dragging the immense logs through the uneven pathways of the forest.

After the turn of the century, the railroad tracks were laid down, connecting Grayling to Kingsley and onward almost to Frankfort. The trains soon replaced the horses, sledges, and "Big Wheels" as the fastest means of transporting lumber across the state. And the Sigma logging camp and way station was an important stop on the journey south.

Sigma was a quiet, sleepy little community. It couldn't exactly be called a farm town, though farming was about the only occupation one could actually do for a living out here. And that was a hard life. The soil was swampy and didn't drain well. Some purposely chose to live in the peace and quiet of this wilderness area. But most of the folks were way out here simply because the land was cheap and it was one of the places they could afford to own a home. And many took advantage of the abundance of wildlife, some even hunting out of season (no one from the Department of Natural Resources ever bothered to check way out there).

Days were quiet and nights were silent. That was the one nice aspect of the little community out in the woods. Very little excitement ever happened. Folks' lives generally followed their basic routines. They worked hard. They played hard. In many cases they drank hard. The community was fairly close-knit; everyone knew each other. It was a rare event when an outsider bothered anybody or anybody got themselves really riled up. At least it was that way until that third week of June in 1987. The haunting of Sigma had begun, and the town's days were numbered.

Lloyd (I)

It was another quiet Sunday evening at Horner's Bar. Lloyd Horner, the owner and proprietor, ushered the last two patrons, Jimmy Dean Holloway and 'Buck' Reynolds, out the door just before nine o'clock and turned the lock behind them. He waited until the headlights from their two pickups flashed the front of the bar on their way home before flipping the switches to the porch lights and the single, lonely neon sign hanging in his single, lonely window. *Give That Man A Blue Ribbon* it proclaimed proudly in its white and blue flickering light during the open hours. Once turned off for the night, the sign was just another mess of tubes and wires hanging against the glass.

Though the sun wouldn't officially leave the world in total blackness for nearly another hour, there were plenty of dark shadows outside Horner's at that hour. Lloyd gazed out the window and across the street at the Dredge beyond. It was hard to see where that great field ended and the dense forest on the far side began. His was the only establishment in town that occupied a corner at the intersection of Lodi Road and C-571. Not that there were very many businesses in Sigma in the first place. Kitty-corner to Horner's was the town's little ball field which hosted the Kalkaska Beer League games every third Wednesday night during the summer. On those nights, Lloyd kept the bar open until eleven or later, depending on the mood of the players and how much cash they were willing to part with. Most every other night he closed up at ten, and called it quits at nine on Sundays.

The inside of Horner's was typical for a small town bar. Dark paneling, dark tile floors, dark tables and chairs. When the lights were low, folks couldn't see how bad the place really looked. The whole place could use a thorough cleaning and fumigation. The once smooth wooden edge of the bar, like many of the tables and chairs, was now dented, scratched, and carved up by an untold number of beer caps. The leather on the stools was cracked and peeling in more than a few spots. Most of the floor tiles needed replacing. The dark hue of the paneling hid most of the graffiti.

Not that it was a dive by any means. Lloyd had been in far worse places down south during his service with the Marines. Of course, looking back now he was grateful he'd missed the really bad action of WWII a few years before he enlisted. Being target practice on a Pacific island sounded fine when you were a teenager but it wasn't so enticing at his current age.

Now in his fifty-eighth year, Lloyd Horner called this bar his home. He spent his waking hours downstairs keeping the spirits flowing and spent his sleeping hours upstairs in his little apartment. He often wondered how many more years he'd be able to keep his legs going up and down between the two extremes of his life. He was in decent shape, but this job was his whole existence, and running a bar would eventually run a man down.

Horner's wasn't a big place; Beer League was his best night by far and squeezing in twenty thirsty players and their entourage meant standing room only. Beer League paid the bills. The other nights wouldn't even pay for themselves.

But Beer League was still a week and a half away, and until then Lloyd would have to entertain the handful of locals who stopped by and forced him to stay open. There might be one or two during the afternoon and a few at night. Pabst Blue Ribbon was the drink of choice, but he also kept a supply of cold Stroh's and Miller High Life for his more distinguished customers. A few years back, some lost college boys found their way into Horner's and wanted Labatt Blue, of all things. Lloyd had given them an incredulous look and pulled out a PBR for each of them. It was the closest he could come to anything blue.

He turned from the glass and gazed across his place. The left wall glowed a rainbow of colors from the old Rock-Ola jukebox. It was silent, considering that no one had played any songs all night. No booths here, only eight small square tables and not nearly enough chairs to fill them. The bar itself, lined up on the right wall, would seat six on the tall, tattered stools. At the back of the room, the hanging light flooded the pool table with dirty yellow light. A cue was still lying on the faded green felt.

Up until two years ago, the small Brunswick pool table was occupied almost every night by the town's only two high school kids. Ricky and Billy Lovett dropped in a few dollars worth of quarters even though they usually brought in their own Cokes. Lloyd didn't care. In fact, he actually enjoyed their company more than the legal Joes who blew smoke in his face or threw up on the floor and more often than not drank themselves into oblivion. Luckily most of those lived within walking distance, or at least they could drive home within a few minutes, the empty roads the only witnesses to their swerving. Way out here in Sigma there was nowhere to cruise to and nowhere to be cruisin' from.

Lloyd smiled at the thought of the Lovett boys. They'd come in wearing their letter jackets, throwbacks to the era Lloyd remembered so well from his own youth. Those kids were polite, respectful. They'd drop a coin in the jukebox for a few country songs, rather than that heavy-metal crap so many kids listened to. The Lovett boys loved to give Lloyd the play by play from their football and basketball games, and the old man would grin, nod his head, and prod them for all the heroic details.

But now those boys were long gone. Ricky graduated in '85 and Billy a year later. They'd departed the little town for points unknown, never looking back and probably never coming back. Ever.

He made his way across the bar, pushing the few chairs up to their tables. He'd given up stacking the chairs a few years ago, after the arthritis started, just as he'd given up mopping the floor. He didn't care what the health department thought. They'd make their cursory inspection each year and get out of Sigma as quickly as they could. It wasn't worth an inspector's time or effort to drive all the way out here or to make a return trip in less than a year's time.

A deep sigh escaped the old man's throat. *Sigma was dying*, he thought. *The old are getting older and dying off, and the few young'uns are escaping as fast as they can.* A few years from now this could all be gone. Just a few abandoned buildings were left along a few dusty and potholed roads. The entire place could disappear and nobody would even miss it. Nobody would know the town was gone. Nobody would know it ever existed.

Buck

Jimmy Dean Holloway's headlights turned off to the right and Buck Reynolds was able to see again. Jimmy Dean always though it cute to tuck in behind Buck and blast his high beams at him over the mile of road they shared before turning down Mecum to home. Considering Buck had pounded back twice as many as his younger drinking partner, the bright light pouring in his dusty back window greatly reduced his already fading vision.

Buck always seemed to pull out of the little parking lot of Horner's ahead of Jimmy Dean. No matter how long it took to fire up his old truck, Buck was outsmarted. Jimmy Dean always seemed to have something that delayed him long enough for Buck to tire of waiting and decide to head home. Then, within a few hundred yards, the kid would be right on his tail with those godforsaken brights on.

Of course, Jimmy Dean had an excuse. His left headlight was burned out and he rightfully couldn't see half of the road without his brights on. Of course, Buck knew that headlight had been out for almost a year now and the kid still hadn't gotten it fixed. Buck shook his head, grunted to himself and managed a half smile. It was just one of the kid's peculiarities. That's what he loved about Jimmy Dean—he was as unique a personality as you could get.

Neither one should have been driving, at least legally. They'd come into Horner's around six o'clock on Fridays, Saturdays, and Sundays, dropping off a few bucks they'd earned at the mill over the past week. Lloyd was still one who believed in a cheap drink, and they could get their money's worth from 50 cent shells or buck bottles of PBR. And, having grown up here on the outskirts of Kalkaska County—which is to say on the outskirts of most any civilization in northwestern Michigan—the two knew the Sheriff's Patrol was lucky if it drove all the way out to Sigma once a month, and certainly then only in daylight. There just wasn't enough action out here to warrant any more frequent visits. Drunk driving on a back road wasn't a crime out here; it was just a fact of life. Besides, there was never any other traffic, and the worst they could hit was a deer, as long as they stayed within the confines of the road. Just like in elementary school, stay between the lines. Except out here, the lines were deep ditches on either side of the hardpan.

Luckily, they both drove fairly slowly, especially because the road's condition had worsened since spring. This summer was one of the driest in recent memory. There hadn't been an inch of rain since the end of April, and the dirt roads were taking the brunt of it. The road commission made the Sigma area its very last priority. Consequently, the heavy rains of April left the washboard grooves, what the locals called "chatter bumps," in abundance. This string of recent arid weather, and the lack of road grading, only made it worse.

They'd been working together for almost ten years now. Buck was still a bachelor, loving his independence. Jimmy Dean, seventeen years younger than Buck, was married right out of school and had four kids by the time he was twenty-five. They'd both started at the Berry Sawmill outside Fife Lake at the same time and had become fast friends. Buck was an adopted uncle to the Holloway kids, and Jimmy Dean's wife, Sherri, actually enjoyed having him over for dinner at least once a week, the dinners being barbecues all summer long. She'd roll her eyes at Buck's antics—the way he rough housed with the kids like a big kid himself; the way he'd harass her, making her grin and feel like a teenager again; the way he and her husband fit together like an old pair of gloves.

Buck still had a few miles to go after Jimmy Dean turned off. The darkness was nearly complete here, where the trees at the road's edge grew their branches wide enough to almost touch their cousins on the other side. Only a thin strip of deep indigo admitted that the sun had yet to totally disappear. A thick fog of road dust streamed out behind the pickup.

His vision was a bit blurry, but Buck was by no means plastered. As long as he didn't drive too fast, he'd be fine. Tired, thinking of the early morning ahead of him, he yawned long and hard, taking his left hand from the wheel to cover his mouth with a fist. His eyes squinted naturally by the action.

That was when he saw it. It wasn't like anything he'd ever seen before. Sure, he was intoxicated, but he'd been driving this road for years now. He'd seen all sorts of wildlife and had taken out his share of raccoons, possums, porcupines, and even deer. But this creature in his headlights wasn't any of those things. It was huge, black, and hairy. In fact, the first thing his brain registered, the way the brain flashes a thought or judgment in a split second, was that it was a mountain lion. But the next thought, after that initial shock flew through his mind, knew that it just wasn't possible. There were no big cats in this area, probably hadn't been any for a hundred years or more. And he knew why that had been his first guess. The creature was hunkering down in the road on all fours, but then it stood up. It stood up on two legs.

And it looked at him. It looked right into the truck with glowing yellow eyes.

He was only doing about 30 miles per hour but instinctively he knew he would hit it if he kept the same course. Without thinking, and probably in conjunction with the alcohol coursing through his system, his right hand, the only one on the steering wheel, yanked downward violently. His body swerved as the truck careened to the right. The creature was gone from his mind in an instant. *This isn't good*, he thought, as the truck's front tires, jacked all the way to the right, skidded into a stretch of deep chatter bumps.

A motor vehicle doesn't have to be going very fast on a washboard dirt road to lose control. Buck was going plenty fast enough. And his sharp jerking of the wheel added fuel to the fire. Plus, his foot was still on the gas. As if there wasn't enough strikes against him, the alcohol had impaired enough of his control to finish the job.

The dark, hairy creature nimbly leapt out of the way, curiously watching as the old Chevy swung sideways past it. The tires caught a pot hole, at the worst place at the worst time, and the entire truck caught air. It rolled as it exited the roadway and entered the line of trees on the right edge. Twice it tumbled completely over until it finally slammed grill-first into a gigantic oak. The bumper wrapped around the tree, the radiator burst open, releasing a shower of hot steam, and the hood peeled back. The truck's momentum stopped in an instant, but Buck's momentum, with no seat belt to check him, catapulted him like a missile through the windshield.

There wasn't even time to raise his hands up in a gesture of defense. His forehead split open from the impact, while the shards of glass tore up his face, hair, ears, and shoulders as his body sailed through the windshield. Several ribs and his pelvis were cracked as he had slammed against the steering wheel on his way through. A fraction of a second later his broken body scraped off the side of the big oak's rough bark, landing a dozen feet from the truck.

Slowly, the creature approached the accident from the driver's side. It walked fearlessly on its hind legs, claws clicking on the hard-packed road surface. The truck's headlights shone on either side of the great oak, and in the left beam, the driver could be seen lying lifeless in the tangle of shrubs and ferns. The cloud of dust had more than caught up with the truck, and the particles wafted their way through the light of the headlamps. The creature looked down upon the driver for a few more seconds before baring its large canine teeth. A low growl emanated from the depths of its throat. It wasn't really loud, but then again, it didn't have to be. Then, as unexpectedly as it had appeared, it dropped to all fours, bounded across the road, and disappeared into the dense forest on the other side.

Jane (I)

A slight wisp of air, still warm and dry from the long summer day, seeped in through the pet door along with the pair of cats. It wasn't too big of a deal, considering that the little floppy door was only open for a brief second and the interior of the little house was just as hot, if not hotter, than the outside temperature anyway. The same could be said in the winter; the little stone house wasn't very well insulated. The stones only seemed to magnify the temperature outside, regardless of whether it was warm or cold. At least Jane's house was back in the shade of the jack pines, which provided shelter from the winds that would whip up and down along the Dredge. Had she bought on that side of the road, as she nearly did almost three decades ago, the interior climate might be unbearable. Thank the Lord for such small favors.

Jane Whitman had survived three husbands, and yet in all of her seventy years she had no children to survive her. No children meant no grandchildren. That whole raising kids business was of little importance earlier in her life. But now, as she entered the long, slow decline through her later years, she secretly wished there was someone to visit her, who wanted to see her and spend time with her.

Whitman was the fourth last name she'd held in her life. Her first husband William Freeman, her school sweetheart from Middleville whom she had married back in 1941, was shot while storming the beach in Normandy. They'd been together less than a year when he had shipped out, never to be seen again. Their love affair was fast and furious, not really much more than two teenagers experiencing their first love, and unfortunately, it was forgotten just as fast. For Jane, life went on.

Her second husband, Pete Conroy, moved her north to Kalkaska County for work in the summer of 1950. Middleville, her hometown, wasn't exactly the heart of civilization, but it was near to a few larger cities downstate. Kalkaska seemed as far from the rest of the world as one could get. Four years later, husband number two dropped dead of a heart attack. Pete had been only 39. Jane, herself just 37 at the time, was already a widow for the second time in her life.

Her third marriage brought her out from the town of Kalkaska and further into the country. Her new husband, Clark Whitman, was a supervisor for the road commission. A native to the area, Clark insisted they buy a parcel out in Rapid City. On his salary, the big house and property was feasible. But when he died in an accident at the shop, Jane was left with a mortgage far too big for her. This time, there was little she could do to support herself. Clark had made good money, but he was too cheap to buy life insurance. So she sold the estate and bought this little stone house out in Sigma. She chose the little stone house rather than the trailer across and down the road a bit (which was bought by Brian Alexander some fifteen years later.)

The cats looked up at her, purring loudly, rubbing their fur against her legs and feet. She knew that they were her children now. They needed just as much looking after as any kids would, and for much longer she believed. At any given time, there were anywhere from four to eight of them in her home. She always seemed to gain cats, but they didn't wander off; they had it too good here to leave for anything longer than a day's time. They'd come and go most days, but they always showed up at dinner time. Just when one of her cats was nearing the end of its life, another (always a younger one) would undoubtedly show up to take its place. Who knows where they came from. There just wasn't enough civilization around this area to properly account for the number of strays that came to call her house home. But at least the cats lived long enough for her to become attached to them, unlike her former husbands.

In the four years she and Clark were together, Jane had come to finally appreciate the peace and quiet of living out in the country. She was originally a farm girl, and returning to nature became a godsend. Sigma was quiet and peaceful, and not much more. The house was paid in full, and her late husband's insurance settlement paid the taxes (they didn't amount to much each year), while her social security covered the bills and kept her warm and fed. At the end of it all, there was just enough to take care of the cats, too. She spent her days walking in the woods, reading, and taking care of her little houseguests, who began arriving almost as soon as she moved in.

In some ways she did envy the many single mothers that seemed to populate the world so recently. Now-a-days a young woman could have a child without a father present. There were even new scientific ways to make it happen, ways that she knew nothing about (and quite frankly, didn't want to know how it worked). Sure it was a lot of work to raise kids; look at those moms who worked two or three jobs to make ends meet. Looking back, she could have done it. At least she'd have someone now. But from where she came, such a lifestyle would never be accepted. Having a child out of wedlock was not only socially inappropriate but it was considered a sin, too. Her ego could have taken it now, but she didn't know if she could have handled it when she was younger.

Now, however, it was these cats who needed her. They weren't as much company as relatives would be, but they were always on time for dinner. And many would cuddle up with her on the couch at night when she sat down for a cup of tea and a good book. She didn't even own a radio or a television.

At least, they were *almost* always on time for dinner. Tonight, only three of the six cats who currently lived with her were at the community bowl. Jane wasn't used to waiting for the cats to arrive; you could set your watch on them. Most days, she was tripping over them as she brought the food to the large oval bowl they shared. Jane waited almost a half hour for the three tardy cats, much to the annoyance of the three who were in attendance. These three didn't mind showing their displeasure at waiting either; they kept a constant chorus of loud, obnoxious meowing along with the scraping of their claws on the edge of the bowl.

Odd as it was, eventually the ones already here did need their dinner. Finally, Jane broke down and fed them. Twenty minutes later, the first customers were satisfied and lying on the couch. Jane looked at the pet door, hoping, wishing that the missing members of her little family would come strolling through. *Late, but not lost mama. We're here now!* But there was no sign of them. She filled the dish, hoping that perhaps the food in the bowl would act as some sort of talisman, beckoning them from the night. Then she pulled up a kitchen chair and watched the door for yet another hour. One by one the present houseguests came in as if to ask, *What's going on? Why aren't you in here, sitting on the couch and cuddling with us?*

One hour turned into two. Still nothing. She rose, padding her way to the back door and opening it, flipping on the outdoor light and peering into the yard. Her eyes moved all across the various flower gardens looking for movement. She even called out for the three missing cats, yet nothing but the light wind whispering through the pines was to be heard. The night was still, silent and stiflingly hot. It was uncomfortable out there, but it wasn't merely the oppressive heat. Something didn't feel right tonight.

Despite the fact that she was out here looking for her cats, she had the unmistakable feeling that she was being watched. It was irrational, but still her skin nearly crawled from the feeling of unseen eyes staring at her from the blackness of the forest. Shivering from her head to toe, she quickly scuttled back inside, closing the door and slamming the deadbolt into place. She left the light on outside, keeping her back yard flooded in a yellow glow.

When her little mantle clock struck ten o'clock, Jane decided she'd had enough waiting. If the cats came back in the night, there'd be a midnight snack for them. If they didn't, well, she could deal with that situation in the morning.

Late in the night, however, when she was woken by that awful, horrendous howling, she wasn't sure she'd ever see the three again. Jane bolted upright in bed and clutched the covers up to her chin with both hands, like a little kid. She didn't move; she hardly breathed, as if the thing that had howled was right outside her bedroom window, listening for her. It howled again: a deep, throaty, violently long growl that made the hair on the back of her neck tingle. Every few minutes, the howl would commence again. Each time, she shivered. It was unlike any sound she'd ever heard before. After a few more, her rational self took back over, insisting that it was quite a ways off, out in the Dredge from the sound of it. That allowed her to slip back down into bed, though she did pull her covers up to eye level.

Even though the sporadic howling stopped less than an hour later, she didn't return to sleep at all the rest of the night. That feeling of being watched slammed back into her with the force of a sledgehammer. She was sure that whatever made that noise had been peering through the trees at her. She shivered again, and this time it was a dozen seconds before her body regained control. By that time, the covers were wrapped tightly around her as if she was in a sleeping bag.

And if there was something out there that could make a noise like that, she thought, *God help anybody who might be out there with it.*

Sigma (II)

10:30 p.m. Rick Butler stood on the back deck of his house and continued calling for his dog. He'd been out here every ten minutes since dark, but there was neither sign nor sound from Dusty. Sure, the golden retriever was apt to go off wandering all over God's green earth. Goldens are known for being adventurous. In the daylight, that is; at night, she loved to curl up in front of the wood stove. Now she'd been missing for almost three hours.

His wife Nancy was still working, a nurse on the night shift at the Grand Traverse Regional Medical Center. They relied on her paycheck much more than his own, and the extra hours on the afternoon shift she'd been picking up lately came in handy, especially since contractors weren't in high demand so far this spring or summer. It seemed like the less he worked, the less he saw of her. Nancy was bringing in more money, but they must have been spending it somewhere, because there really didn't seem to be much more of it to go around.

But right now his personal finances were of little concern. His dog was missing. Finally Rick had enough. He walked down the deck stairs and over to the pole barn, flipping on the light switch, and started beginning to dig around for a flashlight. He'd have to go out looking for her. He considered jumping in the pickup and trying the roads, but the likelihood was greater she was out on the Dredge or in the Au Sable beyond. Probably chasing rabbits or squirrels. He hoped to God that Dusty wasn't after a skunk or porcupine.

Finding the elusive flashlight, Rick strode out into the backyard, the little beam of light leading him into the tall grasses and brambles along the southern boundary of the Dredge.

11:10 p.m. Jack Cooper, the owner of the town's only real store, remembered he'd left the coffee pot on. It was one of those large, industrial-sized monsters that school teacher's lounges and concession stands always seemed to have. In fact, he'd picked it up really cheap at a flea market fund raiser at the Forest Area High School, benefits to the senior class trip of '80. He wasn't sure if the kids had permission to sell the old monstrosity, but he didn't ask, loading it into his van right after paying for it. It was perfect for the Sigma Mercantile and the collection of old farts that hung around the store all day drinking cup after cup of coffee.

The Mercantile served as part grocery, part hardware, part lumber yard, part sporting goods outlet, and basically anything else Jack could squeeze into the little building. Truth be told, it was bursting at the seams. He employed one kid to stock shelves and load the lumber from out back. Jack mostly sat on a stool behind the counter, harassing the old timers who drank his thick, muddy coffee and sometimes played checkers on the little round table in the corner.

Jack lived in the little house next door. Though he owned both parcels, he'd never tried to connect the little buildings. Someday, if he ever had to sell them, he figured they'd do better as separate properties.

He went out the back door of his house, switching on the little sconce so that he could see his way across the yards, and letting the screen door slam shut behind him. He didn't bother to shut the interior door, since he'd be right back. Besides, who would be out this late, trying to sneak into his house? And he'd stopped believing in the Boogeyman decades ago.

Jack had to take his keys with him because the Mercantile did need to be locked at night. He didn't carry alcohol or drugs, but there was always something in the store that somebody needed. And with the number of really poor folks living way out here, well Jack was sure there were bound to be some who'd rather find another way of acquiring something than paying for it. He didn't trust anybody, not even the old farts who kept him company during the day.

Several small night lights allowed him to make his way through the stock room and down the central aisle of the store proper. Yes indeed, the coffee pot was still on, just as he'd left it hours earlier. He crossed his fingers and opened the lid. A breath of relief passed through him. Luckily there was still a half inch of dark liquid at the bottom. Jack could think of little worse than cleaning a pot of scorched coffee.

That being done, Jack made his way back through the stockroom and locked up the store. As he crossed the thirty foot stretch between the buildings, he heard something moving in the woods beyond the back yards. Jack stopped and looked in that direction. The little wall sconce only gave off bright light for about a dozen feet, and it then faded into darkness at about forty (just enough so that he could see where the key went in the backdoor of the Mercantile.) The woods were beyond the range of the light, however, and Jack could see nothing there. He couldn't even see the tangles of brush that were moving.

He continued to stare off into the woods, figuring a critter was out a-wandering, when he heard a low growl roll across the back yard. It wasn't very loud, but it sure was menacing. His eyes opened up wide, and he knew there was an instant where he was afraid he'd wet himself. That growl didn't belong to any small critter. It was unlike anything he'd ever heard in his life.

The growl came again, still soft as if it was a warning. Jack took the hint. He skittered to his back door, which he luckily left opened and unlocked (it was his day for luck, it was!). He shut the door quickly, clicked the lock and set the deadbolt. He hurried to the front door to be sure it was locked up tightly, too. On an impulse, he turned on every light in the house as he went into the bedroom to grab his nightly deposit bag from the safe in his closet. He didn't trust anybody, and each night he emptied the till of the store and brought it home with him. Inside, along with the cash, was a .38 snub-nosed revolver. He checked to see it was loaded, and then he turned off the safety.

Jack returned to the kitchen, made himself a pot of coffee, and sat down at the little table. If anything weird happened, he'd be up for it.

12:42 a.m. Horses and livestock, normally calm and quiet for the duration of the night, paced uneasily in their pens and pastures. They were acting as if a storm was brewing. At Steve Tarran's farm, which bordered the Dredge's northern extremes, young colts who otherwise would be kicking and playing instead sidled up to the mares for protection. The same was true for the calves and the cows. Millennia of motherly instincts kicked in, as the youngest members of the herd were reigned in for their own protection.

2:30 a.m. Nancy Butler pulled her little Chevy into the driveway and parked next to Rick's pickup. When the car light came on, she checked herself in the mirror again to be sure she looked right. The face that looked back at her was a tired one. That was good. If she was supposed to have been working a shift and a half, she had better look tired, just in case Rick was still awake. More than likely, he was fast asleep. But she wasn't going to take any chances.

She grabbed her purse and the gym bag containing her work clothes and stepped out of the car onto the gravel of the driveway. The little rocks crunched beneath her flats. A dim fluorescent light shone from the motion-sensor lamp on the pole barn, lighting her way to the front door. That was the only thing she hated about getting home so late; that white-blue light gave the driveway and the yard a ghostly, creepy, almost otherworldly appearance. It was like being on the moon or maybe some distant planet.

Despite the fact that her rational, scientific mind (she was a nurse, after all) insisted there was nothing to fear out here, even late at night in the deepest of the darkness, a part of her was always scared to be outside when the sun went down. It was a deep fear she carried with her from her youth. There was no noise at all in the woods that night. No insects chirping in the warm night air. No hooting of owls. It was dead silent. It unnerved her. It made her hurry up to the front steps.

Nancy was in such a hurry that she stumbled over the bottom step and fell forward. Her hands caught her with no problem, but to do so she had dropped her bag and purse. The bag was zipped up tight, so it just bounced to a halt near the porch railing. But her purse was still open, spilling its contents all over the cement stoop.

She closed her eyes and swore, not exactly under her breath. The light from the pole barn could just reach around the corner of the house, giving her a little vision. Her hands fumbled, grasping the variety of small items that were scattered all over the porch.

At that moment, she suddenly found herself staring up across the driveway in the direction of the pole barn. Nancy had flipped herself over completely, lying on her back now against the stoop as a sweat broke out on her forehead. Her eyes were wide open in fear. Adrenaline was pumping in her system.

The long, terrible howl was still echoing across the Dredge.

Forgetting the rest of whatever had fallen from her purse, she bolted up the steps, tore open the screen door, and jumped in to the safety of the house. She slammed the heavy front door and leaned against it, her heart thumping in her chest.

Only then did she realize she needed to take a breath.

The howls came again and again. They seemed to be right outside, and they seemed to be echoing through the house. She sank to the floor and crouched, her arms around her knees, which she had unconsciously pulled up to her chest. It seemed an eternity as she hid there in the corner where the door met the wall.

***

All across Sigma Township folks sprang out of bed at the noise. Wives clutched their husbands, who displayed the best false bravado they could; that howl was unnerving even to grown men. Kids screamed for their parents. Dogs, at first braying behind closed doors, later whimpered to the safety of their master's beds. Most thought at first it was a wolf, but the longer it carried on, the less it sounded like any normal kind of animal. Off and on, the deep, throaty howl cascaded through the near total darkness of Sigma. Even after it stopped about an hour later, most folks stayed awake the rest of the night, shaking and shivering, unable to get that horrible sound out of their heads.

***

Jack Cooper dropped his coffee mug, shattering it on the tile floor. Shards on which the image of a lighthouse could still be discerned mingled with the black sludge, now puddling around his worn-out moccasins. But Jack had hardly noticed. His head had snapped upward toward the curtained window of the back door, his shaking hand gripping the pistol tightly.

***

Tom McClusky awoke more from the sounds of his horses than from the howling. He was trained after many years to jump up at any signs of danger to his girls. It would have been the same if their children were still living with them instead of having their own homes and families. A dad was always a dad, even if the kids he had now were his horses. Something certainly had them spooked this evening, more so than he'd ever heard them before. And that was when Tom finally registered the howling and the fact that his wife was suctioned to his arm. He paused for a moment, indecisive. He knew he should go and check on the horses, but his gut response was to just curl back up in bed. Whatever that was out there, it wasn't friendly. After a few seconds, his longtime discipline as a farmer won out. He swung his legs out of bed, much to the surprise of his wife.

"Where are you going?" she whispered forcefully.

He'd already slipped his robe on. "I gotta go check the girls."

"You're leaving me here?" she shrieked again.

He gave her a smile she couldn't see in the room's darkness. "You know I gotta go out there. Somethin's spooked 'em. I just gotta settle 'em down."

She leapt out of bed and threw on her own robe. "Not without me, you aren't."

The howl came again, this time long and drawn out. It was a sick noise, with almost a wet gurgling in its midst. Never had they heard such a sound before, and they'd lived on this farm for years. They looked at each other, now that their eyes had adjusted to the darkness. Neither one really wanted to leave the safety of their bedroom.

***

Scott Hailey jumped right out of bed at the sound and found himself standing in his underwear in his little bedroom. Just like in a cartoon, his knees were knocking and his hands were clutched into a single fist over his bare belly. Goose pimples had broken out all over his skin despite the relative warmth of the night. Regardless of the outward tough-guy persona he showed everyone at school, he really was a coward at heart. At the second howl, he grabbed his pillow and slipped out his door. Within five seconds he had bounded down the hallway and into his father's room. Of course, his dad wouldn't have heard it in his alcohol-induced slumber, even if he could have heard it over his loud snoring; that noxious sound drowned out the howl in a way that nothing else could. Scott, a 15-year-old bully, would never show someone that he was scared of anything, and that included his dad. But the boy knew his father would be sleeping late tomorrow morning. He curled up on the carpet in the safety of his dad's room, knowing he'd be out before his old man awoke. Even the snoring sounded better than that awful howling.

***

Few if any of the folks in Sigma Township slept that first night. The howls and shrieks in the night came and went from all over. Whatever it was, it was on the move. But mostly the sounds were heard emanating from the Dredge. Folks had no idea that it would only get worse. This was just the beginning.

Monday

Joe (I)

Morning came annoyingly early for Joe Randall. Of course, like everybody else, he'd been up since 2:30 a.m. And like everyone else, he still had to work this morning. The sleepiness had been stolen from him in the early hours. Once the howling had finally ceased, he and his wife got up and put on the coffee. Bev also began preparing her famous cinnamon rolls. They usually woke up at 5 o'clock anyway to get the trucks ready for the day's hauling, so a few extra hours weren't a big deal right then. Though he was a little drowsy at the moment, he knew that by mid-afternoon he'd be downright exhausted. You couldn't add on extra hours without feeling them eventually. They'd creep up on you at some point.

The drivers would be in around 5:30, wide awake and ready for the day's work. First thing, they'd inspect their rigs carefully, just as Joe required each day. Then they'd head to the house for coffee. Mondays were special in the stout, cinderblock house because the smell of Bev's baking would roll forth from the kitchen out onto the back porch where the drivers would pick up their day's assignments. Fresh baked cinnamon rolls were a luxury she provided as a special for the boys on Mondays, since she fully believed, "Mondays are always the hardest day of the week." If the boys needed a little extra motivation coming off the weekend, such goodies were the ticket. She squeezed her little frame between their chairs, serving them their first roll personally before leaving the basket on the table.

Neither Joe nor his wife said anything to the drivers about what they'd heard late in the night. Neither one wanted to talk about it anyway, even with each other. Every once in a while, one would glance at the other in an unspoken, knowing manner that only husbands and wives who've been together a long time can do. The worry, the uncertainty, the fear—it could all be seen in their eyes. Of course, the drivers didn't pick up on it; they didn't need to be bothered with such tall tales before heading off to work. They didn't live around here; they weren't up all night because of that loud howling and shrieking in the darkness—it was the stuff of nightmares and legends. Now, certainly the boys would have believed Joe and Bev, but only because they were so close, having worked together for so many years. But they may have wondered about the couple's sanity, too.

By 6:30, the bright yellow Randall's Logging trucks would be warm, the drivers would be full of caffeine and cinnamon rolls, and the day's hauling would begin. Joe's fleet of semi-trucks, earlier lined up like soldiers in the gravel parking lot behind his house, would pull out one by one to head off north toward M-72. As an independent transportation contractor, Joe's trucks would load up with huge logs from the various logging and harvesting sites throughout a five-county area and carry them off to the big mills in Kalkaska, Grayling, South Boardman, and even as far away as Gaylord and Cadillac. On a really good day, he'd have his guys pick up another load near their first drop-off site and deliver someplace on the way back. *Keep the loads full*, he always preached. *If you've got to put the miles on anyway, they might as well be loaded up.* Joe was hired out by as many as a dozen different lumbering companies each year. It was one less hassle they had to deal with, and his reputation for prompt delivery was well known around the business.

Joe gave a brief wave as the last truck pulled out of their wide driveway and onto C-571. Then he turned his 6-foot-4 frame back toward the shade of the house. The sun was already up and quickly heating the world around him. Bev was waiting for him on the porch, nibbling a cinnamon roll.

"It's gonna be another hot one today," he said. "I can't remember the last time a summer started out so blasted hot." Joe picked up the travel mug his wife had filled for him, taking one last sip before heading out himself. He might be the owner of the company, but he worked just as hard as the other drivers, hauling his fair share every day.

"Dry too," commented Bev quietly. She'd be home all day working as both central dispatch and bookkeeper. Usually, her days were fairly quiet. On the rare occasion it was needed, she relayed messages from the drivers if there was an emergency or a deviation in the day's schedule. Today, she sat in silence, obviously fretful.

"Hey," Joe whispered as he grasped her hands and lifted her to her feet. He set the mug down and gave her a big bear hug, like he had been so fond of doing when they were younger. "Last night's over. Whatever that was, it's long gone now, I'm sure."

Bev clung to him like a scared little girl. "You really think so, honey?"

Joe's tanned and lined face gave her the best smile he could muster. The big man didn't smile a lot to begin with. "You betcha. Probably just a wolf or a bobcat. And you know they don't hang around an area long. It's actually kinda funny to think about it now."

She looked at him, face aghast. "I thought it was just awful. I'm not gonna sleep for weeks!"

He hugged her again. "It's okay, honey. It's all gonna be fine. I'm sure whatever it was has moved on by now." He pulled away and headed for the door, grabbing his travel mug from the table.

"You know," she said as he opened the door, "I might feel better if you give me a call a couple times today. Just, you know, to check in."

The big man gave her another smile. "Sure, babe. You betcha."

She stared out the windows as her man lumbered his big frame out to his truck, hopped in, and drove away. She wondered if everything was going to be alright.

Emmonds Farm

Though the sun was hardly up in the sky, the flies were already clustered around the body. Blood rapidly soaked its way into the dry earth, barely pausing to pool up.

Were it not on Mitchell Emmonds' small dairy farm, the carcass might not be recognizable as a young calf, only two months having passed since its spring birth. When Mitchell ambled his way out to the dairy barn as the black sky morphed into a violet dawn color, he immediately knew something was amiss. For one, the cows were terribly agitated. He supposed that was in reaction to that crazy noise he had heard in the night. For another, they were packed up tightly against the barn door, rather than simply milling about in the yard. Though they generally needed milking early in the morning, they were anything but in a hurry. This morning it seemed his entire herd couldn't wait to get inside.

Scowling, Mitchell was preparing to open the large sliding wooden door when a lone cow, a hundred yards off in the pasture, caught his attention. Considering that all of the others were pressed up so closely to the big faded-gray barn, this loner was rather conspicuous.

And then he watched it nuzzle something on the ground, something that looked far too much like a black gunny sack. Only Mitchell knew better than that. Forgetting the immediate needs of the rest of the herd, he squeezed his way out of the throng, strode across the yard, and then picked up the pace as he passed the pasture gate. Within a half a minute, he'd reached the scene of the violence.

Thirty years of dairy farming conditioned him to the perils, the dangers, the deaths that occurred in the natural world. He'd seen countless animals die in all sorts of ways. He'd seen the slaughter and butchering of animals destined for the freezer and the dinner table. He'd even put down many of his own animals at one time or another. But none of these experiences prepared him for the absolute carnage that morning in the hard-packed pasture. Were he a lesser man, he'd have turned aside and brought his breakfast back up. As it was, his eyes could hardly register the damage done to the little calf.

Its mother was staring stupidly down at the sack of bones and skin, nudging it and occasionally giving it a lick. As he approached, Mitchell thought it made a far too human scene.

There was very little left of the animal. It had been slashed open from chin to gullet, and its entrails were nowhere to be seen. Below, the dark patch of earth showed where the blood had seeped out in force. The rib cage was exposed, skin and meat chewed back up toward the shoulder, and the bones appeared to have been gnawed on, as they showed small chisel-like marks and dents stained in the blood. The hind flank was ripped open, and the two rear legs were missing from the hip backward. Only the calf's head was relatively intact, its dark left eye staring blankly up at the oncoming daylight.

Calves are not large, but they're not tiny either, by any means. Whatever had fed on this one had a powerful hunger. Mitchell turned his head from right to left and within a few seconds had located the blood trail heading out across the pasture toward the Au Sable Forest half a mile away. Whatever had done this had obviously carried off a snack for later.

He sighed deeply as he looked off to the forest. Hearing that sound last night, he was afraid something like this could happen. But he couldn't think of any predators, at least in this area, that could dismantle a cow, even a young one, with such savagery. Mitchell had to believe it was more than one attacker to have eaten so much and taken off with both hind quarters. But again, he thought, there were no big predators out here. Coyotes couldn't have done this. Wolves, bears, and big cats were unheard of this far south in Michigan. If he lived in the U.P. maybe, or even in the tip of the mitt. But not here. It didn't make sense.

The mother cow nudged the farmer, who'd bent down to investigate closely. He rose up and led her back to the rest of the herd. He'd have to clean up this mess before any milking could be done this morning. And then he'd have himself a trip out to the forest, following that blood trail with his .410.

Jack (I)

First things first—start up the coffee pot. The old farts, just like clockwork, would storm in within five minutes of the front door being unlocked at 8 o'clock sharp. And they'd start their complaining about five seconds after that if there wasn't a fresh pot waiting for them. Jack knew them well, and though he could care less about their whining, he would be annoyed by the three all day if they weren't pacified. This morning, Jack would be joining them; he'd need the caffeine buzz to keep him going if he wanted to make it through the rest of the day.

Jack paused, running his weathered old hands through the few remaining white, wispy hairs on his head, and wondered which old fart would bring it up first. They all lived within a block of the store, and they undoubtedly heard the howling, too. All four of them were far too old to hide their fears behind false bravado. At some point, age had given them license to do or say just about anything they wanted.

With the till re-stocked and the store readied, Jack sauntered to the front door and flipped the latch and deadbolt. He reached out the door and grabbed the day's *Record-Eagle*. He generally could care less about the news, but he never missed the daily crossword in the back of the paper. Then he turned the *Closed, Please Come Again* sign over to read *Open, Come On In*. He never had huge numbers of customers during the day, but the few who did patronize his business were treated like royalty. If folks had a lot of big shopping to do, they could go to Kalkaska to Glen's or to Traverse City to Meijers. But for those little items, desperately needed at just that moment when a long trip wasn't practical, Jack's store was very accommodating. There was always a run on batteries, toilet paper, dish soap, aspirin, diapers, and any of the other thousands of household items folks might need in a pinch. He wasn't trying to get rich with his store; it basically enabled him to pay the bills and make a halfway decent living.

His one stock boy, Stevie, would show up just before 10. He lived with his grandfather about four miles east on Lodi

Road, and he rode his little rusty bike in every day, rain or shine. *Mostly shine these past weeks,* Jack thought, walking back around the old wood and glass counter. *The farmers here-abouts would give anything for some rain.* Jack paid the boy each day for his six hours of work directly from the till, and Stevie would, on most days, pay a bunch of it right back in exchange for chips, candy, soda, or one of any number of little items from the store. He was always buying some little treasure and taking it home. Jack couldn't imagine where all the trinkets ended up.

Stevie was twenty, though mentally he was still hanging out in the early teens. His grandfather began taking care of him when his parents died in the same car crash that left the boy a simpleton before he was a year old. Jack always had a soft spot in his heart for him. They didn't need any money, the state saw to that. But Jack gave the boy the opportunity to be a responsible member of the community. His role might not be huge, but he did play a role, and he played it well. Stevie was a good boy. He sure did work hard. He kept the shelves spotless and perfectly organized. Strong as an ox, despite his thin, lanky build, he'd be more than happy to carry boxes and crates for Jack. The boy also unloaded the delivery trucks and helped load lumber for customers. And before he left, he always made sure that he cleaned the entire store with great gusto.

Right on cue, the front door opened with the little jingle so common of old mom and pop stores. "Well, if it isn't the three little dwarfs," Jack said with a hint of a smile.

"You know where you can stick your sarcasm, Jack," the old timer in the front said dryly. Fred Waffle waltzed inside the store, followed by Doc Custer. Both of them were long since retired. But whereas Doc lived alone and wanted company, Fred claimed he needed to escape from his wife for several hours each day to keep whatever sanity he had left. "'Sides, there's only two of us. Lloyd's not here yet. Coffee ready?"

"You know where it is. Same as always, you old goats," Jack replied, turning his attention to his crossword.

Fred and Doc grabbed their cups off the little side table that held the coffee pot and filled them with the steaming brew.

"You're losing your touch," Fred hollered across the store after a sip. "This is the thickest batch of coffee you've ever made."

"Yeah, how come the sludge today?" Doc chimed in, taking his accustomed seat at the round checkers table in the front corner of the store. His long, white handlebar moustache wiggled when he spoke.

Jack looked up gravely, his little glasses down at the edge of his pointed nose. "You know why. I thought we could all use an extra shot of the go-fast juice this morning. I don't know 'bout you two, but I didn't get much sleep last night."

The two nodded their heads silently as they sipped their coffee. Each was lost in his own thoughts.

A few minutes later, Lloyd Horner sauntered in. He would hang around until about 11 or so when he'd head over to the bar to prep for the lunch crowd. Each day he'd slap together sandwiches or burgers for the four of them. Stevie would bring the sack lunches back to the Mercantile while Lloyd readied the bar for the couple of folks who wanted lunch and a beer.

Today, Lloyd gave Jack a look that said he'd rather not start a conversation.

Jack was surprised. He thought the three of them would just trip over themselves to talk about that awful noise in the darkness. But here they were, silent and stone-faced about it. And not one of the three was dressed as his usual dapper self.

Usually they were well decked out: suspenders, slacks, button-up shirts. Today they were outfitted in their light flannels, what they usually saved for cool fall days. And Doc was actually wearing jeans—Jack didn't even know he owned a pair. It wasn't often that he underestimated them. From their silence, he could tell they were deeply troubled by it all.

Eric (I)

Of all the folks in Sigma that Monday morning, only Eric Martin was wide awake and refreshed from a great night's sleep. Of course, Eric lived in Traverse City, some thirty-five miles away from the chaos that had ensued the previous night.

Dust kicked up behind his work pickup, an old 1962 Ford one-ton that sported a two-tone paint job that any young man just out of college could appreciate: rusting tan on peeling forest green. It was bound to gain the wrong kind of attention from any young ladies he encountered on the job. Not that he met many single, good-looking young women out here in the wilderness. In fact, he'd yet to meet any women at all in the two months he'd been working for the DNR, either in the woods or anywhere else. Generally, his job kept him hopping seven days a week at all sorts of odd hours. It didn't bode well for his love life, or the lack thereof.

Lately, however, even his work life wasn't boding well for him either. He'd already been written up twice for missing work, and had been docked a day's pay each time. His boss told him not to even bother coming in to the office if he ever missed a day again. Just drop off the truck and leave his keys, badge, and gun on the seat.

He looked back at the dust cloud trailing him. *Man, it's dry out here*, he thought. *I can't remember when I've ever seen land so dry in my life.* He couldn't remember it raining even once since he took this job back in the first week of May. Not a drop.

Driving down Lodi Road, feeling every bump and dip as his teeth rattled (the old truck was rather lacking in the shocks department), his mind drifted back to earlier this morning. He'd checked in at headquarters at 7 o'clock and sighed at the duty roster. He was assigned to Sigma Township for the week. Wonderful. Out in "Redneck Heaven." *The bugs in those lowland swamps would be awful,* he thought. And everybody was apt to be armed and dangerous, even though hunting season was months away.

Sarah, the day dispatcher, saw him staring intently at the board. "You know," she said, putting her clipboard down on the counter, "no matter how long you stare at it, it still won't change."

Eric looked up and gave her a weak half smile. "So much for good Karma."

She huffed, smiling back. "Yeah, right. Why would Karma work for you? If anybody's on the wrong side of it, it's you."

"I think the Warden's just got it out for me," replied Eric, trying to be cute. He did possess a certain sense of charm when he really tried for it. Mostly, though, he didn't try too hard. "This is twice in a month I've been exiled to the boonies."

"Oh, I can't imagine why," Sarah zipped back at him without looking up. "You know, we should all be allowed to come in halfway through a shift every now and then."

"I don't want to talk about it," Eric said flatly. His charm was fading. Normally, he enjoyed Sarah's harassment and even returned his own. This morning, which felt quite different from the norm, he wasn't in the mood. *Why's that?* he asked himself. *Is it 'cause you got what you deserved?*

But she wouldn't give it up. He'd started it this morning, but she wasn't ready to stop the teasing quite yet. The two of them had had a bit of fun over the past two months. It was like they were old friends. The nice thing was that she was married, and Eric knew she was off limits. That allowed him to loosen up a bit, knowing he wasn't trying to impress her. There were no romantic possibilities here, so they could have all the friendly banter they wanted.

Finally, Eric had to hang his head and get his butt out to the waiting excitement of Sigma. *Whoo-hoo!* He'd wasted enough time here in the contact station. Besides, if the Warden, as everyone called their boss, came in and saw him here, there'd be hell to pay. So he bid Sarah a good bye, and she waved back absently, her attention turned to the scanner and the radio transmitter opposite the counter. *Why were all the really good girls already taken?* he asked himself as he headed out to his waiting chariot.

His mind returned to the here and now as he saw the stop sign for Sigma Corners ahead. Quiet as usual. He sighed again. You couldn't fill an hour with a year's excitement out here.

First things first. Part of his job was as a detective, gathering information from whatever sources he could find to investigate if anything shady was happening in the area. The best place to start was always the local watering hole. Since the bar wasn't open yet, Eric pulled the old pickup in front of the Mercantile, cut the engine, and then marveled at the puffing and rattling as it idled to a stop. *One of these days, it's just going to up and die*, he thought. He climbed out and winced as the rusty door hinges squealed in protest.

He'd been here to the Mercantile about a month ago on his first visit to Sigma Township. He counted it the longest week of his life. Trudging through the swamps, swatting mosquitoes and black flies, choking on the dust that rose in great clouds from the roads—yes, sir, that was the glamorous life of a DNR officer!

However, when he strode into the store at 8:35, full of the confidence of youthful authority, he was rather unprepared for the story the four old timers were about to tell him. His whole life was about to change, all because he'd ticked off his supervisor and had been given the Sigma assignment for the week. Karma indeed.

Sigma (III)

Everyone in the little community was up and moving very early Monday morning. Most, like Joe and Bev had their own chores and work to start up anyway. Some, like Jack and Mitchell, had businesses to run. But for the rest, the sun peeking its powerfully bright face over the top edge of the Au Sable Forest brought a final sense of relief from the night's torment. The skies were clear and blue. This glorious morning could almost make them forget the terror they'd felt only hours before. They could almost forget the hours they'd lain awake, hearts racing, eyes darting at every shadow in their rooms. They could almost forget how tired they were from the lack of sleep. They could almost forget the haunting images their imaginations created for them, the terrifying specters that lived in their minds.

Almost.

The people went about their business that morning, trying to forget. No one mentioned it to anybody else. Not that they thought they wouldn't be believed. Not at all. There was no doubt that everyone for miles around had heard that awful howling. They didn't talk about it, because if they did, it became real again. It would escape from their imagination. They'd have to give it a name. And that made the specters real, all too real.

If it were real, they might have to do something about it. If it was real, it might not just fade away like early morning mist out in the Dredge.

Brian in the Dredge (I)

Brian Alexander, Jr., was more than happy to escape the confines of the house, even if it was extremely hot outside. When his father was drinking, which was even more often and more extreme ever since he'd been pink-slipped at the Mancelona foundry, young Brian would be more than happy to be anywhere else but here. His dad, Brian, Sr., had yet to become violent to either Brian or his mom, Marcie, but where there was smoke, there would soon be fire. Most days started with a beer or two for lunch and then deteriorated for the elder Brian as the hours went by. When the nightly news was over, Brian's dad was nearly in the bag, and that's when the craziness in their little trailer would begin.

Marcie worked the dinner shift as a waitress at the Whistle Stop Café in South Boardman a few miles away, and she wouldn't be home until around 8:30 or so. Brian, Sr., was often passed out by then. She wasn't there to see the damage he'd done in the hours before.

Once it was a broken living room lamp. Another time, it was a hole in one of the radio speakers. The worst of the accidents was a month ago, when he tried to walk over to Horner's (stagger over was more like it) and instead fell right through the porch railing. The flimsy two-by-four was no match for Brian, Sr.'s 240 pounds. He was a large man and his gut had been growing steadily since his layoff.

But worst of all was the verbal abuse that Brian, Jr., had to endure. His dad, when sober, was an okay father. Nothing truly special, but he did teach the kid to play catch, sat through endless summer little league baseball games, and even showed up at a Cub Scout meeting or two. But when he was sloshed, as he was regularly now-a-days, he became downright mean.

School had been out for two weeks, and in that time the younger Brian had become adjusted to the wild summer life expected of a 13-year old who would much rather be outdoors than in. Escaping his father was a good enough reason to leave the house, but even more so was the inexplicable call of nature.

Despite the wildly awful noises he'd heard the night before, Brian, Jr., was one of the few in town (they'd been kids mostly) who'd been able to fall back asleep. However, it was a restless sleep, in which monsters of all sorts chased him through dark, dismal streets and haunted corridors. He'd run on and on, and every time he peeked his head back over his shoulder, he'd see nothing but dark fur and long, piercing claws reaching for him. Periodically in the dreams, he'd hear that roaring howl, and he'd awaken, covered with a fine bead of sweat.

But morning sent those fears and bad dreams off with the departed night. Brian arose, a little tired, but otherwise ready to attack the world with a genuine energy and an excitement that only a young teenager can muster. A quick bowl of Cheerios and he was out the door.

The Alexander home (house trailer actually) was situated just a quarter mile north of Sigma Corners and the town proper. Their small front yard, shaded by huge and ancient oaks and maples, held the usual collection of junk that is unfortunately associated with trailers: an old and rusty Thunderbird (its days of ripping up pavement long gone) up on blocks; a collection of several broken or busted boards and two-by-fours that were once long ago meant to become a picnic table; a tire swing hanging on an old and frayed rope from a no longer sturdy oak branch; a bathtub (one clawed foot broken off and missing) filled with dirt and flowers, dying from the intense heat and drought; and large mats of weeds at the edges of the unkempt yard that threatened to overtake everything each year.

However, the scene drastically changed on the other side of the trailer. As the backyard opened to the Dredge, the view was spectacular. A mile or more of tall grasses and wildflowers that dotted the great meadow glistened like a sea of sparkling gold as the morning sun barely clipped the tops of the Au Sable Forest to the east. The grasses rippled in the light breeze, waves upon waves bending the long stalks. Many hours later, as the sun set, the rich earthy tones of the grasses would emerge, the reds, oranges, and tans against the shadows. Just behind the yard, huge sunflowers would peek their silky, round heads over the grasses in early August. It was truly a million-dollar view.

Brian played outside every day for as long as he could. His few brief forays into the house were just to find lunch or snacks. Sometimes he'd even wrap himself up a few peanut butter and jelly sandwiches in the morning to take with him, so he wouldn't have to return until just before dinner. He was always as quiet as possible; his father's attention wasn't exactly wanted.

Halfway out on the Dredge, Brian, Jr., had built his fort. With the considerable time available to him this summer, it was already well underway. Stevie had sneaked him a few of the old crooked or split boards from the Mercantile that no one would buy. And he'd searched all through town, picking through the busted lumber pile out behind Mr. Randall's, as well as snatching up any stray boards he'd found hiding in the neighbors' yards. Of course, being a polite and respectful boy, he'd asked the homeowners first, mustering up the courage to walk right up to each front door. He'd always liked his neighbors, and they liked him. He'd never had any problem exchanging niceties with them; he'd known them all his life. But it was something different to have to go and ask them to give up their possessions. Most had no problem with it; some were even glad that this enterprising young man would help them clean up their yards. But he always felt a weird sensation asking all the same.

Plus he didn't want his dad knowing what he was up to; all it would take was a phone call from an upset neighbor to make his dad put a quick end to Brian's summer adventures.

But his dad didn't find out, and within a week's time, he had enough boards to begin his project. Tools and nails were never a problem. His dad certainly wasn't up to putting them to any use this summer. Each day, he'd grab his school backpack and fill it with a hammer and an empty peanut butter jar filled with nails from the little storage shed in the side yard. He'd also toss in any prized possessions he might need from home: a sandwich, if he was ambitious in the morning, a Choose-Your-Own-Adventure book from his collection, a few of his Star Wars figures, and of course, his toy guns and army gear. Many great hours were spent building his fort and planning his adventures, all in an effort to leave the troubles of home well behind.

The fort was constructed beneath and attached to a mature apple tree that had yet to bear fruit in Brian's lifetime. The many low-hanging branches were sturdy enough to support him when he climbed up into its boughs. He never really got very high up, but that was okay. The lowest branches spread themselves wide and he used these as the skeleton for his fort. A few old landscape timbers were sunk carefully into the ground a few feet away and nailed to his assortment of boards. The going was slow, but time was on his side this summer. At this point, three walls were up, the only small entrance existing beneath the apple tree's lower branches and beside its trunk.

Brian's goal this week was to fashion a roof on the top, save for an opening he could use to climb up the tree without leaving the safety of the fort. Every fort needed a lookout spot, after all. That way, he'd have plenty of warning if Scott came along. He wanted to avoid that bully even more than he wanted to avoid his own father.

Scott Hailey was two years older than Brian and had picked on him since Brian had started school. A full head taller, and of course, much more muscular than Brian, Scott instilled the sort of fear that only bullies can. Brian had never been assaulted by the bigger boy, but there were plenty of threats, name-calling, and teasing. Brian, short for his grade anyway, lived in mortal fear of Scott. They were two of only three total students that the school bus picked up way out here, and lucky for Brian, he sat closer to the front and he was dropped off at home first.

The third student was the object of Brian's secret crush, Bonnie Eastman. She was dropped off by the bus a mile before Brian on the other side of Sigma Corners. Bonnie was a grade younger and was the prettiest girl he knew. She wasn't a knockout or anything, simply a cute girl who lived on the south end of the Dredge. But she would be something someday when she was older, he just knew it.

Often times, Brian's adventures ended up revolving around saving Bonnie from all sorts of dangers. If he was the knight, she was the princess; if he was the swashbuckling hero, she was the damsel in distress. However, the most prevalent adventure was rescuing Bonnie from Scott, who more often than not, played the part of the villain. That was rather fitting, because she was the unfortunate object of his attention in real life. Brian hated to see Scott drape his arm around her neck or shoulders, blow into her ears and light brown hair, and make comments about her being his girlfriend. Bonnie, much younger, cringed and shrank away from him in disgust, which really got the bully going. Scott would always turn up the volume and the teasing, making sure everyone could hear him clearly. When she would try to get away, Scott would act offended, before cursing and finally insulting her in some awful manner. *He really couldn't get the hint*, Brian thought. *Even if she was anything but disgusted by him, that was no way to get her to like him. Even if she doesn't know I exist, at least I don't treat her that way.*

This went on several times a week for as long as Brian could remember. He wished so desperately that he could really save her, that he really could be heroic and brave enough to stand up not only for her but for himself too.

Eric (II)

Later on, as evening drew on toward night, Eric Martin knocked back another swig of his beer. Most of the other officers had since retired to their homes, leaving he and Todd Lindell to close up the sports bar. After the day he'd had, the others at the Grand Traverse DNR Office were more than happy to take him out in an effort to help him forget all that he had experienced. It wasn't every day that a DNR officer found a body in the woods.

While the staff was around, no one brought up the incident. They just kept buying rounds in the hopes that Eric would find a way to drown his memories in beer. He obviously didn't need to be reminded of it.

Now that they were alone, Todd carefully brought it back up. Sometimes it helped more to tell the story than to hold it inside.

"Wild, huh?" Todd said, breaking the uncomfortable silence between them.

Eric stared into the bottom of his glass for a while before refilling it from the pitcher. "Yeah, man," he responded slowly and quietly. "I never thought I'd be pulling bodies out of the woods today."

"You wanna talk about it?" Todd asked cautiously, taking a sip of his beer.

Eric took another long pull. Then, wiping his mouth, he said, "Sure, why not? I was headed out south of Sigma..."

***

The road became worse as it left the little town farther behind. If he hadn't been there a few weeks previously, Eric wouldn't have believed it was possible. The chatter bumps and potholes became more intense as the road wound into the wilderness.

The crashed vehicle caught his attention immediately. Folks might be a bit uncouth around here, but they didn't park their trucks half in the ditch and half wrapped around a tree. He pulled the rusty DNR truck to the side of the road and clicked on the emergency flashers, which were one of the few features in the old beater that still worked well. Not that it would matter much way out here; he hadn't seen a car yet in the last twenty minutes of driving and he didn't think it likely that he would now. If he was the first one on the scene of this accident, it must have been hours since another vehicle had been by. If he hadn't driven way out here, it might still have been hours (or even days) before it was found.

Cautiously, Eric approached the accident. The windshield, a gaping, bloody hole splintered and pushed outward, caused his heart to drop. That wasn't a good sign to start with. Nearly every inch of the vehicle was dented, scratched, and flattened from its roll. The side mirrors were smashed right into the metal of the truck's side. As he stepped around the truck, his attention was drawn to the body in the woods. Eric sprinted, knocking the roadside ferns about, until he was right above the dead man. Eric had absolutely no experience dealing with dead bodies, and he was no medical expert by any means, but even he could that tell this guy was long gone.

The eyes were the giveaway, opened wide and staring upward, glazed over. The entire face and head was a mess of jagged scars, dried blood, and wet, matted hair. More cuts and blood covered the ripped clothing. The head, arms, and legs were splayed out at impossible angles. He'd been a goner from the moment he rocketed through the windshield. The landing only sealed the deal.

As he waited for the ambulance to arrive, Eric surveyed the scene. The tire tracks in the dust showed the truck's path toward destruction. But it was another set of tracks that caught his eye. Eric walked over to them and bent down to peer at them carefully. They were vaguely familiar, similar to tracks he'd seen, but on second glance, they were also as foreign as if a UFO would be parked next to the wrecked truck. Something about the tracks just didn't seem right, especially to a person who was trained to identify the marks of animals that lived all around the Midwest.

The ambulance and the local sheriff's patrol were painfully slow in arriving at the scene of the accident. Eric waited for over an hour, kept company by the stiff in the ferns. He knew he couldn't touch the body in any way, pending the investigation by the sheriff's deputies. He couldn't even put a sheet over the body. And no matter what he did to occupy himself during that time, his attention was always pulled back to the victim and the strange tracks.

***

"Man, that's harsh," Todd said when his partner was done. "Any idea what caused it all?"

Eric had that far away look again. "The EMTs suspected alcohol played a part. The victim had left the little bar in town just a bit before. Probably going too fast, lost control, you know how it happens."

"Yeah," Todd knew. This might be the first time they'd had to personally deal with a drunk driving accident, but they both knew such things happened all the time. "It just seems so odd, you know, he made it quite a ways from the bar. And there are a number of tight curves on that road. How come he didn't bite it earlier?"

Eric had thought of that, too.

Todd continued, "Must've been lucky. Up to a point, that is. His luck ran out."

"Yeah," Eric commented, draining his glass. He could afford to pound them back, as Todd was his chauffeur home. "But you know, I found the strangest thing as I looked over the scene."

Todd gazed over his glass at his friend. "What's that?"

"Footprints," Eric said slowly and deliberately. "Footprints in the dust of the road. No cars were through there, so there was nothing to disturb the scene. I saw footprints. Well, not actually human footprints. These were a canine's prints, they seemed like a wolf, but they were odd, too."

"How's that?" Todd asked, intrigued.

"There weren't enough of them," Eric stated flatly. "They were spaced a few feet apart, but you've seen wolf tracks, they always bunch up when the four legs are moving. They're always close. These were wide, almost like, I don't know, almost like…" He trailed off.

"Almost like what?" Todd pushed.

"Almost like there weren't enough feet to make enough tracks." He'd neglected to tell his friend about the story the old timers told him at the store earlier that morning. His mind couldn't stop connecting that hideous noise in the dark with those unidentifiable tracks. But that was a mental connection he'd keep to himself for now. He wasn't about to tell his fellow co-workers just yet and have them think he'd lost his mind. But Eric also couldn't keep it all in; he'd feel better if he could confide just a little in Todd, who was probably the closest friend he had on the DNR staff. However, the ambulance and the sheriff's car wiped out the evidence when they arrived, so there was nothing to back up Eric's story or his musings.

"One other thing," Eric said, looking around for a moment to be sure no one else was listening in on their conversation. That wasn't very difficult because they were the only two left in this section of the bar. "They weren't the nice, finished off prints of a wolf, either. Usually you can see the back of their paw, the footpad, you know, really well. In these prints, the print was elongated, almost as if it was dragged. Or as if the paw was long in some way, longer than a normal wolf's track should be."

"That's absurd," Todd said, leaning back in his chair.

"I know, it should be," Eric said, locking eyes with Todd. "I know it sounds crazy, but the tracks almost looked human in a way, you know, the way human prints will trail off toward the heel, especially if the weight is on the balls of the feet.

"I know, it sounds crazy. Maybe it is. But I know what I saw. Something ain't right out there. I'm not sure I want to go and find it out, but some part of me does. I want to go looking for whatever made those tracks, you know? To see what it really is."

Jimmy Dean (I)

Just as Eric and Todd were closing up the bar in Traverse City, Jimmy Dean Holloway was closing down Horner's. Lloyd kept it open for an extra hour until nearly 11 o'clock, just for Jimmy Dean, who hadn't come in until after 8. But finally, he had to send the mourner on his way. It didn't make much sense to stay open for one customer, especially since it was now nearly pitch black outside.

There was no wake for Buck. There was no place for mourners to gather, not that there were any mourners. He didn't have any family anywhere in the area, and the closest of his friends was Jimmy Dean. A short funeral ceremony was scheduled for Wednesday afternoon at the request of the Holloway family. Buck was not the religious type, and it had been years since Jimmy Dean had been to church. But his wife insisted that a proper burial was needed.

Once the kids went to bed, Jimmy excused himself and headed to town. His wife completely understood; he needed a little time to himself. And if there was any place to both drown his sorrows and to remember his good friend, it was at Horner's. They'd certainly spent enough time there together.

Jimmy Dean thought it very strange when Buck didn't show for work that morning. His partner hadn't missed a day in all the years they were working together. Jimmy Dean had been doing both of their jobs when the foreman called him into the little office at noon to deliver the bad news. Jimmy Dean had taken it hard, but despite the news, he still finished his shift. His family needed the income. His wife knew about Buck by the time Jimmy Dean had arrived home; word always travels like wildfire in a small community.

By 10, Jimmy Dean was halfway in the bag, and Lloyd knew that if he stayed much longer, he'd either have to drive Jimmy Dean home or get him a pillow to help him sleep on the floor. So while Jimmy Dean was still able to function and before it was dangerously dark outside to drive home, Lloyd kindly escorted the mourning fellow to his truck. Jimmy Dean hugged the old man, whom he had known for years, and Lloyd held him for a few moments while the last of the tears ran down the young man's cheeks. No words needed to be spoken; few had been said in the two hours while Jimmy Dean was saddled up to the bar either.

Lloyd slowly walked back inside and locked the door as Jimmy Dean's pickup pulled out onto C-571. The swamp-gas of the neon lights in the window blinked and then melted into the darkness of the bar's interior. Jimmy Dean didn't see it; he was concentrating his best through wet and puffy eyes. A moment of clarity hit him—it just wouldn't do to join his old friend a night later. He took a deep breath and let it out slowly. His hands held a death grip on the steering wheel, his knuckles already turning white from the effort.

The single, solitary pickup bounced along the rough road until the last light from the open air of the Dredge ended and the forest to the south began again. The road continued to worsen until he finally turned right on Mecum Road.

This deep in the woods, the impending twilight was completely blocked by the overhanging branches. There might be a half-hour of dim light left in the world above, but down here, it was pitch black. Jimmy Dean's headlights bounced up and down as the truck hit the bumps and dips, flashing the road, the high banks on the side, the thick tree trunks that loomed far too close to the edge (certainly too close for his good friend Buck).

He released his right hand to wipe his eyes, and when his fingers returned automatically to their former location, he saw the creature.

There was no time to avoid it, no time to swerve out of the way. Jimmy Dean did all he could to slam his feet on the Chevy's brakes, but it was too late.

That moment of sobriety he'd had a few minutes ago rushed back at him with alarming speed. Everything seemed to slow to a near stand-still. He saw it all clearly.

The bright headlights created twin spotlights for a cinema-like show featuring a star unlike any ever created in a Hollywood special effects department: The creature wasn't quite on all fours, and yet it wasn't quite standing on two legs either. Jimmy Dean was rather amazed by this. It was sort-of halfway in between, transitioning, in the process of standing upright. Its long arms (or front legs) were hanging down, knuckles just above the hard packed road, the claws at the end of each front finger (yes, they were fingers, visible even from here) clicking and scraping at the dust. It was completely covered in dark fur. The creature's shoulders and head were turned toward the oncoming vehicle. It opened its muzzle, revealing long, sharp canines. Pointed ears wiggled in the light. Jimmy Dean was sure it was some sort of gigantic wolf, and yet that face, formed by the muzzle and the glowing yellow eyes, was surprisingly, even shockingly, human. Horribly, it seemed to be grinning evilly at him.

The pickup then slammed into the creature with enough force to drive it backward along the road for a good fifty feet. The creature spun and rolled, tumbling over itself in a number of seemingly crazy, acrobatic spirals, until it finally landed in a heap.

The truck, too, finally came to a bumpy stop. The dust, once following the pickup, now came rushing forward, bathing the road all around in a thick fog, nearly obscuring the creature in the headlights. Jimmy Dean exhaled and took in a huge breath; he hadn't realized he'd been holding it in for some time now. His heart was racing. He had to wipe his eyes yet again to be sure he was seeing all of this correctly.

Breathing rapidly now, Jimmy Dean looked out the dirty windshield of his truck as the creature began to rise from the road. Its head and torso emerged slowly in the dusty fog like a spirit rising from the graveyard. The creature appeared stunned, but it turned its face once again in the direction of the headlights. Jimmy Dean's eyes widened in fear and shock. Its eyes, still glowing that horrid, bright yellow-gold, narrowed as it furrowed its forehead and brows. Jimmy Dean was sure it was a look of anger and pure hatred. It staggered, almost drunkenly in his direction, trying to regain its balance and its bearings. The muzzle curled up again, fangs bared. It was simply terrible!

He certainly wasn't going to stick around here to see what it was. He punched the gas and the pickup roared to life, rear tires spinning for a second in the dust before it jumped forward and shot past the creature, leaving it far behind him on the road. Jimmy Dean was going far too fast for the road conditions, but he didn't care. He wanted to get as many miles as he could between himself and that awful thing back there.

Sigma (IV)

As the sun had begun to settle behind the trees on the western edge of C-571, the residents of the area had become more and more edgy. For the first time most could remember, the farmers actually brought their livestock into the barns for the night, carefully locking the doors. Pets had been called in early, and though most whined about being stuck indoors, their owners were very reluctant to let them back out.

The darkness completely took over the land, and everyone was nervous.

Folks, already extremely tired from their early rise this morning and the long day, waited to see what this night would bring. An unusual number of lights were on in the town's homes, even in rooms that were empty or unused. Outdoor lights were left on all night.

Only Jack Cooper and Lloyd Horner completely closed up their businesses and left them in the darkness. They weren't about to run up their electricity bills, especially since no one would be in either the bar or the Mercantile.

Once home, Jimmy Dean locked the doors of his house tightly for the first time ever. Most folks way out here didn't even have keys for their homes, and locking them when they were home was never even an option. But this night, Jimmy Dean was scared more than ever before. He even pulled the curtains closed on the windows in the living room and dining room. He then went down to his bedroom and settled into bed, desperately hugging his sleeping wife. He, however, didn't sleep at all that night.

McClusky Farm (I)

Like the other farmers on the Dredge, Tom McClusky brought his horses and chickens in for the night. The horses resented it greatly, but he figured that they'd appreciate the safety and security later in the night if that wild howling began again. If nothing else, it would give him peace of mind.

His chickens, normally free-range and running wild around the yard, were gathered up and ushered into their coop. Tom knew something about losing a chicken every once in a while; if one wandered too far into the Dredge, it was bound to become a meal for the many scavengers that were home to the area. But that unnerving howl the night before was quite unlike any scavenger he'd encountered before. Whatever made that noise sounded fully capable of making a meal out of several of his hens. Losing one chicken happened occasionally; losing more would be unacceptable and certainly unprofitable.

With over an hour of daylight to spare, the livestock was safely tucked away. The barn door, though not locked, was latched tightly. And the coop out back was secured. Tom paused in the rapidly diminishing daylight, removing his John Deere cap and running his rough, callused fingers through his graying hair. His eyes moved from the latched barn to the coop and then out to the Dredge beyond. Already the dark shadows were creeping westward from the Au Sable Forest. His fingers crept down the back of his head and around his neck to the neatly trimmed beard on his chin. He continued to stare out into the wilderness, partly curious and partly worried about what might be lurking out there.

His rational mind told him there was little to be concerned about. It was more than likely a bobcat or a loony coyote. Maybe even a sick or deranged animal, that did happen every once in a while. If it was suffering, it might make such a noise. It could even be a bear that simply needed directions to a much more remote environment farther north in the state. He'd never heard a bear before, and he was pretty sure such animals didn't make a noise like the one they'd heard last night. But one couldn't be sure.

And most likely, it was a just a one-time event. Whatever animal made that shriek was probably miles away by now, probably having moved on many hours ago, before the daylight even poked its rosy head over the trees of the Au Sable. Or if it was injured or sick, it may even have met its maker by now.

However, Tom's irrational side, normally buried deep beneath his disciplined, farmer's mind, sent up question after question to his brain, questions he was unable to answer. *So what is it? What could make that noise? What if it does come back? What if it decides to hang around a bit?*

His eyes were suddenly drawn by the tall grasses of the Dredge, lightly swaying in the breeze that blew down from the north. Even in mid-June the grasses were already four feet high. Anything could be lurking out there, hiding in the tall grass. Anything could be watching him right that moment, looking him over, studying him, searching right through to his soul for weaknesses and frailties. The intense, glowing eyes of a predator boring its gaze into him, trying to decide if he'd be a better snack than a chicken.

A shiver ran down his spine. He gave a short, half-hearted laugh. Spooked himself silly, he did! That wasn't normally like himself, creating ghosts and specters in his head. In his fifty-odd years, he wasn't one to be spooked, especially by something that probably only existed in his mind.

Yet, that forest was daunting. There was a lot of wilderness out there, certainly acres and acres of land where no humans had tread. Shoot, there weren't even roads out in to most of that space. Come to think of it, very few even hunted out in the Au Sable Forest. Thousands of acres of dense pine and cedar forest lay unexplored, a forest so thick that a man (and not just a squirrel, mind you) could cross from one side to the other without having to put his feet on the ground. Considering that it was interspersed with swampy lowlands as well, it was a relatively un-appealing place to visit.

Tom shivered again despite the high heat of the day (it had topped out at 94 degrees, for the third time this month already). He gave one last glance at the Dredge that night, eyes squinted, before retiring to the safety of his house.

***

Like most of the other residents of Sigma, Tom and his wife awoke to the shrill, piercing shriek at 12:24 a.m. They both sat upright as if they had been expecting the sound at any minute. They had, in fact, hardly slept. Both of them had lain awake for a long time, lost in their own thoughts, wondering and waiting. This time, they didn't have to wait too long into the night.

The howl came again, and they both realized it was quite a ways away, surely farther north on the Dredge, at least near the middle of town or even beyond.

They had no idea that their farm had already been visited.

***

All across Sigma, though the local farmers thought they'd secured their farms tightly, nothing could stop the carnage on this second night of the siege. The creature belonging to that awful, bloodcurdling scream was not to be denied.

Tuesday

McClusky Farm (II)

Tom McClusky stared, his mouth open in disbelief, at the scene before him.

The faded paint, once a bright red, was scarred with deep grooves that could only be claw marks. Together, they formed slashing arcs across the weathered board siding. Tom walked closer to the building and traced the scars with his fingers. Four cuts in unison, four distinct claw marks. And they were wide, certainly wide enough for him to scrape his own fingernails along in the grooves. He couldn't think of any animal in the north with claws that wide.

Tom was still dead tired from the lack of sleep on Sunday night, and there had been no sleep after 12:30 last night. His eyes were already blinking excessively. He'd have to catch up on his sleep somehow, and soon. Tom hadn't taken an afternoon nap since the end of the NFL season last winter. Normally the days of spring, summer, and fall were packed from sunup to sundown. But today might just be an exception. *I might need a nap*, he thought, *before the afternoon gets too far underway.*

Tom had certainly seen claw marks before. As a youth, he'd hunted black bear a few times in the Tahquamenon region of the Upper Peninsula, and the bears always left their calling card in such ways. But these marks were very different. For one, they covered a wide span, nearly five feet in total from one end of the scrape to the other. And, strangely, some were very high up on the side of the barn. Tom reached up, tracing them again with his fingers. From his six-foot frame, his hands stretched up another foot and a half. Whatever made these marks could stand and reach up at least seven and a half feet. *That's one big mother*, Tom thought. Black bears weren't known for reaching that high; they preferred to stay on four legs and only scraped the trees they could basically hug when standing. Besides, the long arcing of the marks indicated something with long front legs; otherwise, the creature responsible would simply fall over from extending too far up. His mind kept returning to the thought of a major predator hanging around their little community as his eyes kept returning to the height of the claw marks.

Whatever made these marks, whatever made that awful noise again last night, it certainly wasn't going away on its own. It was here for a purpose.

How he and his wife had slept through this onslaught he'd never know. The vandalism must have happened while they were asleep but before the howling occurred farther on down the Dredge. At least the horses were okay. Being in the barn, their frantic neighs would not have made it all the way to the farmhouse.

Luckily, the barn doors were still bolted tightly, though they were scraped up even worse than the side wall. But they had held, and the horses inside were all accounted for. And they weren't even all that riled up this morning. Since they were fine, Tom went back outside, sighing once again over the extent of the wreckage.

But despite the damage here, things were even worse on the back side of the barn. Tom followed the scrapes around the corner and stopped dead in his tracks. His left hand shot up to cover his mouth which had dropped open for the second time this morning. The homemade chicken coop was a disaster. Bloody feathers plastered the walls and ceiling. A pair of loose feathers still fluttered about in the slight breeze. The floor was the worst—feet, legs, and bony carcasses lay strewn about, like islands in a thick pool of deep red goo. The chicken wire covering the coop was shredded. Huge, gaping holes were ripped into the sides as if by some gigantic can opener. Most frightening of all was that the damage seemed effortless.

All around the coop, errant feathers littered the hard packed ground, the otherwise dry soil now stained a dark rusty color. Of the chicken carcasses, there was no sign, other than the bits and pieces strewn about in the coop and yard.

He'd butchered his own chickens for dozens of years, but never in his life had he seen such carnage as the scene before him. It was inhuman. *Predatory*, his mind spat at him. *Something, some predator, came here and fed. And you're seeing the awful results of that feeding.* Yet, he'd never seen, never heard of any predator or scavenger that made such a god-awful mess.

A moment later, the light breeze changed direction and he received a brief smell of the violence before him. The alkaline smell of blood and entrails mixed with something heavier, something musky, dirty, and yet deeply offensive. It was like the worst case of wet-dog smell he'd ever encountered, like a wet dog that was buried in compost and came back from the dead up through the soil. Tom's gorge rose, and he turned away, planting his hands on his knees and vomiting up his dinner from the night before. There was little left in his stomach, and he choked a bit on the bile.

He spit, then wiped his mouth on his sleeve. *You reap what you sow*, his father had always told him. And now he'd have to clean up this mess before his wife came outside and saw it. Her reaction wouldn't be nearly as nice as his was.

His eyes rose and followed the trail of blood out into the Dredge. *Somewhere out there, something is watching us*, he thought. *Something is preying on us, our fears, our farms, our very lives. This thing isn't going anywhere.* And of course, the worst thought entered his mind: *we're going to have to do something about this thing.*

Sigma (V)

Jimmy Dean fell asleep on the job and nearly severed his left hand. Only a last second reaction saved the hand, though he did suffer a fairly long cut. Docked a half-day's pay, he was sent home early, where he collapsed on the old pull-out sofa in his living room. His body didn't even notice that he was lying down upon a half an army of G.I. Joe figures. Fortunately for him, his wife had taken the kids shopping for the afternoon in Traverse City. He had garnered a grand total of four hours of sleep since the howling began on Sunday night, and this was the only way he could put his mental stress on hold. Grief over his dead friend mingled with the impossible sight he'd seen the night before. He knew that the creature he saw in the headlights was real and not a figment of his alcohol-induced imagination. And he knew that the creature he saw was the originator of those horrible nightly screams. But beyond that, he had no idea what to do with this information. Who could he tell? Who would believe him?

***

Nancy Butler was sure that today was the day. Or probably the day. When it came down to it, leaving her husband was harder than she initially thought.

She'd intended it to be a quick departure; leave him a note on the table, load up the car with the essentials (already packed, of course), and skip town. But now that the moment was upon her, she kept finding reasons to delay it. She'd wanted to leave last Sunday night, but she had still found herself heading home after work. Considering the rude homecoming she'd endured, she cursed herself for not leaving him that night.

Their marriage was not only on the rocks, it had scraped bottom. Rick still seemed oblivious to it, and that made her even more sure it was time to split.

Plus the new love of her life had given her a spark she hadn't felt in years. Their affair had been underway since mid-winter, when Nancy started telling her husband she was picking up extra hours on the afternoon shift.

Her lover had convinced her to run off with him. Leave it all behind her: the unemployed husband, the run-down house in the middle of nowhere, the life that was stealing her youth.

While Rick snored loudly, Nancy threw some more of her clothes and personal items in yet another bag and dragged it out to the trunk of her Cavalier. Already the trunk was nearly full, and she had to squeeze it in.

Besides, things around here were getting a bit too uncomfortable. That nightly howling was getting under her skin. She didn't think she could take one more night coming home late in the darkness and wondering if she'd hear that again. And would it be closer next time? And what on earth could have made such a horrific sound? She was sure she didn't want to stick around to find out.

Yes, maybe today was the day. *Carpe Diem*, she'd learned that somewhere along the line.

***

Stevie knew exactly what was out in the darkness of the forest. He'd heard the song, and he believed it.

His grandfather took out his hearing aids each night before retiring to bed. He didn't have to worry about hearing any crazy sounds in the depths of the night.

Though Stevie had only heard the howling in the distance last night, it was something else that had spooked him so badly that he'd wet the bed for the first time in fifteen years.

Outside the thin panes of window glass, scratching sounds could be heard. Stevie recognized two distinct noises—one was the sound of scratching on the dry, hard-packed ground of their backyard. He was pretty sure it was toe claws grating on the multitude of pebbles and rocks. The second was the sound of fingernails on a chalkboard. Only this, he knew beyond a shadow of a doubt, was not fingernails, but instead claws scraping on the little barn-shaped utility shed behind their trailer.

The song had first been played on the radio on April Fool's Day. Stevie knew that for a fact. He almost didn't make it to work that day, certain that the Dogman was going to jump out of the woods and knock him right off his bike. The forest seemed a bit creepier to him since that song started playing, a bit more dark, dank, and foreboding.

He hadn't set foot in the woods all spring or summer.

And now, hearing those awful sounds in the darkness (and yes, it was very dark at their home—they didn't have any of those fancy outdoor lights), Stevie knew that the creature had somehow left the confines of a song on the radio and had emerged into reality here in his little town. The Dogman had come to Sigma.

Eric (III)

His footsteps stopped crunching on the twigs and the dried leaves of yesteryear. The extremely dried leaves. *God, this whole place could go up with the slightest spark*, Eric thought.

After walking for what seemed like miles in the Sigma wilderness, he should have been glad to take a rest. However, what caught his eye was anything but a pleasing sight.

It was a beautiful mid-morning. Shafts of sunlight stole their way down through the thick canopy of branches and leaves, illuminating the forest floor in scattered patches. Little spider webs connecting the forest's large fiddle ferns still dangled droplets of dew in mid-air, catching the rays of light and sparkling like tiny diamonds. A pair of whippoorwills called to each other every thirty seconds or so, as if playing tag, in the tree canopy above Eric.

He paused before bending down to examine the carcass on the ground before him, swatting away a score of blackflies. His DNR training immediately identified it as a yearling doe, though there was little left, making the determination a bit more difficult. It had been dead only a few days, that was for sure. And it had been brutally ripped apart.

Judging by the remains and his past experience, Eric guessed the doe was probably a hundred and twenty pounds. His next guess was that there was less than 20 percent of it left.

Eric's attention then turned to the surrounding area. There was blood for a few feet around, indicating that this was the site of the kill. The doe was alive and pumping blood like a champ when it was finally done in. Eric found it interesting that there was no blood trail. He checked carefully to be sure. A young, healthy doe could push on for quite a ways, even after being injured.

It wasn't shot, and it hadn't died of any accident. What he saw here was an attack, contained in close quarters. He was positive of it.

So what could attack a doe without warning, drop it immediately, and consume nearly the entire animal in only a few short days?

You know what it is, his mind said. *The same thing that's been scaring these folks at night. The same thing that was at the scene of that pickup wreck.*

You don't know that for certain. It was just that single paw print, and even that's history now. It was wiped out by the proper authorities.

And yet his mind kept telling him this was related. He just knew it had to be.

Eric brushed his hand past his ear, swatting away an annoying mosquito. *Just wouldn't be the swamp without the bugs attacking you whenever you stop*, he thought. *Even if the swamp was mostly dried up.*

He took out his small pad of paper and jotted down several notes as he made his official examination. Best thing was to document everything this time. His first job was to ensure that this wasn't a poaching incident. That part wasn't too hard. There was nothing to indicate that the animal was killed by a human. By the huge amount of blood splatter, it also didn't seem to be natural causes. So what could take down a powerful animal, giving no opportunity for escape? There was no great predator here in northern Michigan that could do this. Sure there were predators in the world that could kill a yearling, but not around here. But unless the animal was sick and dying already, there was little other explanation for its condition.

Maybe that's it—it was already dying, he thought. *That would explain it.*

Yeah, right. And maybe tomorrow I'll be promoted to Sergeant, and the Warden can bring me coffee every morning.

His notes on the carcass completed, Eric then made a careful examination of the surrounding area. Slowly he strolled around the site, his boots careful not to disturb anything. His eyes darted from ferns and soil to branches and leaves, looking for any clues. He'd covered a wide swath of area and was nearly back where he started when he noticed the track in the soft soil beneath a covering of ferns.

Eric's eyes widened as he recognized the impression left behind like some clue in a mystery case. It was the same track he'd seen a day ago on a dirt road several miles from here. It was the same track found in the vicinity of a vehicle accident that claimed the life of a local man. It was the same track that had bothered him all last night and most of the day today.

His finger slowly traced the air just above the track, being sure not to touch the soft soil.

Sure it looked like a wolf or coyote, or at least some sort of canine. Any conservation officer could identify it easily. That wasn't the problem. The problem was that wolves didn't belong this far south in the Lower Peninsula. There were a few breeding pairs in the U.P. but none here, let alone in Kalkaska County. And the second problem, Eric soon realized, was the size of the track. It was nearly twice the size of what a regular wolf track would be.

Considering that he was on foot, he didn't have everything he'd need for collecting evidence. Eric looked up and sighed, thinking of the long trip he'd have walking back to his truck, and then returning all the way back here again. Since there was no way he would be able to drive any closer to this spot, he'd have to carry an evidence bag as well as his plaster casting materials. That way he could preserve a copy of this creature's tracks as evidence.

His sigh changed quickly though as a smile spread over his face. Sure, it might be a hike back to the truck, but he was going to get the evidence he so desperately wanted. This was a situation unlike any he'd ever imagined, a situation that conservation officers everywhere dreamed of—yet despised. This was actual evidence of an as-of-yet undiscovered creature. The implications were huge. And though he was the one who had discovered it, this needed to go over his head very quickly.

The lab at Michigan State was going to go nuts over this one!

Brian on the Dredge (II)

It was a rather tight squeeze inside Brian's fort on the Dredge. He and Stevie were playing with a couple of the Star Wars figurines that had taken up permanent residence in the fort. Though Brian was fairly small for his age, Stevie was a child in an adult's body; he consumed nearly half the square footage of the little outpost.

They were in the midst of an adventure where Luke and Han (played by Brian) were saving the princess from a loud, howling (and still unseen) monster that was living up in the tree that held up the fort's roof.

Stevie liked the creature characters better, so he played with Hammerhead and Bib Fortuna. Stevie also didn't quite get the concept of the good guys against the bad guys, so he had no problem with the villainous side of the adventure. He was just tickled that he had someone to play with. At least he would have something to do after work other than just return home; his grandfather was very nice, but he wasn't really a "friend" with whom he could play.

"I know what's making all that racket," Stevie said quietly, absently.

Brian perked up, his eyes locking with Stevie's. A long moment passed before he asked, "So, what is it?"

"It's that Dogman, just like in that song on the radio." Stevie's attention returned to Hammerhead blasting away at the tree trunk.

Brian was a bit confused. "What's that song, Stevie?"

Stevie smiled, his crooked front teeth standing out on his amicable face. Then he playfully reached out and pushed Brian's shoulder with his open palm. "That Dogman song they play on the radio, silly! Channel one-oh-three point five, today's classic country favorites!" He looked sideways at Brian. "Don't you like country music?"

Brian gave a little snort of laughter at Stevie's simple honesty. "My dad only listens to the classic rock station, and he says country songs aren't good for nothing." Brian kept giggling. "He says if you play a country song backward, you get your house back, your truck back, your wife back, and your dog back."

Stevie didn't quite catch onto the joke, but he did respond to the younger boy's doubling over with giggles. The older boy couldn't help but start laughing himself. Before long, the two of them were rolling on the matted grass floor of the fort as only middle school age boys can do. Stevie might be ten years older, but his mind was on the same track as Brian's.

Finally, as they regained their composure, Brian was able to ask Stevie about the song he'd heard. "So, what's a Dogman, Stevie?"

The older boy paused in his play and gained a look of seriousness. "Oh, it's really scary. It's a monster out in the woods. I heard the whole thing and remembered it all, yes I did.

"The Dogman looks like a huge wolf, but it walks around like a person too. In the song, there's screams in the night, howls and grunts, just like we're hearing out here at night."

Brian was amazed by Stevie's story. "What else does the song say?"

Stevie actually did a fairly good rendition of "The Legend," the ballad of the Dogman, though his singing left a lot to be desired. He got all of the stanzas correct, even if he did miss a few of the words in the song. Brian got the gist of it.

"There's folks that get scared to death, and even animals, too," Stevie finished.

"Is it true?" Brian asked. His mind was already connecting the images from the song with the occurrences that were happening around Sigma.

"It's gotta be true, it's on the radio, isn't it?" Stevie retorted. To him, it was the gospel.

Brian sat amazed. "Wow," he finally managed to say, his voice trailing off. "That's something, isn't it?"

"I hope I never meet the Dogman, no sir, I sure don't," Stevie said gravely. "That song scares me something awful every time I hear it."

"Do you think that's what's really out here? Is the Dogman really here, Stevie?"

Stevie gulped and hunched his shoulders. "I dunno. I hope not. It sure doesn't sound very nice, does it?"

Scott on the Dredge

Scott Hailey kicked the old, rusted can squarely on its side, propelling it into a graceful arc. It landed in the tall grass of the Dredge, about twenty feet away. A divot of dry gray soil, struck up by the toe of his faded Nikes, sprayed fine dust that settled its way to the ground before him.

There was plenty of junk out here to kick around in the Dredge. And it was better pickings than the junkyard behind Randall's, which consisted mostly of old cars and washing machines and such stuff. Sure, you could sneak out there when Tough Joe wasn't home and take out your aggressions on a large piece of metal. Scott had done everything from swinging an axe into a stove's glass front to pounding away on sun roofs with a hammer to sharp shooting side mirrors of cars with his .22 rifle.

But Scott preferred being out in the wide open air of the Dredge. It made him think of the wide open spaces out West. Some of the junk here actually traced its roots back to the turn of the century. Old beer bottles, made from the thick, brown glass that could take a beating before busting were here in abundance. Once, he'd even found a partially intact wagon wheel, or at least a few spindle spokes and part of its iron clad rim.

Rather than destroy things he found on the Dredge (unless it was an old can), Scott spent time examining them with all the care of a trained archaeologist. Of course, he'd never be mistaken for an academic; his grades at school were dismal, and he generally didn't care much for book learning or studying or homework. But he was anything but a dumb kid. His interests were just in the real world—exploring in a hands-on fashion.

But beside the ancient treasures, there were plenty of more recent artifacts. Beer cans, broken clay pigeons, empty shotgun shells. The Dredge was a testament to typical redneck sports.

You never knew what you'd find out on the Dredge.

True to form, Scott saw a figure (well, actually just a head above the tall grass) off about a hundred yards in the distance. Scott immediately knew, judging by the person's height and ball cap that it was Brian Alexander, Jr. *What's Brian doing out on my field today?* Scott mused to himself. *That little pansy should be indoors playing with his toys.*

Scott was a bully because his dad was a bully. Though this fact had never crossed his mind, it was the truth nonetheless. He endured his dad's teasing and pushing around, and then turned around and did the same to other kids.

But his attention was caught by another figure a ways off in the other direction. Above the grass, he could see a head with a ponytail sticking out the back.

His face lit up. Now this was more interesting than messing with Brian. With a half grin on his pimply face, Scott turned to walk south through the Dredge.

Eric (IV)

It was the right place. It was the right location. He'd walked the same path. He could even see his own trail of breadcrumbs, the scuffling of the leaves where he'd tread earlier.

Eric recognized the huge, ancient oak with its gigantic main branches reaching ever skyward. He remembered it well because of its unusual shape. He even named it the "hanging tree" because it looked the part.

He saw the ferns he'd bent over on his way through. Eric even occasionally saw one of his own footprints.

But what he didn't see was any evidence of the carcass. Even the quintessential track was gone, wiped away into oblivion.

Unable to believe it, Eric continued to canvass the area. He was certain he was in the correct spot because the blood splatter was still visible on the ferns and on the dried leaves. However, his evidence was gone.

Sure it had been nearly six hours since he'd been here. Earlier, when he had gotten back to his truck, he found, of course, that the Plaster of Paris had been there so long it had hardened into a white brick. *Probably been there since Nixon was in office*, Eric thought to himself, angrily throwing the solid chunk into the bed of his truck where it smashed into a thousand dusty chips. Several song birds were scared up by the loud clang, and Eric swore loudly in the otherwise quiet woods.

Since a plaster cast of the monster track he'd found was the key piece of evidence, a trip back to headquarters, though he hated to leave, was absolutely required. Driving wildly down the narrow dirt road, Eric practically flew back to the office. Once there, much to his dismay, the Plaster of Paris was out of stock and currently on back order with the supplier.

Eric threw his hands up in disgust before Sarah smugly suggested that he call one of the other on-duty officers and borrow some. Todd Lindell was happy to meet him for a late lunch, Eric's treat. All in all, it seemed a small price to pay.

Returning as quickly as he could, the old truck skipping crazily over the rough roads, Eric managed to park at the same spot. He practically jumped from the cab, swinging his day pack over one shoulder in a hurry to get back to the site.

As it turned out, all that run around was for naught.

Now the sun had closed its distance to the horizon. Shadows began to creep across the forest floor. According to his watch, it was only 6:45, though it felt much later because the light had difficulty penetrating the thick canopy of leaves.

Eric swore again, loudly enough to echo between the large, ancient tree trunks. He just couldn't believe that his evidence was all gone. Just gone.

It didn't make any sense. How could the carcass and the track just disappear? Obviously, someone had been here. *Or something*, that pesky voice said in his mind.

Suddenly, Eric straightened up and carefully looked around him. Other than his swiveling head, his body went rigid. Despite the hot afternoon air, a deep chill wracked his body. He suddenly wanted to be someplace else. Fast. It didn't matter that he was armed and trained to deal with most anything that he could happen upon in the outdoors, be it human or animal.

The day just seemed a little too dark, the night a little too close for comfort. If something had been here, in broad daylight, it could come back. It could be here watching him right this minute.

Eric shivered again and spun a complete circle, looking off into the thick foliage of the forest. He even glanced upward to the tree boughs, searching carefully for a sign, a manifestation of what he was sensing.

He just couldn't shake the feeling that he was being watched. Eric wasn't one to be easily spooked, nor had he ever been. He was always the kid who could watch the axe-murderer movies, those with the blood and guts and the suspenseful forest jaunts at a blood-bathed summer camp.

But it was quite another thing to be living with real terror.

He'd seen the size of the track, twice even. He knew it was huge, bigger than any wolf on record. And he'd seen the deer carcass. Despite the fact that neither was here now, Eric's mind could envision several manifestations of the creature that had initially left these clues for him. It was not a pretty picture.

An immediate decision was made. Eric sidestepped his way back to the trail, mindful to monitor the environment around him. Crickets continued to chirp their lonely song as night approached, while a solitary chickadee called far above in the branches hidden from the forest floor.

Head swiveling on his shoulders, the young officer quickly made his way back through the woods. He did not out right run back, but he was breathing heavily and sweat stains soon covered his khaki shirt.

Every noise in the depths of the forest drew his immediate and undivided attention. The snap of a branch off to his left nearly caused him to leap several feet backward.

The sun continued to descend. The shadows of the huge, menacing trees lengthened. The ferns and undergrowth lost their bright luster.

Finally the truck came back into view. Eric could hold out no longer; he sprinted the remaining thirty yards to the relative safety of his vehicle. He didn't even bother to unload his pack, but climbed into the cab still encumbered with its bulk upon his back. Digging into his pockets, he finally freed his car keys and was fumbling with the ignition when the long, low, forlorn howl cascaded through the forest.

It came again. It wasn't all that loud, but the sound carried. It was a lonely, deep and moaning sound that made Eric's skin crawl.

He froze, scared out of his wits. His mind raced with apparitions of all sorts. He was sure the sound had come from the trail behind him. It didn't sound all that close, but the woods had a way of disguising its noises. It could be far off in the distance or right nearby.

Either way, Eric wasn't going to stick around. Sure he had a natural curiosity to find out what kind of creature could have left such evidence. But his penchant for survival far outweighed his curiosity. Some instinct, deeply hidden away, had come roaring back to the surface. It insisted that he get out of here at once.

His fingers tightly gripped the ignition key until he had calmed himself. He then easily fired up the old beast and dropped it into gear. He tore off down the dirt road for the second time today, kicking up a cloud of dust and gravel, obscuring the environment behind him.

Jane (II)

Two sleepless nights in a row only put a slight damper on Jane Whitman's attitude. Unlike many of the other residents of the little town, she could easily nap her afternoons away, making up for the lack of sleep. It was one of the few perks of being retired and living alone—no job to go to and nobody to be accountable to, or for. However, her afternoon siestas were still plagued by horrible nightmares the likes of which she had thought she'd left in her early teenage years.

Just as troubling (if not more so) as the haunting howls that filled the dark night was the disappearance of two more of her cats, her little darlings, in the past two days. Jane nearly worried herself sick over their vanishing. Somehow she knew that they were gone for good, probably at the hands of whatever was making that awful noise on the Dredge at night.

Only Simba was left. *Good old Simba*, she thought. He was the oldest of her houseguests, her only children. Simba had also been with her the longest of any of the cats so far, nearly fifteen years now. Probably the reason he was still around now was his physical stature. Simba weighed in at almost twenty-five pounds. Neutered long ago, Simba had grown quite fat, his own saddlebag stomach nearly dragging on the ground. The chubby, tan, tiger-striped kitty rarely ever left the house; he certainly knew he had it too good to leave.

Of course, Simba was Jane's favorite. He always cuddled up with her on the couch at night. The other cats would even defer the best spot when he sauntered into the little living room. Simba was the outright king.

Darkness had fallen once again on the little village. Like the other residents, Jane left her few room lamps on all night long. The diffused yellow light spilled lazily from the little windows of her stone cottage, windows that should have been open to the few cool night breezes. Now they were closed and tightly locked. Even the back door was closed and bolted, the screen door useless and certainly not living up to its potential. Normally the back door was open so that the cats could use the kitty door to come and go as they pleased. But things were different now; things had changed drastically in the once peaceful country setting of Sigma.

Jane wasn't sure how long it would take before that spine-tingling sound erupted again this night. It hadn't just been coming from out on the Dredge, though that was where it always seemed to begin from and return to. The howling had been heard all around. Listening carefully, Jane had been able to tell if it was nearby or far off. And sometimes it had seemed to be coming from everywhere at once, as if it pierced right through the walls of her home and down into her very soul. It had echoed powerfully over the open air of the Dredge and through the myriad of thick tree trunks in the Au Sable. When it was close, as it had been last night, she had just known that the maker of the noise was circling her own home, just off in the woods beyond her backyard.

She hadn't slept either of the previous two nights, and she didn't anticipate any more rest this evening. It was just a matter of when it would begin. And she wondered what pets around town would disappear tonight, or if the creature making these truly terrible shrieks would up the ante and take out something even bigger.

Simba had eaten more than his share of dinner this evening. Jane continued to put out more food in the vain hopes that her other darlings would return, but the only one to show up was Simba, who helped himself to generous portions from the community bowl.

Comfortable on the couch, Jane stared out the small living room window at the lighted yard outside and waited anxiously for the noises to begin again. On Sunday night, she had been awakened by the howling around 2:30. On Monday, it had started up around 12:30. Jane was waiting to see if the noises would be even earlier tonight. She had an eerie feeling it would.

She was nervously sipping at a cup of herbal tea, thinking of her missing pets, when it suddenly hit her. She looked down at her side, and the cup of tea wavered in her hand. Simba was not in his usual spot. Jane was so used to him being there cuddled up against her hip that she hadn't thought to look for him.

Her eyes opened wide in fear, and the corners of her mouth trembled. She sat forward on the edge of the couch cushion, her eyes darting around the room. From her vantage point she could see most of the little house. But Simba was nowhere to be found.

Jane stood up and called his name a few times, becoming more and more nervous as the seconds ticked by on the weathered old maritime clock on the mantle.

And then she heard it, that awful sound from the nightmares of past nights, and she froze in mid-step. It wasn't a howl this time; it was more of a deep growl. It sent chills down her spine, and the little tea cup slipped from her old fingers, spilling its liquid contents all over the hand-woven rug. The noise was very clear, though she judged it a mile or more away on the Dredge.

But her Simba was missing, and that was the immediate danger. Fearing the worst, Jane searched all over the little house. She frantically called his name over and over but to no avail.

The growl came again, and then in mid-roll it changed pitch and became the high, dreadful howling that Sigma had not quite gotten used to. Jane's hands flew to cover her ears in an attempt to block the sound. She cringed, her eyes shut, her mouth letting out a small, frightened squeak.

When she was sure that it was over, Jane glanced out the living room window at the pool of light in her yard. There, just at the edge of the shadows, she saw two little eyes glowing back at her. She froze, feet anchored to the floor. Her heart began hammering in her chest as her breath caught, stuck in her throat.

After a few long, tense seconds of staring, Jane watched as the creature stepped its way into the flood of yellow light. Her breathing resumed harshly (she thought she might begin to hyperventilate), but her tense body relaxed as Simba waddled his way into the part of the yard that she could see in the surrounding darkness. One frail hand made its way to her heart, feeling the rapid beating beneath her nightshirt.

This moment of relief passed instantly as she realized her baby was out there with that creature. She watched another few seconds as Simba lazily plodded his way around the yard, seemingly uninterested in going inside or in whatever being produced that awful screeching. Jane realized she had to go get him right away, before the owner of that howl decided to head their way.

She quickly slipped on her robe and shuffled her slippered feet toward the kitchen, wondering how on earth Simba had made it outside. The kitty entrance was in the screen door, not in the solid oak door, which was now closed and locked.

Jane turned the deadbolt, opened the door and called for Simba through the screen. The fat cat continued to lollygag his way around the edge of the light, swatting at june bugs and nibbling at dandelions. Jane called twice more, but the cat either couldn't hear her (not likely) or chose to ignore her (she'd bet her monthly social security check on that one).

Nervously, the old woman creaked open the screen door a few inches, glancing around the yard. Only a few peepers and of course the buzzing of the june bugs broke the silence of the summer night. She tried calling for Simba one last time, but just as before, he went about his business, seemingly deaf to her voice.

There had been no report from the Dredge—no howling, screeching, or growling for several minutes now. Simba was still wandering around the edge of the light, and Jane was worried that he might disappear at any moment.

Jane took a deep breath and made the decision. Carefully, quietly, she slipped out the screen door, stepped down the two cinderblock steps, and made her way across the yard to where Simba was playing.

Sigma (VI)

The heyday of Sigma was long past. The town proper probably reached its highest population in the mid-fifties. Not long afterward, the train tracks that ran east from Traverse City to Grayling were pulled up. The logging business had finished its long tour in Sigma, and the town suffered a long, slow suffocation.

In 1974, the Sinclair went belly up. There just wasn't enough business here to warrant a gas station any longer. The pumps were taken down (though the underground tanks were still buried there, unbeknown to the EPA and the DNR), and the building was eventually sold to Joe Randall. With no zoning codes in effect, Joe turned the gas station store into his own home, and he moved his hauling business into the large vacant lot behind.

The little town barbershop, long since closed, resided in an annex on the left side of the Mercantile. It was never boarded up, and the single, solitary window was so caked with road dust that no one could see inside. Not that there was much to look at anyway. It mostly served as a long-term storage shed for Jack Cooper's store. Jack owned the rights to it, considering that it was a part of his building. But since the old barber had died, he'd not had much interest in merging the two and expanding the store. It just didn't seem right.

Permanent residences were a rarity in Sigma, even in the times of the lumber camps. In the times past, the Mercantile building served as the basic "company store" and Jack Cooper's house was the home of the camp foreman. The loggers stayed in a series of simple log cabins, which were torn down sometime around 1955 so that the ball field could be built.

A few other small houses near the center of town were erected by industrious business owners who thought to capitalize on the captive work force. However, these newcomers soon realized that there was little they could offer the lumberjacks, and that these roughnecks had little cash in hand to partake in goods or services. Most of the salaries were kept on the ledgers, exchanged at the Mercantile, and finally paid out in full at the end of the season for those who returned south to their homes.

The loss of the railroad and the lumber camp devastated the area. The property values plummeted. Folks who could moved away, and quickly. Before long, house trailers comprised the only new homes going up in Sigma.

A few farmers built on the vast expanse of the Dredge, but the soil wasn't good for much except the wild grasses already growing there. The land was fine for raising livestock, but ranchers had to buy their winter hay from other spots in the county. It just wouldn't grow on the Dredge.

The only folks moving into Sigma were either those who had no other place they could afford to go, or those who chose to disappear from society.

Disappearances would soon become a more common occurrence in town.

Bonnie (I)

Her dolls and stuffed animals stared at her across the dark bedroom. Some folks might have been unnerved by dozens of tiny, plastic eyes staring—cold and lifeless—back at them. However, they didn't cause any fear or panic for Bonnie. She was used to them. They were comforting. They were a source of strength, of stability.

She didn't have to see what happened out in the living room after she'd gone to bed. She could hear it well enough through the thin walls, and her mind played out the scene like it was some after-school TV special.

In her twelve short years, her father had never hit her. But the day was coming soon, she was sure of that.

For the time being, her mother took the brunt of his physical abuse.

He yelled several times, each a step up on a rising crescendo that would end with an audible "smack" that signaled her mother receiving a reminder of who was the boss. Then he'd yell at her for interrupting whatever he was watching on TV because he had to deal with her. Bonnie could almost hear her mother, tears spilling down her cheeks, pleading, "I'm sorry, I'm sorry," over and over.

Her father was especially irritable these past few days, mainly because of the noises they'd all heard at night. He wasn't sleeping well, and even a few drinks didn't seem to do the trick. The echoing howl seemed to funnel right into their trailer, which was situated near the Dredge at the south end of town. She didn't know her father to be afraid of anything, but these noises were aggravating him to no end.

Bonnie's mother, however, was terrified more by her husband than some noise out on the Dredge. At least the owner of that sound wouldn't pop into their house and slap her around for burning dinner or forgetting to pick up a new case of Milwaukee's Best.

And to make matters worse, there was Scott. Tears welled up in her eyes as she thought back to this afternoon. There she was, out picking wildflowers on the Dredge, and out of nowhere, that bully shows up. She'd hardly showed that he scared her—she wouldn't give him the satisfaction. But what a creep! Sneaking up on her through the tall grass.

And then the teasing started up. "Whatcha doing, Little Miss Pretty? Pickin' flowers for me? Aw, that's so nice of you." Before she could stop him, he'd grabbed the handful of delicate, colorful flowers from her hands.

"Give 'em back, give 'em back now! Those are for my mom!" She'd cried. And then a few tears did well up in her eyes. He was a bully and she was sure he was a lot worse too. There was no way she wanted to be alone with him, especially way out there. She certainly didn't trust him to keep his hands to himself. And there was nobody else around. There were a lot of times on the school bus that he'd sat next to her and put his arm around her as if he cared for her. *If he truly cared,* she thought, *he'd just leave me alone. He's so icky.* She pretty well knew what Scott was interested in, and she wanted nothing to do with him.

He kept up the teasing, of course taking it all too far. "Whatsa matter? You lose your flowers, Little Miss Pretty? Here, I give 'em to you. From me."

Between sobs that came freely, she tried to shout, "Don't call me that! Don't you know I hate that?" But it all came out as a high pitched mumble. She swatted the flowers from his hand, and they fell slowly, petals floating in the still afternoon air. In doing so, she fell back on her butt. That made her sniffle and cry even more.

Scott stepped back, momentarily stunned. But he regained his composure quickly. "Silly girl," he sneered, curling one side of his mouth. "Like I'd give you flowers anyway." He grunted, then turned and stalked off through the tall grasses, leaving her sitting on the hard soil of the Dredge.

Lying in bed, as she'd done so many nights before, Bonnie wished her life was different. She wished she could be swept away from all of this to a place with no fear: a place with no abusive fathers; a place with no abusive schoolmates; a place with no horrible howling that kept her up all night.

She cuddled up with Mr. Hutchison, her old, ratty stuffed bunny. He'd been her constant companion since she was a very little girl. A few small tears rolled down her cheeks, and though she'd probably get a few hours of sleep, she'd be up again soon.

Jane (III)

"Simba, come back here!" Jane whispered through her teeth as loudly as she could, as loudly as she dared.

Still, the kitty evaded her attempts at capture. For a fat, over-the-hill cat, Simba was still rather spry and nimble. And evasive.

Jane tightened her hands into fists, shook them at her waist, and swore under her breath. It was rather unlike her, but things were taking on a new sense of urgency at the moment. Since she had left the comfort and safety of her home, the howl had come twice again, reverberating through the sultry night air.

Now here she was, in her slippers and pink night robe, cautiously avoiding the june bugs that buzzed and scuttled around the yard. A few crickets nervously chirped at each other in the darkness. She'd been calling for the kitty for several minutes now, trying to be both unobtrusive yet authoritative. Simba, however, went on his way exploring the little intricacies of the grass, the weeds, the various insects that hopped away from him. He did give Jane one brief glance that was more contrary than acknowledging.

"Simba," she called again, this time at a normal speaking level. She stopped and darted a few glances all around, having startled herself.

Finally, Simba turned his head and stared back at her. He settled down on his haunches, legs turkeyed up beneath him, green eyes glowing back toward the far reaches of the porch light.

Jane rolled her eyes in both exasperation and relief. She wasn't nearly as nimble as she had been twenty years ago, and attempting to keep up with the cat was trying indeed. It seemed that every time she got within a few feet, he'd scamper away to another part of the yard. But this time it looked like he was ready for her, ready to be picked up and comforted and brought safely into the house.

At least that was what Jane was thinking. She'd never imagined how wrong it all was about to go.

Her whole attention was turned toward Simba, wanting only to get ahold of him and to get back inside. She'd been pressing her luck already.

Her luck ran out.

As Jane came within a few feet of the kitty and bent over to pick him up, Simba's face wrinkled up. His eyes flashed angrily upward, and his mouth opening, teeth bared, in a warning hiss.

Jane's first thought was that the little ingrate was hissing at *her*. She looked down indignantly at her baby and straightened up a little. *Well, excuse me for trying to save your little butt*, she thought. *Maybe I should have just left you out here.* Except she knew she couldn't do that, she wouldn't do that.

Simba hissed again, this time loudly, and a moment later, the cat bolted up from its squatting position and sprinted away into the forest darkness opposite the house. It happened so fast, all in one motion, that Jane stumbled a step backward in surprise.

Behind her, a low, slow growl built itself up as it crossed the small backyard.

And then she noticed the large shadow looming over her own, which seemed so small and feeble in comparison. It was upright, like that of a very large person. And yet it was as inhuman as could be. Sharp points, surely its ears, extended from the shadow's head. Its shoulders were hunched, and its arms were extending outward in a monstrous bear hug. The darkness overtook her, completely blocking the light that shined from outside her back door.

Simba hadn't hissed at her or run away from her. Playfully avoiding her was the least of his concerns.

But unlike her cat, Jane Whitman had little to defend herself. She was far too slow to even try to escape.

The growl came again. It was right behind her now, deep and throaty. She felt the beast's breath tingle the hairs on the back of her neck like some evil breeze.

Tears dripping down her cheeks, lips quivering in terror, she cowered, her hands raised, her fingers interlocked behind her head in a gesture of futile protection.

Jane had no last wish, no desire to see and face her attacker. She didn't have to wait long. The darkness, that repugnant smell of musky fur and rotten flesh, enveloped her.

Wednesday

Sigma (VII)

The lack of sleep was rapidly catching up to the residents of Sigma. Three nights in a row, the horrendous howling and shrill screeching, or just the fear of whatever could be making that awful racket, kept everyone wide awake. Some folks hid in their bedrooms, covers pulled up over their heads, refusing to peek out. Others gathered their families and huddled in a centralized room of the house. More often than not, loaded firearms accompanied the scared residents. Parents cuddled their children on their laps, whispering soothing words and lullabies. Everyone was living in a state of perpetual fear.

Some folks had only managed a handful of hours of sleep over the past three days. Half-lidded, bloodshot eyes peered out at the world. Feet shuffled slowly as they walked, and more than one person nearly tripped over themselves in an embarrassing manner. Clocks and watches were glanced at often throughout the long day, but the hours, minutes, and seconds ticked by in slow motion.

***

Jack Cooper's Mercantile ran out of coffee and No-Doz. Over at the small table in the corner, Doc and Fred had dozed off, each leaning up against an adjoining wall. Lloyd never even showed up. Jack would have run the two of them off if either one began snoring or had spilled any coffee, but luckily, they both slept like the dead. Jack wished he could join them. Instead, he pounded cup after cup of the black sludge that had replaced his normal half-way decent brew. He tried the morning crossword but his brain wouldn't work right. He ended up doodling all over the puzzle, not noticing that he'd created a sinister face in the little black and white boxes. Beneath the counter he kept his .38 fully loaded, the safety clicked off.

When the old timers finally awoke from their naps, their conversation was soft, muted. Of course, it revolved around the noises in the night, the awful howling that kept everyone awake. Not one of the three conjectured a guess as to the identity of the mysterious nocturnal stranger. At least, that is, they wouldn't make a guess out loud. It was as if mentioning the creature might make it suddenly appear.

Unbeknownst to them, Stevie, who was diligently stocking and dusting the shelves, closely tuned in on their conversation. His hands slowed over the cans and bottles as he pretended to be busy and instead eavesdropped on the old men.

The old timers might not know what the creature was, but Stevie did. Everything, each and every clue, fit. The howling that sounded like a wolf, the appearance after dark, even the stories he'd heard from folks who stopped in the store the past few days.

"You listenin' in on us, boy?" a voice hollered from across the next aisle.

Stevie was flustered and his hand knocked over a few bottles of mustard. None were broken, but the noise gave him away. He raised his head over the shelf and responded in his slow voice, "No, sir, I'm just workin'."

A moment of silence hung in the store, and then the three old timers broke out in laughter. It was a pleasant sound inside the quiet building in contrast to the seriousness of the week so far.

Embarrassed, Stevie worked his way to the back of the store.

Laughter was hard to come by in Sigma these days.

***

Lloyd Horner finally fell asleep as the sun was rising over the Dredge and didn't get around to opening the bar until 4 o'clock. It didn't matter, though, because not a soul in town was interested in a burger and a beer; everyone was willing to even forego nourishment to get some rest.

***

Jimmy Dean Holloway wasn't the only one in the area who decided to leave Sigma, though he was the first. After a second day out of work, he convinced his wife that they needed to get away for a while. He suggested going to her parent's home in Greenville. They were constantly begging Jimmy Dean and Sherri to bring the grandkids by to visit, and, besides, they had a pool for the kids to play in.

Sherri was immediately skeptical. It wasn't normal for her husband to want to spend time with his in-laws. But Jimmy Dean convinced her that it was time for some time off. In their years together, he'd never outright lied to her like he did this afternoon. He told her the mill was giving him the rest of the week off for bereavement. He told her the mill foreman told him that Buck was as good as family. He told her that he was encouraged to take a few days off and get himself together.

Truth was, he wasn't sure he ever wanted to come back.

She bought the story. Her husband's appearance the past two days had iced it. He was definitely taking his friend's death very hard. And he wasn't sleeping. He looked terrible. Living quite a ways out of town, they'd only heard the howling one night, and that was from a distance. It didn't mean much to her, and she had forgotten about it quickly enough. Sherri and the kids had slept well, and she thought Jimmy Dean had been up all night, nervous and edgy, because of Buck's accident.

There was no way he could tell his wife what he had seen. He didn't want to frighten her or the kids. And after a hard night at Horner's, as well as dealing with the death of his good friend, she might think he'd been seeing things anyway.

He knew what he'd seen, even if no one else might believe him.

Though he had never heard that song on the radio, and he didn't know the name of the creature, Jimmy Dean knew beyond a shadow of a doubt that he'd seen the Dogman. He'd lived to tell of the encounter.

And he wasn't going to press his luck. He and his family were getting out of town right after Buck's funeral. Getting out while the getting was still good.

Joe (II)

Joe Randall was sipping his second mug of hot coffee when Gary burst in through the back door nearly out of breath. Gary Atkins was always the first one in each morning at 5:30, just like clockwork, but he usually he spent the first ten minutes examining his rig. From the look on his face today, Joe knew he wasn't running in just for coffee.

"Joe," he said, a strained look of concern on his face, "you need to come see this. Outside, quick."

"What is it?" Joe's deep voice responded.

Gary appeared sick as he shook his head. "You gotta come see the trucks, man."

Joe set his mug down on the faded yellow tablecloth and followed Gary outside. The big man didn't know what to expect, but he could see that Gary was agitated.

The first thing Joe noticed once when he had staggered tiredly out the back screen door was the vandalism to his truck fleet. Of course that caught his attention right away; the trucks were his life. Two of the big rigs were leaning over precariously, their tires slashed on one side, the rims flat on the gravelly ground. Another was leaning forward, its front bumper nearly touching the ground. And on the left flank, the grill of the truck was ripped wide open, revealing the dripping guts of the radiator and the pooling green liquid on the ground below. Joe paused in the yard, mouth open in disbelief, his hands planted on the hips of his blue jeans. It just wasn't possible.

He walked quickly over to the line of trucks, his boots kicking up little dust clouds from the extremely dry gravel. Starting with the truck he drove over on the right, Joe and Gary walked all around each vehicle, inspecting the damage which they soon realized was even greater once they moved in closer. Each of the trucks was scraped a number of times by claws, by the looks of it. The marks were in unison, four parallel streaks curving together in graceful arcs. These slashes, carved so deep into the metal sides that they nearly went all the way through, were seen all over the vehicles. The paint had been scraped away from the indentations, revealing the silvery-gray underbody beneath the yellow exterior.

Joe slowly ran his own fingers along one of the sets of claw marks. Even though his hands were huge, he still had to spread his fingers wide to match the slashes. Whatever made these had some gigantic paws, alright. And judging by the depth of the carvings, the claws at the end must be something right out of a horror movie.

"Are they all the same?" Joe asked absently, staring at his own fingers, trying to match the claw marks.

Gary, who was now over at his rig, nodded. "Same thing for 'em all."

Gary swore, then hunkered down on his haunches to inspect the front tire on his truck. The rubber was sagged flat, pinched between the ground and the thick rim. Distinctive slashing marks covered the upper portion of the tire, from the sidewall to the thick, heavy treads. The tire had been completely shredded.

"What the hell could have done this, Joe?" Gary asked incredulously. He was now poking his index finger into one of the slashes in the thick rubber.

Joe shook his head slowly "I have no idea." But that wasn't exactly true. He'd had his suspicions already, and they were intimately tied to the horrible noises they'd heard the last three nights.

Considering that he and his wife were up almost all night, Joe couldn't believe he wouldn't have heard something like this going on in his own backyard. The howling was one thing, but he should have heard if something was ripping up his fleet.

Echoing Joe's thoughts, Gary looked up at his boss, asking, "You didn't hear anything last night?"

Joe turned his head quickly, from the truck down to where Gary was hunkered near the wheel well. His disbelief was quickly replaced by anger. Joe's neck, and then his face, turned a deep red, replacing the normal tan. His mouth puckered up as his lips turned inward, pressing against his gritted teeth. The big man's dark eyebrows met and together pointed down toward the bridge of his nose in a scowl. He swore under his breath, then turned his head and spat onto the dry ground.

"You'd think I would have, wouldn't you," he said. He was angry at the vandalism, he was angry at himself for not noticing it happen, and he was angry at Gary for pointing it out.

The rest of the drivers would be here any minute, and there was no hiding this damage from them. Only one truck appeared fit to drive today, and it was just as scarred up as the others. This mess would take all day to set right. And he'd have to get on the horn to cancel most of the jobs he had lined up for today. This was going to cost him big bucks, not to mention really ticking off his employers.

Plus, there was his wife to think of too. He'd done his best the past few nights and days to put her mind at ease. So far Joe and Bev had only heard that awful howling and screeching at night. But this incident right in his own backyard brought it far too close to home. She was scared enough by the recurring noise in the night. When she found out that something had attacked their home, she would most certainly freak out.

Joe let her sleep in yesterday, and today as well, to make up for being awake all night. Her duty as the dispatcher wouldn't be necessary until after mid-morning, and Joe was making the coffee himself the past couple of mornings. He was obviously wrong about the thing moving on; it seemed here to stay, at least for a while. And now it was getting too close for comfort.

His attention returned to the fleet. He needed to make some quick decisions. One truck could probably head out on time. With the help of his other drivers, they could replace the tires on a second truck with the spares he had on hand. But he'd have to wait until after 8 o'clock for the service station in Kalkaska to open before they could get more replacements. And all that may have been wishful thinking, providing they didn't encounter any further damage that wasn't immediately visible.

But in the meantime, he'd have to field the questions his drivers were sure to be asking. What caused this? What kind of thing has claws that could make so much damage? *And how could those claws be strong enough to carve up the trucks and completely shred the thick rubber sidewalls of those heavy-duty tires?* He'd deal with those questions when they came up, but he realized that he didn't have any answers that he could give them.

Gary was still staring up at his boss, who was running his fingers through his thick, wavy hair in stunned silence. "What's your plan, Joe?"

"Clay's truck seems fine, so he can take it on out. As soon as the other boys get here, we get the tires fixed on yours and you head out, too. You've got to get over to Frankfort. Better late then never. The rest of us'll head to town and pick up some parts and more tires. We might get two more up and running by noon if we hustle."

Just then, the still of the morning was cut short as two more vehicles pulled around Joe's house and into the parking lot, kicking up clouds of dust as the drivers hit their brakes, staring in disbelief. The drivers didn't need to see their boss standing out front, arms crossed, to know their day was going to be a long one.

Eric on the Dredge

Eric heard the two boys playing, and as he reached the fort, he smiled. He could remember building forts and tree houses in the woods behind his own house when he was young. Fond memories flooded back into his mind, and he paused, eyes closed, lost in thought.

His attempts to gather evidence having been thwarted yesterday, Eric decided he should start gathering statements from everyone in the area. Surely, someone had to have seen or heard something. Of course, the folks in town had told him all sorts of stories about the awful noises in the night. But beyond the boogeyman tales, he'd been unable to see any definitive evidence. So he had decided to start walking the Dredge, considering that was the source where most of the noises seemed to be emanating from.

Reaching out to grasp one lower branch of the apple tree, Eric kneeled slightly so that he could hear the boys behind the slat-board walls. Ever polite, he cleared his throat so as to not spook them, and then knocked on the outer wall. "Hello there, it's Officer Martin with the DNR. Would you mind coming out for a minute?"

A brief moment of silence was followed by whispers inside the fort. Then a tentative voice asked, "Are we in trouble, sir?"

The officer smiled again and chuckled to himself. It was the first response by most everyone he encountered on the job. It was just human nature. Folks either got defensive or had a guilty conscience about something. With kids, however, you never knew what response you'd get.

"No, no, no, I just have a few questions for you," Eric said soothingly. "I'd squeeze in there with you, but I don't think I'd fit."

Stevie giggled. He knew there wasn't room for another soul inside the fort. Pretty soon Brian was laughing, too.

"Okay, we're coming out," Brian said. Then he and Stevie crawled past the apple tree and beneath the doorway.

Eric was a bit surprised to see one boy and one man emerge. However, he soon realized that Stevie was just a boy in a man's body. He was a bit impressed that Brian had the wherewithal to spend time with a person like Stevie.

"What questions do you have, sir?" Brian asked tentatively. He still was afraid that they were in trouble for something. Maybe it wasn't okay to build forts on the Dredge. He hoped not. Of course, he didn't want to get in trouble and have his dad brought into it. And he didn't want to see his hard work building the fort to go to waste.

The officer looked down at them and tried his best, most confident and most reassuring smile. Eric was a head taller than Brian, and nearly the same height as Stevie, who stood with a slouch, his head slumped a bit as his eyes wandered around. It was a nervous habit he displayed when he was around authority figures. He remained silent.

"Well, for starters, I'm Officer Eric Martin, and I keep an eye on the wildlife around these parts." He offered his hand, and each boy shook it in turn, giving him their names.

Then he continued, "Mostly, I make sure nothing bad is happening. I look out for the animals and the plants, and make sure folks are following the laws in the outdoors."

Brian looked down at the ground. "Is there a problem with my fort, sir?" he asked dejectedly. He was sure the boom was about to be lowered.

Bursting into good-natured laughter, Eric said, "No, your fort is fine. It looks really good. You've spent some time putting it together, haven't you?"

Brian nodded, looking up, his face brightened. "I was afraid you were going to tell me to tear it down or something."

"Nothing like that. In fact, you should be proud you've done so well."

Both boys looked at each other and smiled. They gave their thanks for the compliments.

"I was wondering if you boys have heard or seen anything unusual around here lately. In the last few days perhaps?" Eric then asked them calmly.

The two boys again looked at each other, differently this time, and Eric knew something was up. They looked slightly panicked, slightly nervous.

"I think that maybe you know something you should tell me," he said patiently. "You two could be a great help to me, you know."

The boys wanted to help. But they weren't sure how to bring it up. It was one thing to talk about it with each other. But they never thought an adult would believe them.

"Well, sir, I don't know if you'll believe us..." Brian started before trailing off.

Eric sat down on the grassy soil of the Dredge with his legs crossed and gave them his best smile. "Try me," he said.

Brian looked at his companion and nodded his head. "Stevie, tell him about the song."

"What song?" Eric asked slowly.

"He can say it all by heart," Brian said proudly. "Every verse, too. Just wait until you hear it. You'll be impressed!"

Brian looked from Brian to Stevie and raised his brown eyebrows. "Please, by all means, impress me."

Lloyd (II)

It never took long to clean up the bar, especially in the middle of the week. There just wasn't enough business to make much of a mess. Since the next beer league game wouldn't be for another week, a Wednesday night should have been quiet.

However, each night this week had found another couple of souls downing drinks in Horner's. Flavor of the night remained the Red White & Blue, and the bottles of liquor on the back wall hadn't been touched. Still not much for clean up, just the collecting of the bottles; no glasses needed washing.

Lloyd still closed up at ten each evening, and he'd be locked up and upstairs and ready for bed twenty minutes later. This week's sudden rise in nightly attendance didn't make for much more work on his part.

Despite the fact that he left the upstairs lights on, the bar would become just as dark as the street and the woods beyond. Sigma had no street lights, and at night, the only light visible in the otherwise pitch blackness was what spilled forth from people's homes.

Tonight at closing, Lloyd would usher nearly a dozen men from the bar, insisting they could stop back again tomorrow night to pick up where they left off. These guys were surly, irritable; obviously hoping a few drinks would help them find sleep easier and more soundly than they'd had the past few nights. Each man had his own theory about the creature in the dark, and throughout the night Lloyd had nodded his agreement as he wiped down the bar and pulled cold, fresh bottles from the fridge below.

Of course, the notable absence of his two best customers weighed heavily on Lloyd's mind. The death of Buck Reynolds was a tragedy. He was one of the really good guys in the world. Lloyd still felt partially responsible for his accident three nights ago. But the thing was, Buck really hadn't polished off that much beer that night. It didn't make sense. Buck had driven home safely in a far worse condition on many occasions. And Jimmy Dean Holloway had to have followed him most of the way (with those annoying high beams on) every time. Surely,

Jimmy Dean would have noticed if Buck was having difficulty staying on the road the other night.

There had been no public funeral, just a short ceremony today. Lloyd had slept in and missed it. Not that he and Buck were tight by any means. But he had liked the man and tonight, as he listened to the endless drone of the patrons, he wished he'd been there this afternoon to pay his respects.

That brought up the other missing customer; Jimmy Dean hadn't made an appearance in Horner's tonight or the night before. If there ever was a regular, it was Jimmy Dean. He'd stop in, even if for just one beer on his way home, like clockwork, every night. Lloyd wiped out the inside of a pilsner glass before slinging his dingy bar towel over his shoulder. *So where in the sam hill was Jimmy Dean?* he thought.

Lloyd wished the pair was here tonight. He'd enjoyed their company much more than the groups currently assembled here before him. He finished the wipe down and turned his attention back to the customers seated at the old, alcohol-stained bar.

"It's a bear, I'd bet my next paycheck on it," Gordy LaJeune insisted, pounding his fist on the bar top. His faded Tigers baseball cap slipped down a little on his nearly bald head, and he absently pushed it back with the hand not splayed on the bar. "I'd know that sound anywhere. Used to go a-bear huntin' up by Newberry, don't ya know it. Soon's our blue-tick treed 'em, those critters'd start up that howlin and screamin'."

Phil Barnes, a skinny character wearing an old, green army fatigue jacket, crushed out a Camel and said to no one in particular, "I'd say it sounded more like a bobcat. Each time you hear one, its screamin' is a little different. I've heard 'em shriek like babies, that high pitched, long wailin' they do. Sends chills right down my back, I tell ya."

Gordy stared down the bar at Phil. "There's no bobcat in the world with a call that deep, you idiot. You think we all haven't heard 'cats before? There's tons of them around here. Hell, if not for them, the damn squirrels'd take over around here."

"How many bobcats have you heard lately?" Wade Thompson posed over the top of his longneck. He'd slugged back the fewest of the men in Horner's, and he was probably the only one who hadn't started well before making his way into the bar tonight.

That caught the younger man a bit off guard. "Well," Phil started out gruffly before becoming a bit perplexed himself, "I haven't heard too many this summer, come to think of it. Not until this thing kicked up on Sunday, anyway."

"Yer both full of it," Wade Thompson said from down at the end of the bar. "That's a wolf out there. Anybody with half a brain can tell from the howlin'. No bobcats means they've been scared off. And yet there's no squirrels here either, are there? Any of you been seeing them little rodents much lately?"

Heads shook around the bar. Come to think of it, there hadn't been much seen in the way of wildlife seen around Sigma lately.

Gordy wouldn't let his end drop. "That thing's a bear I'm tellin' y'all, nothin' but a black bear that needs directions. It's wandered off from its rightful home in some deep, dark wilderness up north and ended up here." Gordy flung his arms, telling the geographic tale. "If we could get that DNR feller to stop wastin' his time measurin' trout and botherin' the fishermen and to pay attention to the bigger issues we got around here..."

But he was cut off abruptly. "Shut up, you old fool," called Jeff Higgs from a side table. He was a hot-head who lived a few miles off of Mecum road, just a couple of turns from Buck Reynolds' place. Jeff always had an opinion to give, and he most often thought little of what anybody else said. "It isn't any of those things."

"So what do you think it is, big mouth?" called back one of the old timers, all of whom were losing patience with this rich "youngster." Jeff was a very young retiree from the Muskegon area, having recently moved into the area and built a fairly expensive log home between South Boardman and Sigma. He was relatively disliked by the long time residents because of the way he threw around both his money and his philosophy.

"Yeah, city boy, enlighten us with your great wisdom," Gordy uttered from across the bar. He was chewing on a toothpick and snorted at Jeff, wrinkling his nose at the transplant.

Jeff turned in his seat and nearly sneered at the line perched at the bar. He took a deep, slow pull from his longneck, and then set it back down carefully on the square, wooden table. "I spoke with that young DNR fellow today," he began matter-of-factly. "He's already found tracks and some signs from a large predator that doesn't match any known species up here. The tracks look like a canine, he says, but they're twice the normal size. He can't identify it yet, but he's checking with the lab in Lansing to compare it with what they have on file."

Jeff took a puff off of his fancy, fat cigar and then tapped the ashes into the table tray. His thick goatee and mustache wriggled as he spoke. "Mark my words, they're not going to match it with anything normal from around here." Jeff looked from one end of the bar to the other, slowly, making eye contact with each of them, completely at ease with himself. His long, blond ponytail, hanging down under the black biker bandana atop his head, only enraged the crowd more. He definitely didn't fit the typical dress code in Sigma. "There's something else here."

A few tense seconds ticked by in the bar. No one moved. Breaths were held. Only Jimmy Buffett broke the silence through the Rock-Ola's speakers, avidly searching for his lost shaker of salt, as each man was just as lost in his own thoughts.

"You and that snot-nosed DNR kid are full of crap, pal," Gordy said over his shoulder. He'd returned to his drink, facing the variety of dusty liquor bottles that lined the back of the bar. "He wouldn't know his crack from a hole in the ground."

"And you couldn't see the difference between a bear track and a tire track, you old blind fool," Jeff shot back toward the bar.

At one point, Lloyd worried that a fight might actually break out. But the men managed to keep their strong opinions in check. The bartender, the only sober one in the room, managed to carefully steer the conversation from one patron to another, just when things started getting really heated.

"Fellas, fellas, let's just relax a bit here. Maybe it's that Dogman they're always talkin' about on the radio," Lloyd offered, calming the conversation down a bit. That brought a mixture of laughing, sputtering, and various cursing from the assembly. Various stories of the Dogman started flying around the bar, mostly in the form of jokes to be played on the tourists.

A few minutes later, the bar once again lapsed into silence.

"I tell you what," Wade said slowly and carefully, "if this continues another night, we might need to have a gatherin'. Maybe it's time we take the bull by the horns. Maybe we need to go out there in force and make whatever it is shut up. Then we all could get some real sleep."

Again, heads nodded up and down the bar. Even Jeff was in agreement, though his was more undercover. His gaze was focused out past the cigar smoke and on through the dusty windows of the bar to where the street met the darkness and the Dredge beyond. *Time for a bit of action*, he thought to himself.

The Dredge at Night

Bright yellow light flared across the wide open stretch, skirting the tops of the tall grass. The spotlight, Brad's Christmas present, was a million candle power, and it could easily reach well over halfway across the Dredge even from C-571. From up to a mile away, the light could just barely illuminate the thick screen of trees on the edge of the Au Sable Forest.

Three Kalkaska High School seniors-to-be were hitting the back roads this evening, shining for deer. Brad rode shotgun while Travis drove his mom's Cherokee down the bumpy road in the total blackness of the Sigma night. Popped up through the sunroof, like some gunner in a tank turret, was Justin, who tonight manned the spotlight. When the thick glass of the sunroof was removed and tossed in the far back part of the Jeep, one of the three could stand up through the opening and shine the fields so much more effectively than from out the window, especially since the back windows were those child-safety types that only went down about six inches.

Riding in the "gunner's seat" was an honor that the three of them always argued over. But since they'd been out shining a night or two each week since mid-May, they'd had plenty of time to share. However, standing up through the hole in the roof also had its disadvantages. There were plenty of bugs out in

June, and the gunner's clothes and face required a good wiping from the high-speed impacts. And speaking of speed, the cool air blowing by, even on a normally warm night, often required a jacket or sweatshirt to be worn by the man outside the comfort of the Jeep's interior. Plus, on some of the back roads, low-hanging branches proved to be an obstacle that caused a gunner to drop back inside, often at a second's notice.

With little else to do on a weekday night, the three would spend a few hours cruising the dirt roads and trails shining for deer. There was nothing illegal about it—they weren't hunting by any means. Technically, they had to quit at 11 o'clock, but the likelihood of meeting an officer of the law way out here was slim to none. It was simply entertaining to spot the deer and keep the night's count. At points along their route, which was generally the same through the country each time, they'd see anywhere from eight or even up to ten deer at a time. Some were on the edge, others further back in the pastures, and even some right on the roads themselves. But when they headed south, crossing M-72 toward Sigma, the Dredge would always be the jackpot. Herds of dozens of deer were all over the gigantic field's six-and-a-half mile length. The night's count would rise well up over a hundred deer by the time the Dredge ended in the forest to the south.

However, this evening carried a not-so-pleasant surprise. For some unknown reason, the Dredge was eerily empty. As they neared Sigma Corners, they'd not seen a single animal out on that barren land. That was anything but normal. They'd been through Sigma quite a few times already since school let out, and the Dredge was always full. This didn't make any sense to any of them.

The Jeep cruised along the Dredge, the spotlight picking out nothing of interest in the field. After a few minutes, the town proper approached. Justin cut off the light as they drove past the town's little houses. He certainly didn't want to shine somebody's living room. A few seconds later, he dropped back down into the little backseat of the Jeep.

"Man, it's weird. There's nothing out tonight," he said to his partners in the front seat. "Usually, we shine a ton of deer out here."

Brad was busy, staring intently at the houses that slowly floated past. They kept the Jeep at 30 miles an hour or less so that they didn't miss anything. He jabbed his thumb out the window. "What's really weird is that all the lights are on. Look at 'em all."

All three boys noticed the abundance of house lights, spilling their yellow glow out of nearly every window. They'd have more success counting the lighted windows than the deer around here.

"Yeah," Travis agreed, nodding. He sipped at his Pepsi, and then put the bottle back in the cup holder. With his thumb, he scratched the side of his face in deep thought. "I can't remember this many people being awake this late. None of the times we've ever been through this place."

The boys lived in Kalkaska itself, and though they fancied themselves as rough, tough country boys, the real wilderness way out here, miles from home, was always a step or two beyond the level of civilization they'd come to appreciate in their own small city.

The Jeep passed the crossroads and continued south past the closed-up bar and the dilapidated ball field where Travis's dad played softball every few weeks in the summer. More houses were lit up like Christmas as they passed through the edge of town. Justin rose back up into the open sunroof, stretching his legs as the spotlight again lit up the Dredge. He slowly scanned the great field from left to right, forward and back across the high grass, looking for the reflection of the eyes. The eyes always gave the deer away—two little points of light would be staring back, reflecting the high-powered beam. However, this pass produced no results. The Jeep worked its way to the south end of the Dredge, and still they saw nothing.

They'd never struck out at the Dredge before. Justin dropped back down again and said, "Let's double back and go over it one more time. I just can't believe there's nothisng there."

"As warm as it is, they ought to be out in force," Brad said. "We should have counted over a hundred by now. What gives?"

The other two boys were silent. They didn't have an answer either.

Travis swung the Cherokee around, making a tight turn in the narrow road. He'd always admired his mom's Jeep and its ability to turn on a dime. That feature had gotten them out of many tight spots on the back trails. Put together the tight turn radius and the four-wheel drive, and it was much easier to mess around out here. They usually didn't use the 4x4 unless they were in deep mud or climbing hills or something else equally challenging to teenage boys.

The red Jeep retraced its tracks north this time. Again, Justin shined the field. Again, nothing appeared. They drove through town again, and again they pondered the preponderance of house lights. A few moments later, the land was nothing but pitch black around them again.

And then, about halfway between Sigma and M-72, heading north back the way they'd come from Kalkaska, they finally found something. Or actually, something found them.

"Cut it," Justin called down to the driver below. "I've got one!" Not quite halfway out on the Dredge a single pair of eyes glared back at them.

Travis slowed the Jeep to a crawl, fully applying the brake and stopping the vehicle before putting it into park. Justin kept the spotlight trained on their target. All three boys looked out into the field intently.

The eyes, unblinking, shone back as a brilliant golden color. The eyes were just a few inches below the tips of the tall grass, which hid the rest of the animal's head and features. The boys watched those eyes, waiting for it to turn and run so they'd get a better look. But it never moved.

Justin gave a cursory look to the left and right of the eyes with his spotlight, but there was nothing else around. When he returned to the where the eyes were first sighted, they were gone.

"Where'd it go?" Brad asked from the shotgun seat.

"I don't know," Justin replied. "It must have ducked below the grass. I'll keep panning and see if it shows back up."

The beam of light continued its slow sweep across the tall grasses, standing still in the calm night air. A full minute passed with nothing.

Travis put the Jeep back in gear and prepared to continue on when the eyes reappeared. Justin caught them again in the spotlight's bright beam. This time they were only about fifty yards away.

"Guys, they're back," Justin said, excitedly. "It's gotta be a big doe, judging from the height of the eyes. That grass is high already this summer."

All three boys were entranced by the golden orbs that reflected back at them. Justin kept the beam right on it, waiting for it to move. The animal's features still could not be discerned while it hid in the grasses' natural camouflage. Of course, the best guess any of them could come with was a big doe.

The eyes were hypnotizing. The boys continued to watch the points of light in the field, not noticing that they were getting closer. The grass slowly parted as the creature pushed its way forward, though its head was still obscured. The distance between them was cut down to half, then half again, and yet the boys were still absorbed by the calm serenity of the golden eyes, eyes which did not blink.

It turned out to be Travis's foot that saved them. His left foot had fallen asleep, and to shake off the pins and needles, he stretched it out. The foot slipped off the clutch, sending the Jeep lurching forward a few feet, and stalling out in the road.

Justin, consequently, moved the spotlight off of their quarry. But as it turned out, the light wasn't needed.

The boys were still looking out at the field, now very dark except for the two eyes which were now glowing on their own. It was one thing for an animal's eyes to reflect the beam of the spotlight; it was something altogether different for eyes to be giving off their own unearthly glow.

Brad cocked his head at the sight, squinting his eyes and nose. "What tha…"

The beam of the spotlight, one million candle power, swung back to its position, and the boys finally caught a glimpse of the creature in the field. It was moving toward them, not in a run, but in a steady, purposeful advancement. The distance was decreasing with each second.

A dark head emerged from the thin stalks of grass. It was very dark, covered all over with thick, coarse black fur that seemed almost wispy. Two pointed ears twitched, picking up sounds from all around it. And then its face fully appeared to them all.

Travis's mind immediately told him he was looking at a werewolf. A real, honest-to-God werewolf. He'd seen plenty of monster movies, loving the classics the best: Lon Cheney, Michael Landon, and all the others who donned the werewolf suits throughout the history of film. And of course the special effects of more modern movies were enough to give children nightmares for months. On the outside, he'd shown false bravado in the cinema. But on the inside, Travis was deathly afraid of these unnatural creatures. The deepest, darkest parts of his mind surfaced now, laughing at the rational side of him, which still insisted that this must be a nightmare. Such creatures didn't really exist. And besides, there was no moon at all this week. Werewolves needed a full moon to exist. *This couldn't be real,* half of his mind said, over and over. But the other half kept telling him, *I told you so! I told you they were real!*

But this was no nightmare that stalked its way toward them. It was real. All too real.

Brad's thoughts went back to his early youth. The stories of the Three Little Pigs and Little Red Riding Hood played themselves out at high speed on the cinema screen in his mind. Time had stopped for him as he saw that eternal villain, the wolf. Of course, the wolf in both stories was a horrible, bloodthirsty monster, which truly scared the daylights out of little kids who hear such tales for the first time. He flashed back to the fear and trepidation he'd had for so many years, a fear of a wolf that could walk and talk, eating up little pigs and old grandmothers.

But this was no story book character coming for them. A happily ever after ending wasn't guaranteed out here in the dark wilderness.

The monster that approached had the features of a wolf—the muzzle, the ears, the scraggly fur around its face. And yet, impossibly, it was walking upright through the grass. It couldn't be. And yet it was. It walked like a man, it was shaped like a man, and it had human characteristics. The boys could see where its neck met its shoulders, and its front arms were pushing the grass aside.

But most peculiarly, the boys watched as it opened its mouth, revealing long, sharp fangs. Its muzzle first curled up in a snarl, and then it almost seemed to be making a horrible, evil grin at them as it came closer and closer to the road and their Jeep.

The dark head dropped back down, its sharp, pointed ears just visible at the tips of the tall grass. A low, husky, guttural growl emanated from the field, rumbling like thunder toward the Jeep. It was the sort of sound you'd hear in a monster movie. It wasn't the kind of thing you'd expect to actually hear in real life.

Only Justin, who'd kept the beam directly on their stalker, was not overcome by a paralyzing fear. He'd shouted down at Travis twice to get them out of there, but the driver was unresponsive. Finally, he kicked Travis in the shoulder, slamming his body against the driver's side door.

The growl came again, louder and more imperative this time. The boys had received their second warning. There might not be a third.

That got Travis's attention, breaking the spell. He turned the car key but nothing happened. In a panic, he stared in disbelief at the steering wheel, the illuminated dials, the key.

"Clutch, idiot!" Justin yelled, now dropping back inside the Jeep. The light fell to the floor, shining up at the back seat. Brad was already shrinking back from his window, where the glowing eyes, large and distinct even in the blackness of the field grass, were still approaching them at a steady pace. Only a few more seconds and it would be on top of them.

Travis pushed in the clutch and tried the key again. The Jeep fired right up.

"Go! Go!" both of the passengers yelled at once in unison.

Travis hit the gas, and the engine revved way up before his left foot caught up and released the clutch. The Jeep bolted forward, Travis working the stick shift up to third in barely three seconds. The vehicle tore down the road, just as the creature leapt the final dozen feet onto the dirt where Brad's window had been.

Justin was staring out the back window as Brad and Travis looked into the side mirrors.

The glowing eyes were now on the road directly behind them, following their narrow escape. The boys all breathed a sigh of relief as they noticed the twin points of glowing light were shrinking smaller and smaller, finally fading into the blackness.

The Jeep, now up to fourth gear, flew on through the night, putting miles between themselves and the specter they'd left behind them. The boys all had trouble sleeping that night, and they never did return to Sigma or the Dredge to shine deer again.

Sigma (VIII)

Brian Alexander, Jr., again dreamed of the monsters chasing him through dark alleyways and forest paths. But this time, as some eternally dark and distressing creature was about to grasp his shoulders from behind, he awoke to a loud crashing sound in the dark. He sat up in bed, fingers clutching the sheets in a death grip, staring at the bedroom's only small window. The shades were drawn, so he couldn't see outside (and of course, nothing could see in either!). But that didn't stop his imagination from conjuring up haunting images of Stevie's Dogman out in the depths of the night, destroying homes on his way in to devour the inhabitants.

When the first of the howls began, Brian slid back under the covers and grasped his Star Wars pillow tightly in his arms. Before long, the pillowcase was soaked from his tears, as he silently screamed in terror.

***

No one noticed the absence of one little old widow. Jane Whitman's house lights remained on all day and into the night. It wasn't unusual; everyone's lights were on all night these days. She never had any visitors, and she made only the very occasional trip to the Mercantile. Jane's old sedan sat parked in the driveway in the same space it occupied every day, all day long. There was nothing unusual to report—her home appeared to have kept the status quo every day as long as anyone could remember. She was rarely seen by anybody in the village anyway; she was a recluse, who regularly kept her front door closed (and locked). To almost everyone, she was just the crazy cat lady.

No one would know she was missing. No one came to her home that day to find the back door open, only the tiny screen door keeping the bugs outside.

No one would see the one pink slipper caught in a bramble of blueberry bushes.

No one came to feed the one remaining house guest, an overweight cat whose belly nearly dragged on the floor. By the next day, Simba would realize that there would be no more food available here and that it was time to move on to greener pastures.

***

Folks had laughed and joked all spring about the Dogman. A crazy song, fit for April Fool's Day. The more it played, the more they found it amusing. Imagine that, a monster in their backyards. It was laughable. Laughable in the daytime, when the bright, hot sunshine ruled the land.

But nobody laughed, nobody joked now. Nightmares in Sigma had become far too real.

Some loaded bags, and some loaded guns.

And everybody stayed awake.

Thursday

Brian on the Dredge (III)

Brian Alexander, Jr., sat on the dirt floor of his fort on the Dredge. He'd been there for over two hours now and was waiting patiently for Stevie since 4 o'clock when his friend would leave the mercantile. It wasn't right for his older friend to be so late. Every so many minutes, Brian would stop and listen carefully for any sign of Stevie. But so far, there was nothing.

Luckily, his attention was turned to one of the many adventures involving Han, Luke, and Leia, who were just stand-ins for himself, Stevie, and of course, Bonnie. The figurines had assumed these roles more and more often as the summer went on, and this week they'd become permanent fixtures in Brian's mind. Maybe it was having Stevie there to join the adventures with him. Maybe it was his father's decadence. Maybe it was the haunting world of the deep night and the horrible nightmares. Whatever it was, Brian had retreated to a safer place, a place where the good guys win and the bad guys (especially those monsters that howl late at night) get thumped a good one before meeting their doom.

A twig snapped outside. Brian stopped, frozen, Luke in one hand and Han in the other. He listened carefully. There came a crackle of dried leaves from beyond the back wall.

That wasn't quite right—Stevie always walked up the road from work and would then enter directly into the Dredge from the west. Through the fort's door, Brian could always see him pushing aside the tall grasses as he came near.

These noises, however, came from the east side of the fort. It couldn't be Stevie. Brian wanted to call out to be sure, to find out who it might be, but he held back.

Suddenly, Brian was deathly afraid. His mind was racing, picturing the creature, the Dogman, stalking its way toward his little fort, which now seemed so tiny and vulnerable. The little jumble of old, warped boards would never keep such a monster out. Brian's skin went cold and clammy, and a slight sweat broke out all over his body. He'd stopped breathing in an attempt to be perfectly still, perfectly silent.

Brian could now hear the footsteps, fairly quiet until they crunched something else, as they closed in on the fort. A few seconds later, the crunches moved from the back of the fort to its side. Brian did his best to squirm his way silently to the far corner. His heart was racing in his chest. Another second and something would be peering in his door, the only way in and the only escape. There was no place for the boy to go; he'd backed himself right up against the weather-worn boards of the wall.

And then a face appeared in the doorway. As keyed up as he was, his eyes only saw the faintest glance of long hair before shutting tightly, and his mind finished the rest for him. Brian screeched and flung his arms up over his eyes and head in the only protective gesture he could muster.

His yell was answered by another from the front entrance. But it took Brian a good long second before he realized that it wasn't a deep howl, but the high pitched scream of a girl. Brian stopped abruptly and dropped his arms. His eyes showed him, not the horror of the Dogman, but a sight he never thought he'd ever see in his life.

Bonnie was kneeled down at the fort's entrance, her palms up covering her own face, screaming back at him.

"Stop that!" he called to her. "Please stop that. I'm sorry, I didn't mean to scream at you."

Bonnie stopped just as abruptly as he had. Slowly, she pulled her hands down her face until they simply dropped in her lap. She wasn't crying, but she looked on the verge of tears. Brian had scared her pretty badly.

"I thought you were something else," Brian said apologetically. "I'm sorry, please don't cry."

She sniffled a few times, and then gave him a weak smile. It might have only been a half-hearted attempt, but to Brian it lit up her whole face. And it instantly pulled him out of the funk he'd been in all day.

"What are you doing here?" he asked carefully.

She looked at him, and then a tear did well up in one eye. The story came pouring out of her like a torrential river. There was no one she could tell it all to, no one to listen to her, and it had built up until the dam finally burst. "That bully, Scott, you know him, he won't leave me alone. I keep trying to avoid him, but he finds me and I just wanted to pick some flowers for my mom, and I had to hide so he couldn't see me. And then I saw this place and I wondered whose it was and so I came over here to see, and then you started screaming and I, I, I just couldn't help myself." The whole thing came out faster and faster until she was nearly hyperventilating. Little streams of tears were coursing down her freckled cheeks.

Brian sat unblinking, staring at her as she rattled on the story through sobs and sniffles. He wasn't sure if she was done or if he should say something. So he said the only thing that came to mind. "You can stay here if you want. It's safe."

She stopped and took a deep breath, exhaling slowly. Then she smiled, a wide, genuine smile, and began to crawl inside. "Thanks," she said. Bonnie didn't say much else for a while; she just leaned back against the cool boards and closed her eyes, lost in thought.

Brian stared at her, the former adventures of his action figures a distant memory. He'd never had the courage to go up and talk to her; he never thought he'd do it. And yet, here she was, right in his own fort. Brian's heart felt two times bigger that afternoon. They didn't' talk much; they didn't have to. They were just there for each other, providing comfort in companionship—a couple of kids, just hanging out. It was so much better than being alone.

Later, when Bonnie asked him to walk with her to town on an errand she had to do, he wasn't sure his feet actually touched the ground.

Eric (IV)

The Warden gave Eric a dreadfully sour look from across his green, 1950s industrial desk. "Yeah, next thing you'll be telling me it's that damn Dogman running around out there."

"All I'm saying is there is something unusual going on in Sigma," Eric nearly pleaded. "I don't know what it is. If you'd seen the size of that track I found, the remains of that doe…"

He was cut off by his boss's deep voice. "And yet you are unable to produce the evidence for all of us to see. Your so called theory isn't holding water. There are plenty of large predators out there. Coyotes, bear, bobcat, any one of those could have been responsible."

Eric quickly countered, "There's no coyote or bobcat anywhere in the world that could take down a yearling in the space of only five feet, not without the doe putting up some sort of fight or running. There was no blood trail. It didn't have a chance to run or fight."

The Warden exhaled deeply and dramatically. He gave the young officer a look of pure annoyance. It was getting close to quittin' time, less than a half hour till Miller Time that is. He really didn't need this crap at the end of the day, especially from the snot-nosed kid who'd been more bother than he was worth since he hired on.

"Boy, you don't know the number of prank calls we've gotten since that nonsense song started playing on the radio," he spat. "Dogman this and Dogman that. And guess what— we've seen the Dogman at the Clinch Park Zoo! And I've even been getting these stupid Polaroids that supposedly show Dogmen! Just look at these."

His boss reached into a squeaky middle drawer, pulled out a manila envelope, and emptied its contents onto the desk. He then arranged the dozen or so photographs so that Eric could see them.

"Look at this one," he pointed to a snapshot. "That's some student in a werewolf mask. And this one, a kid beneath a bear skin rug. So fake it almost looks real, huh?

"And of course, my all-time favorite," the Warden went on, practically shoving a photo into the hands of the young officer. "Spot the dog goes Hollywood!"

The Polaroid showed a black lab wearing plastic yellow sun glasses and a brown, leather bomber jacket. Beneath its paws were a Frisbee and a chew toy. Labeled in plain blue pen was nondescript handwriting that said, *Dogman on Vacation* '87.

"I tell you what," the Warden went on, "I wish I could get my hands on the guy who wrote that crap. That song, this whole thing's been nothing but a headache for me! And now you want to try and make up a serious case for a monster in the woods. I ask you, kid, how old are you? Don't you think it's time to grow up a bit?"

Eric knew he wasn't getting anywhere here. In silence, he accepted the chastisement, though he really didn't listen to the rest of the Warden's tirade. True, Eric nodded in the right places and hung his head in mock obedience, but inside he was already trying to formulate a plan to find and bring in some evidence from the field. Someplace out there, there must be some sign of this creature.

And since the Warden had so assigned him this week, Eric would do his duty and make his presence known in the Sigma woods, even if he had to camp out there the next few days.

The lecture finally over, Eric made his apologies and practically ran for his truck, excited to begin some real work.

As he pulled out of the headquarters, he gave a cursory glance to the Smokey Bear sign out front. The old, faded sign held by the paws of the famous DNR mascot gave a bright red warning. In bold letters it read FIRE DANGER: EXTREMELY HIGH TODAY. Hung a few chain rings below that was another sign that read NO BURNING: FINES DOUBLED FOR ANY VIOLATIONS.

It was a sobering reminder of the dry weather that had plagued northern Michigan for the past two months. *Any spark could set this whole place off,* Eric thought before turning his attention back to the matter at hand. Any spot up north could go up quickly if a fire were to start somehow. But he never thought he'd actually see it happen.

He clicked on the radio and listened as Bob Segar and the Silver Bullet Band played out the "Fire Down Below." Eric smiled, thinking the song was rather appropriate.

Brian and Bonnie (I)

The screen door opened easily, though its spring creaked a little in the quiet of the afternoon. Only a light breeze blew through town, giving the maple leaves a light rustle. Soft, little hands held the screen door open as a brown-haired head poked in.

"Mrs. Whitman?" Bonnie called into the house. "Mrs. Whitman, are you here ma'am? It's Bonnie Eastman."

Bonnie stretched her neck into the doorway and chanced a look around. The house seemed empty, lifeless. A smell of old cat food wafted out the door to the kids. She looked back at Brian, Jr., but he was more or less useless here. He only shrugged his shoulders and held up his hands. He hardly knew the old woman, and he'd certainly never been in her house before.

The young girl cautiously stepped into the shade of the home's kitchen. Brian was a few steps behind her. On the surface, it seemed like the same place she'd visited old Mrs. Whitman on many previous occasions. But then it hit her—no cats. Usually she was mobbed by the old woman's cats; that was what drew her there like a moth to a flame. Sure, Bonnie enjoyed the company of Mrs. Whitman, but it was really the many cats she liked best. And normally Mrs. Whitman would answer the door herself, chattering away as if she'd saved up a week's worth of words just for her little guest.

Today, there were no cats and no Mrs. Whitman. The stone house was stone dead. Only a few flies darted around the room, trying their best to escape through the glass panes of the windows.

Brian was extremely nervous. Deep down, he felt like they were trespassing, even if Bonnie was often a guest in this house. He touched her arm, gaining her attention. "Do you think we should be here? I don't think she's home. I mean, wouldn't she have met us at the door?"

Bonnie felt the same vibe from the home, and yet she felt compelled to check it out further. "Maybe she's hurt or something. She is old, you know. I hope there hasn't been an accident. We should check it out to be sure."

"If you say so, I guess," Brian answered tentatively. His voice hadn't risen much above a whisper. He still didn't feel right being here. The house had taken on a creepy feel. It suddenly seemed much larger inside than it looked from the outside. As his eyes surveyed the room and the adjacent doorways, he could imagine any number of horrible things hidden in the home's nooks, crannies, and shadowy corners.

She shot him a glance of annoyance at being second-guessed. "I do say so. She's a nice lady that I like a lot. If something's happened to her, we should help."

Brian shrugged in compliance. Truth was, he'd follow her anywhere. Here she was being very brave, and all he could think of was Stevie's Dogman. He was scared of the creature in the song, and he'd never even heard the song before! But the way Stevie whispered the lyrics, telling the story in a way that chilled Brian to the bone, his mind was already picking out spots where the Dogman might be hiding.

They walked across the kitchen linoleum and stepped into the living room. It was still as empty as they had feared. Everything seemed in its place, nothing suggesting that there was anything wrong. Nothing, of course, except the missing lady and her missing cats.

Bonnie continued to poke around the house, checking Mrs. Whitman's tiny bedroom and bathroom. When she came back out of luck, Brian again shrugged his shoulders.

A noise from the other room startled them both. They spun immediately to face the kitchen. Brian felt the warm comfort of Bonnie's hand slip into his own. Although he was scared to death at that moment, he was elated, too. He couldn't tell if his racing heart was due to fear or the electric touch of her fingers against his. A small spark of bravery rose its way through his body, and he took the slightest step forward and in front of "his" girl.

Scott Hailey appeared around the doorway to the kitchen. Both kids exhaled in relief, but it was rather short-lived. Scott was no Dogman, but he could be a monster in his own right.

The older boy smiled, though it appeared more like a sneer. "What're you two doing in here?" he asked. Then his eyes narrowed and he shot them a dirty look. "You're not kissin' my girl, are you Brian?"

Despite his deep desire to do just that, Brian flushed and stammered back, "No!" Immediately, he wished he could have said something clever and dauntless. He wished he could be the same valiant character he always pretended to be when playing with his Star Wars figures. He wished he could stand up to Scott.

Bonnie, on the other hand, was not at a loss for words. "What're you doing here?" she asked defiantly, eyes squinted in anger and quite possibly disgust.

Scott walked fully into the doorway and leaned an elbow against one wall, propping up his greasy head with his palm. His black, faded AC/DC t-shirt, already a size too small for the big boy, tightened around the sinewy muscles of his upper arms. "I saw you two sneaking around the house and wondered if you were up to no good." He took a long moment to look the two youngsters over. "Guess I was right. Breaking and entering is a serious crime, you know," he said in a smug, know-it-all tone of voice.

Bonnie scowled at him, wrinkling up her lips. "We weren't breaking in. The back door was open. Besides, we're here checking on Mrs. Whitman. I always come over on Thursdays, not that it's any of your business."

Brian wavered between disgust at himself for his lack of gallantry and being impressed by her courage in the face of certain danger. Here she was, standing up for the two of them, when Scott could easily thump them both. Usually, Brian avoided the bully at all costs, and if an encounter did happen, he made himself as small and meek as possible. Scott usually left him alone, though only after a bit of serious teasing.

But here they were, stuck together within the confines of the little house, and Bonnie was egging him on. Well, at least he'd only beat up Brian. Who knows what he might do to Bonnie after that.

"So, if you're here to see the old lady, where is she? Or did you lock her up in a closet someplace? Probably tied her up and gonna rob her, weren't you?" Scott's eyes narrowed to slits once again. His attempt at portraying a detective was actually more amusing than intimidating.

Bonnie's voice faltered a bit. "We don't know where she is. We were checking to see if she was okay, but we can't find her."

"Likely story," he said, taking a long, slow look around the room, taking in all of its contents, appraising them. "Have you looked everywhere?"

"Well, yeah, duh," she shot back at him.

The two kids waited while Scott made his own cursory walk around the room, briefly checking the areas they'd already been to. Then he stopped at a door by the bathroom that was slightly ajar. Scott slowly opened the heavy wooden door. "What's back here?" Cool air, a very nice contrast to the hot afternoon, emerged from the darkness below.

Bonnie's face flashed bright crimson in anger. "That's the basement, retard. And I'm sure Mrs. Whitman doesn't want you snooping around her house. Not any more than you already have."

"Basement, huh?" he asked, now intrigued. "What do you say, Bri? Let's go check it out."

Brian had no interest in descending into a dark, dank basement with Scott, even if Bonnie went with him. He only swiveled his head, looking from the cave-like entrance to its rickety staircase leading to the unknown depths, and back to the older boy.

"You two aren't chicken, are ya?" Scott asked, leering at them, his pimply face leaning forward.

"No, we're not chicken," Bonnie sneered back. "There's just no reason to go down there. Besides, Mrs. Whitman's not here, and we should probably go tell someone. It isn't like her to just go and leave the back door wide open."

Casually looking around the room, Scott slyly asked, "So, have you seen her anyplace up here?" He knew the old lady was no place to be seen up here or they'd have found her already.

"No," Bonnie replied a bit flattened. She was quickly losing control of the situation.

"Then maybe she's down there," Scott said, shrugging his

shoulders. "Maybe she's had an accident down there and needs some help. Didn't think of that, did ya, Little Miss Pretty."

"Don't call me that!" Bonnie hissed through clenched teeth. "You know I hate that!"

Her tough act didn't faze the older boy. He slowly sauntered over to them and planted his hands on his hips. He gave them both an ugly grin. "She could be down there in pain right now, maybe even needing a doctor. Do you want to take that chance?"

"Well, no," Bonnie stammered.

"Then it's settled. Bri, you lead the way."

Brian's eyes widened in fear, and his head snapped back. "What? No way."

"Yeah," Bonnie said, "What's to keep you from shutting the door behind us and closing us in down there?"

Scott seemed to calculate a new plan in his head for a second or two. Obviously, deep thought wasn't natural for him. "Okay, Brian first, then me, and then you. If I'm between you two, you can't lock me down there either."

Brian and Bonnie exchanged glances. There was little either of them could do. They didn't want to go downstairs, but for the first time in his life, Scott might actually be right. They should check for Mrs. Whitman down there, just to be sure.

"And if I'm between you two, you can't go off kissing in the dark," Scott joked. "Not that she'd want to kiss you anyway, Bri."

A deep flush of anger rose up Brian's neck, right to his face. He gritted his teeth but could find no response to the older boy's taunting.

They descended the stairs, one by one, slowly and carefully in the order agreed upon. Every other step strained in a long, agonizing creak. Brian gripped the round, wooden banister tightly, and his eyes slowly became adjusted to the dim light. Within a few seconds, the three of them were off the stairway and on the cement floor.

The air of the basement was definitely about twenty degrees cooler than upstairs. Though it should have felt really good on such a hot day, there was a different quality to it. It became apparent to them that the basement hadn't been used by Mrs. Whitman in a long, long time. A thin layer of dust caked everything but the steps. The skin of all three of them broke out in goose bumps, and not just from the chill in the air. It just didn't feel right down here.

It didn't seem to matter much to Scott, who immediately began sifting through the hodgepodge, looking for anything of value. He went from pile to pile, blowing the dust off of old records, while moving stacks of faded newspapers and boxes of canning jars.

At one point he even held up a silver coin he'd uncovered someplace, trying to get a closer look at its face in the dim light that managed to steal its way down there.

Brian and Bonnie stood on the cold cement floor looking around the overcrowded basement. For the second time that day, Bonnie's hand slipped casually into Brian's, and he couldn't help but be more than a little pleased. Despite Scott's digging on him, he was the one she looked to for comfort. They stood that way, like little lost Hansel and Gretel, for almost thirty seconds taking it all in. They could hardly believe the jumbled piles that covered most of this lower room. Indeed, the piles formed narrow aisles that zigzagged throughout the room. Bonnie, in particular, had trouble believing that nice old Mrs. Whitman could have collected so much stuff and just left it down here to rot away.

Then they slowly began shuffling across the room toward another door, this one built into a partition. The wall that divided the basement and created this smaller storage room at the back was fairly solid, made from thick rough-cut lumber. Truth be told, it had been milled this way not fifty yards away on the Dredge almost a hundred years ago. It was true two-by-four construction, and certainly not kiln-dried like today's lumber. The wall itself was made of thick, true one-inch oak planks, and this mighty structure did in fact support a great deal of the home's upstairs weight.

Cautiously, Brian reached out his nervous left hand (thankfully, it wasn't shaking) and pushed the heavy oaken door. The two peered in at another wildly jumbled collection of junk, piled up along the walls nearly to the narrow casement windows at ground level.

There was no way Mrs. Whitman was down here. It looked like no one had been down here in years. Thick strands of cobwebs stretched between each floor beam above, meeting those attached to the walls and various pieces of furniture, boxes, and odds and ends strewn about the basement. The air was stale and musty, like that of a long lost tomb. And yet there was another deeper smell behind these, one they couldn't quite identify. Its pungency made the nose twitch and wrinkle up. This particular smell was almost like a different layer of existence, overpowered by the odor of old, cracked stone and wet earth, but not completely covered up by it.

Then Brian remembered. The zoo! That smell, the one in the layer beneath, reminded him of the Clinch Park Zoo! It was the smell of the big animals, the smell of thick, matted fur, of sweat and raw meat. Brian didn't have long to dwell on the happy memories of their trip to the zoo, because his mind was already processing this new information. He thought, *Why would this basement smell like the zoo? Because some big animal had taken up residence here.*

In answer to his thoughts, a low rumble reverberated through the basement. Brian's first thoughts were that it was thunder or maybe the house shifting somehow on its foundation. His eyes darted to the stone walls, which held up the floor joists above. They were still as solid as before. And it was a clear, blue-skied day outside, with not a cloud in sight.

But as the noise continued, it changed to that of a deep snarl. Some big animal *had* taken up residence here.

It was unclear where the sound came from, and with all of the junk piles, it seemed to echo from everywhere. Glass bottles vibrated in their boxes. A few ancient newspapers slipped off a trunk and hit the floor, disintegrating immediately into a puff of dust.

Bonnie squeezed Brian's hand tightly. She'd moved in close to him, though he hardly noticed.

Scott had frozen in mid-squat, hands digging deeply into a flimsy box of old tools. His breath caught in his windpipe, and the corners of his mouth curled downward in terror. All three of them had heard that sound before, though at the time they had been safe in their beds behind locked doors. Somehow, late at night, there was a dreamlike quality to the howling out on the Dredge. It wasn't really real to them. Sure, they'd heard it and were frightened by it. But tucked beneath their blankets, the three kids still always felt safe. The growling was always a ways away, not up close and personal like it was now.

It was here with them. Their nightmares had become real and invaded the day.

The noise came again, and this time the three of them could pinpoint its origin. A short wooden door, no more than four feet high, was set into the stone foundation on the other side of the stairway. And that door was slowly creaking its way open on old, rusty hinges.

A furred set of dark fingers reached around the edge of the root cellar door, the claws scraping on the wood. The other hand emerged, gripping the door jamb, claws easily digging into the wood, a moment before the creature pushed its way out into the basement itself. Because it emerged hunched over, it became an even more impressive and grotesque monster as it stood up to its full seven-foot height.

Brian might not have ever heard that Dogman song before, but he knew exactly what he was staring at across the dark, cluttered basement.

Though Brian might not have been quick to defend himself in a battle of witticism, he did make an important decision at that moment. It only took the briefest of glances at the monster to prompt him into action. It wasn't something that he planned, it just happened. He gave Bonnie a hard shove, and she rolled head over heels into the back storage room. He then spun and slammed the heavy door shut, turning the lock.

The girl landed a few feet away, but she righted herself quickly and stood staring at the door, her face a mask of pure terror. Brian backed several feet away from the door and stood next to her. This time his hand took hers, the fear causing her fingernails to bite into his skin.

A thud racked the door, and Scott's terrified screams echoed through the basement. Further behind him, loud crashes signaled the creature's advance. Piles of discarded junk were falling and crashing all around the basement.

"Let me in! Let me in!" the boy outside screamed over and over outside the door, his hands trying their best to turn the handle. He'd been left on the other side! It wasn't intentional, a means of payback or even Karma, but only an act of self-preservation on the younger boy's part.

Bonnie grasped Brian around the chest, burying her tear-streaked face and screams against his shoulder. Despite their previous poor relationship, despite all of the role-playing he'd done with his Star Wars figures in which Scott personified evil and met a bitter end, despite all of that, Brian still wanted to let Scott in. But his body wouldn't respond. It just didn't respond at all. His feet stayed rooted to the spot, his body weighed down by the frightened, sobbing girl.

The door shook from Scott's efforts, but it did not give. And then his words turned to pure shrieks of agony and pain.

And then it was already too late. A few seconds later, the last bloodcurdling scream was cut off by the rolling thunder of the creature's growl.

Brian and Bonnie looked at each other in pure horror, realizing what had become of Scott.

But the moment of silence was interrupted abruptly as the heavy door shuddered in its frame. The creature was slamming into it with all its might. Despite its stout construction, the door (and quite possibly the entire wall) wouldn't last long.

Bonnie cried out again in fear and panic, tears rolling down her flushed cheeks. She was unable to move. This just couldn't be happening.

Brian, on the other hand, had taken to action. He climbed the pile of junk stacked atop an old desk and a few wooden crates, desperately trying to get the single, small basement window open. He'd flipped the lock, and yet it still wouldn't budge. The window was a bit too high for him to get good leverage on it for a real, full-body push.

The monster hit the door again, and this time a loud crack

split the air. It sounded like the entire wall was going to give way. Both kids looked up as a puff of dust fell from the ceiling at the top of the wall.

More frantic than ever, Brian turned back to the tiny window, startled so badly that he nearly fell back off the desk and crates. A dark shadow had covered the dim daylight coming in through the casement. His first thought was that the creature had doubled back on them and that it was now going to burst through the glass. Brian's left foot slipped and he hung suspended in mid-air, his arms circling madly trying to keep his balance.

At the last moment before tumbling over, Brian was able to plant his foot down on a firm spot, his arms leaning forward to catch himself against the stone wall. Forgetting what startled him previously, he looked up to the window and there, through the grimy glass, he saw a face, a familiar face, peering back at him.

It was Stevie!

"Open the window, Stevie!" hollered Brian. "Quick!"

The older boy gave the casement a good shove, but it wasn't going to move that way. It held firm and fast.

Bonnie shrieked again as the creature hit the door. The doorframe creaked, ready to give in at any moment. Brian, nearly hoarse now, cried imploringly at Stevie, "Please, get it open!"

Stevie dropped down to his butt, his worn-out jeans scraping on the gravel that ringed the stone house. His knees were drawn up, his hands dug back in the stones for leverage. Stevie loaded up all the strength he could muster, gritted his teeth, and grunted as he kicked forward with both legs.

Luckily, Brian saw it coming, and he hopped back down

to the basement floor. A second later, the glass of the window shattered inward from the impact with the heels of Stevie's thick cowboy boots.

Just as the glass shards were hitting the cement floor of the basement's back storage room, a loud crunch emanated from the door. Bonnie screamed again as splinters flew in all directions. The creature had finally broken its way through.

A muscular arm covered in thick, black fur and tipped malevolently with long, sharp claws extended through the opening. It reached in, snatching and pawing the air, trying to enlarge the hole. The other claw could be seen at the bottom corner of the break, prying more of the door loose. It continued to growl in deep gnashing sounds, teeth biting at the air. Though the basement was dark behind the creature, Brian and Bonnie could both see the outline of its huge head and the glow of its eyes, peering at them. The two were rooted to their spots, entranced by the deep golden hue staring at them from the darkness.

Stevie broke the spell. "Come on, you guys!"

Brian, shaking himself out of the entrancement, reached out and grabbed Bonnie's slender wrist and pulled her to the junk pile beneath the window. She was still sobbing hysterically and he had to nearly drag her up high enough so that Stevie could reach through the window and pull her to safety. Tugged by Stevie's great strength, Bonnie slipped through the window with only a few minor scrapes from the remaining shards.

Still, the monster struggled with the door, though new cracks were constantly enlarging the opening. The heavy iron hinges strained under the intense pressure. Luckily for the kids, it had given up slamming against the door, which would have certainly caved in with only another impact or two. As it was, the creature's upper torso was nearly through. Brian watched as its claws continued to pry and dig at the door, while its maw snapped and growled, frothy spittle flying through the darkness.

And then it was Brian's turn. He reached upward with both hands as Stevie heaved and strained. Brian was heavier than Bonnie, and bigger around the middle. It would be a tight squeeze. He looked back one last time as the door finally gave way. But the Dogman was lost in the dust and rubble, as most of the jamb and partition wall tore loose as well. Several plank boards snapped from their previous place on the wall and flew across the room. The overhead beam, once supported by the wall, slipped from its anchors in the stone foundation and dropped down upon the creature. A large cloud of dust, splinters, and the piled junk of ages past flew from all directions as the floor above began to cave in.

There was a horrible second where the younger boy thought he'd be stuck in the opening, trapped in the disintegrating house, but he then popped out into the hot, dry late-afternoon air.

It really was a miracle that neither one had been sliced to ribbons on the protruding glass shards at the window's edges. Rumbles and groans emerged from the interior of Mrs. Whitman's house, and though no damage could be seen from the outside, the three knew that the insides were falling into the basement. Little puffs of dust shot out from the edges of every window and from under the eaves. No one else was around to see the destruction; they were the only ones to know what had happened there.

However, there was no time to stop and take a count of their blessings. Stevie was already pulling them across the side yard to the street and the Dredge beyond. The two youngsters were powerless to stop their feet from running to keep up. Though exhausted and still scared out of their wits, they didn't stop running. The three slipped through the tree line and into the tall grass. They hoped Stevie knew where he was going, because everything had become a blur to them. The weeds split around them, parting momentarily before closing back over their path.

And then they stopped, gasping just a moment for breath, before they were violently yanked down into darkness. Startled, memories only a few minutes old flooding back to her, Bonnie tried to scream, but was cut off by Stevie's hand covering her mouth. Brian's head was spinning, and a dull ache was creeping across his brow from temple to temple. His legs were burning and there was a stitch in his side that felt like he was being branded with a red-hot poker.

Only then did Brian realize they that were in his fort. Stevie had brought them to the only place he knew that was relatively safe. True, it might not hold up to the onslaught of that creature back there, but they could take a moment to recover from the ordeal before, deciding what to do next.

Looking up into the older boy's face, Brian tried a weak smile. Stevie returned it, genuinely, and reached out his arms to hug the two younger kids.

Lloyd (III)

Darkness fell again on the little town, and folks were not just edgy—they were downright petrified.

As always, Lloyd first locked the door. Then he hit the neon lights in the window. Finally, he gave the tables and the bar top a quick wipe down. He'd already scooped up the bottles as his patrons were leaving tonight, keeping each for the deposit when the beer man came on Friday. Every penny counted.

The pickups had rattled away right after closing, their taillights fading to tiny red specks in the distance. Lloyd was completely alone in the bar.

Despite the added folks in the bar this evening, there wasn't much to clean up. Lloyd had it all set within twenty minutes, bottles stacked in the back, the till emptied, even a quick mop job in the john. He was about to head through the back corridor to the stairway, when something caught his eye outside the window.

It must have been a trick of the lighting for Lloyd's old eyes to be able to see across the bar, through the dirty window, and out into the street beyond.

And what he saw chilled him to the bone, frightening him in a way he'd never been before in his life. He'd seen some very bad things, but nothing to compare with this. There, at the edge of the dim, fading light from Allen Wallace's house trailer across the street was a dark figure lurking in the shadows.

He could see it, walking on two legs in a hunched-over way, its arms dangling out in front of its chest. No trick of the light, it appeared fuzzy at the edges, indicating that it was covered in fur. The head above the thick shoulders and back was topped by two pointed ears. And very distinctly, a long muzzle like that of a dog or wolf poked out from the figure's face.

Lloyd stared unblinking at the creature as it stole its way along the edge of the street and toward the ball field.

Very slowly, Lloyd's hand reached up to the room's light switch. The creature's head seemed to be swiveling slowly from right to left. As soon as its attention turned to the ball field and the Dredge, Lloyd flicked the switch off, entombing the bar in darkness. He could still see out the dirty windows, and was still rooted to the spot.

The creature's head snapped to focus directly toward the bar, and in the blackness of that face he could see the glowing yellow eyes, piercing the night, penetrating the double-paned windows and stabbing right into the heart of Lloyd Horner.

Distance wasn't an issue; Lloyd could discern the pure malevolence in that glare even if it had come from over a hundred yards away. And those glowing eyes. Somehow they were even worse than the physical, hulking appearance of its frame. They were like tiny, twin keyholes right into the door of hell itself.

Lloyd wasn't sure how long he stood there, feet fixed on the same squares of tile, facing the creature. All he knew for sure was that his legs eventually went numb. His heart kept racing, and he was afraid he was going to have an attack.

After what seemed like hours, the creature turned its attention back toward the direction it had been originally stalking. In a moment, it disappeared from view.

The old man quickly walked to the front of the bar where he could see out the corner of one dirty window. His body was shielded by the wall, but he inched his head out so he could see the street and yet be inconspicuous.

It was completely empty. There was nothing there.

Lloyd blinked a few times, and then shook his head. He couldn't believe he'd only imagined the whole thing, but there was nothing outside to be seen.

Lloyd crept his way backward to the stairway to his apartment, his mind swimming with indecision. Should he call someone? Should he report this? And, of course, what exactly would he say? *I just saw the boogeyman in the street outside my bar.*

Please, send help. He imagined a phone call with 911 going very badly very quickly.

And Lloyd was very frightened, the last of his courage spent taking those steps to the front window and back. It took everything he could muster to climb the steps to his apartment where he felt at least a little bit of safety. He thought he'd never sleep again.

Later on that night, when the loud crashing and howling erupted a bit down the street, Lloyd only pulled the covers up over his head, trying his best to block the awful sounds with the palms of his hands tightly around his wrinkled ears. He knew something truly dreadful was happening to one of his neighbors, but he was paralyzed with fear and unable to do anything to help. His legs went numb and violent shivers wracked their way through his body. Over and over, the uproar outside continued.

The face in the window would not leave his mind; that phantom visage remained burned in his memory the way a bright light will leave its impression on the insides of the eyelids.

And it was sad indeed. Though undoubtedly one of his neighbors, one of his acquaintances, perhaps even one of his friends, was involved in the chaos ensuing beyond, Lloyd's only thoughts were those of self-preservation. Having looked the devil square in the eyes, he counted himself beyond lucky already. He certainly wasn't going to tempt fate again this night.

Bonnie (II)

Bonnie cried herself to sleep that night. Her father at first wasn't interested in why she was sobbing; he only hollered at her to keep it down so he could hear Al Kaline and George Kell call the Tigers game. Tanya, her mother, tried her best to comfort the girl, holding her tightly. Bonnie wouldn't say what had happened, couldn't get out the words to tell her mom (not that she thought her mom would believe her anyway). She only sobbed and clung to her.

The only words she could get out that either parent could recognize were, "Scott...dead." These she repeated over and over. Her mother knew whatever this whole thing was, it was bad. Whether her husband would slap her around for interrupting the game or not, she had to take the chance.

Wayne Eastman was very angry at his wife's intrusion, but it was pretty important news. Then he proceeded to yell at her for not telling him sooner. He called up Scott's father, John, who sobered up immediately at the news. The two men weren't necessarily good friends, but both had shared beers at Horner's on occasion. And though both took out various degrees of aggression on their families, each still had an obligation to the safety of their kids. They could smack around their kids, but nobody else had better try such a thing.

Of course, Scott wasn't home. John didn't know where he was or the last time he'd checked in. The kid did have a lot of freedom, but he was always back home by dark. And now it was almost eleven o'clock. He was far overdue.

Minutes later, John Hailey rapped on the screen door, a shotgun in one hand and a red plastic flashlight in the other. Wayne brought him into the small kitchen, where Bonnie was interrogated, forced to tell whatever she knew. Anything that might help. Wayne did everything but slap the girl (as he often slapped her mother), trying to force her into divulging more information. But the girl was beyond useless to them. The only new piece of information they could get out of her was "Mrs. Whitman's house."

The two men looked each other in the eyes, and a silent decision was made between them. They'd both be going out to find the boy.

A minute later, Tanya watched as the two men strode out the front door walking toward town, the beams of their flashlights bobbing up and down in the darkness outside. Once they were out of the yard, she slipped over and closed the door tightly, locking both the handle and the deadbolt. Then she led Bonnie down to her bedroom and held her until her cries finally (and mercifully) ended in a troubled sleep.

She stayed up all night, waiting. Though she didn't hear the crashing in town, Tanya did hear the sinister howling in the deep darkness. A few hours before dawn, she tried to call John Hailey's house to see if they'd returned, but the line was dead.

She waited.

Neither man returned.

And when the sun came up, she wasn't all that unhappy.

The Mercantile

A loud crash from beyond the living room's single-paned windows shook Jack Cooper violently awake. He'd fallen asleep on the recliner, and he nearly tripped over the little oak coffee table in agitation and dismay as he leapt to his feet. Though he saved himself a tumble to the floor, he did rack his shins awfully hard on the table's edge, sending streaks of pain up his legs. A cry stifled, he rubbed the thin skin covering his bones and gritted his teeth. He left the store at exactly 5:05 in the afternoon, having locked up a few minutes early, and made it as far as his living room before the tiredness overcame his weary body. Every minute of sleep he could get this week was precious, and he'd had no trouble passing out immediately on the old Lazy-Boy, even if it wasn't as comfortable as it was twenty years ago.

The smashing sound of wood splintering tore through the quiet night again, and he was able to finally orient himself to his surroundings. His house, his living room, his aching shins. The loud clamor came from outside, from his store next door. He cringed; a noise that massive could only mean something major had been destroyed.

Still in the khakis and button-up plaid shirt he'd worn that day, Jack reached past the *TV Guide*, its cover displaying the triumphant headline "Los Angeles Lakers—NBA Champs," and slipped his fingers around the handle of his revolver. Instant courage flooded his system as he held the manly weapon. *This must be what Dirty Harry feels like*, he thought to himself, stifling the urge to smile. Confidently, he strode to the front door, forgetting that he was just an old man in a little town, forgetting that he was no match for anything that could smash its way into his locked store, forgetting that he hadn't fired that pistol in years. Next to the door he grabbed the little red plastic flashlight from the top of the coat rack. He was going to protect his little part of the world.

And then that loud crashing began again, though this time it was more muted. It obviously, had come from within the store this time, and it continued on for ten seconds or longer. Jack noted the variety of noises emerging from the darkness next door: the metallic clatter of cans bouncing off the linoleum; the sharp tinkle of glass breaking; the popping of wood splintering apart. His brief moment of machismo left his body, seeping down his legs, which would have knocked his knobby knees against one another if they weren't spread so far apart.

Jack, his .38 wobbling in his shaky right hand, turned the deadbolt. His front door creaked open, a slow and steady mechanical squeal that pierced the night, momentarily eclipsing the droning buzz of the myriad of insects flying in the glow of the yellow porch light. Jack winced, squeezing his eyes and scrunching his nose as his left hand squeezed the flashlight in his fist. Whoever (or whatever) was next door would certainly be alerted to his appearance. A few moments of indecision caused him to pause in the doorway, one foot out and one still behind the weathered stoop. *You can still go back inside*, he thought to himself. *Go on back in, lock the door, and pretend you didn't hear anything. You've got insurance; there's nothing in your store that can't be replaced.*

He peeked his head out past the screen door and looked over to the right, to where the Mercantile stood, a darker black block in the deep of night. Only the faintest light diffused its way over to the store's front from his porch light. The building waited for him in the darkness. *You, however*, his mind told him, *well, that's another story.*

In the end, his false, foolish bravado won out. It was his store, after all. He wasn't about to let someone or something break into his place.

He left the stout front door open and slipped out, careful to quietly shut the screen door so that hundreds of bugs wouldn't be dancing around inside his house when he returned. Pistol pointed outward, he slowly descended the four wide steps to the yard. The front of the store was still hidden in shadow. He kept the flashlight off so as to not give himself away. Besides, he wouldn't need it until he reached the store front.

One foot planted squarely in front of the other, Jack tiptoed his way across the yard, his shoes making little squishy noises from the wet dew already settling on the grass.

More racket from inside the Mercantile caused him to stop at the edge of the building. Somebody was definitely inside, ripping up the place from what he could tell from the outside. In the midst of the furor, a loud crash echoed outward, followed by a few seconds of pings and tingles. Jack could only imagine one of the large heavy shelves being pushed over, its contents spilling all over the floor, glass smashing everywhere.

Jack's eyes were finally adjusted to the night, and he surveyed the scene in front of him. His jaw dropped, his brain refusing to believe what he saw. The door to the Mercantile wasn't just smashed up or busted in; it was completely missing! Even in the darkness, he could see that the door jamb and trim had been violently splintered inward. A few small pieces of wood were strewn about the cement walkway leading to the curb. One hinge lazily pointed into the cavern-like doorway; the other two were missing, along with the heavy front door itself.

Taking the next few steps forward proved the most difficult that Jack had ever trod in his entire life. More crashes, the sounds of upended boxes, bottles, and cans, reverberated from within the depths of the dark building. Jack gulped, took a deep breath, and forced his feet forward until he was looking directly in through what was left of the entrance.

His pistol held in front of him like some sort of talisman, Jack raised the flashlight up to eye level and clicked it on. It was only a cheap plastic light, the kind that kids typically took along on family campouts. Its beam, nervously jittering from his shaking hands, only shined in a few feet with any sort of intensity. Indeed, the utter mess he could see was reflective of the reports he'd heard earlier. But the damage appeared to be even worse than he'd imagined.

The front door, a solid two inches of ancient oak, was impaled eight feet away on the upper corner of the nearest shelf, the sharp metallic edge now protruding through the splintered plane of the door. Large chunks of wood lay everywhere.

Jack shined the light from left to right across the room. The shelving units on the right side of the store were indeed pushed over into the aisle nearest the cash register. That was quite a feat, considering each weighed upwards of eight hundred pounds when fully stocked. Of course all of that stock was now littering the floor. The cans and bottles that were still intact had ceased their rolling and now lay motionless, their labels facing upward, as if accusing the owner of allowing them to be disturbed in such a manner.

All noise inside had ceased. The only sound came from Jack's rasping breath; he sounded like he'd just run a marathon. His heart was pounding in his chest, adrenaline coursing through his old body.

He hadn't noticed that he had stepped through the shattered doorway and was now standing in the midst of the wreckage. His light went over to the cash register and saw that it was fine, one of the only items in the store untouched by the tempest.

The beam of the flashlight weakly illuminated the middle aisle and its contents, previously so neatly sorted, stacked, and stocked by Stevie, that were now strewn across the floor.

Jack's feet continued forward, acting totally on their own. His body simply followed, though his mind was screaming for him to get out of there, to escape while he still could, to quit this investigation. Beads of sweat formed on his brow and the back of his neck, both from the warm night air and the intense fear that enveloped him. His hands continued to shake, and it was evident that he'd have to be right on top of the intruder to actually shoot with any accuracy. His worn out loafers crunched on glass shards, potato chips, and what were undoubtedly M&Ms or possibly Reese's Pieces. More than once he nearly lost his balance on something slippery or stepped down on a can, which then tried to roll its way out from under his feet. Still he moved on, against what was surely his better judgment.

Ten long seconds later, the little flashlight's white beam of light reached the back wall where the refrigerators separated the stockroom from the rest of the store. On the left, his light panned the floor to ceiling units, which appeared to be untouched with the exception of something foamy (probably the two-liters of Faygo that were on display at the end of the aisle) streaking its way down the glass.

Then the silence was interrupted by a low, raspy rumble. Jack at first thought one of the store's window air conditioners had turned on. But as his light moved to the right side of the store, where the front counter turned the corner behind the meat counter, he soon realized that this noise came from something that was certainly not man-made.

Jack stood, rooted to the linoleum, loafers soaking up spilled root beer and red pop as he looked at the display case, when a huge, dark shape rose up from behind the glass. His light was focused on the glass where the fresh cuts of beef, pork, and chicken should have been proudly displayed for the customers. But the case was nearly empty; only red smears were left on the plastic trays inside.

Again, the deep growl emanated from the back corner of the store and Jack was able to shakily raise the beam of the light up the display case glass to its stainless steel top and past the little digital scale. Jack didn't want to see what was there, but his hands acted independently of his brain, just as his feet had brought him all the way to the rear of the store. He had to see it, whatever it was that had caused so much destruction to his store. Instinctively, he knew he wasn't going to be seeing a person there; no man could have done such a wrecking job. No man could have cleaned out the meat case so thoroughly.

The beam of light finally rose past a thick, hairy torso and stopped at the creature's shoulders and head. Jack's eyes bulged, his nose crinkled up, and the corners of his mouth peeled back and downward in an awful grimace. It was the most horrendous sight he'd ever seen.

Three nights of enduring that awful howling on the Dredge in the middle of the night had provided the old man with plenty of specters to run wild in his mind. But nothing he could have imagined prepared him for the monster he saw before him. It towered over him, standing seven feet tall. Its arms, long and powerful, reached forward and leaned on the top of the meat case like some evil butcher serving up the finest cuts in hell. Jack noticed that there were the remains of two bloody steaks clutched in the claws of each hand—and they were hands—for they definitely weren't paws on the end of its arms.

The head of the creature was distinctly canine in resemblance, though its triangular shape was larger than any coyote or wolf Jack had ever seen. A long muzzle extended from the face, and the huge mouth was open, a few scraps of meat caught in the sharp fangs. The shoulders were wide and hunched as its head extended forward and slightly down. It was completely covered in a dark black, coarse fur that was matted and unkempt. In fact everything was dark, everything, that is, except the eyes.

Jack's open mouth worked up and down in a silent scream as he watched the creature gulp down the last mouthful of meat it had previously held in its claws.

The narrow, pointed orbs glared maliciously back, reflecting Jack's light. The bridge of the snout furled, distinct eyebrows narrowing the eyes in a far too human look of anger and even possibly hatred.

The old man could take it no longer. He wasn't exactly sure what he'd find over here when he left the safety of his house. But he sure didn't think some monstrous demon would be waiting for him. He forgot the manly bravado he'd had earlier. He even forgot he was carrying a weapon.

He simply couldn't look at it any more, and the flashlight beam lowered slowly back to the display case as the strength left his arms.

But his attention was still held by those eyes, which continued to glow a hellish, flaming gold, creating their own light in the pitch blackness.

The next second, Jack's thin, wispy hair was blown back by the incredible, throaty roar from the creature. Echoing through the small store, the thunderous blast was like being far too close to a passing train. Jack's nose was assaulted by the acrid, disgusting smell of rotting flesh and raw meat. He never noticed the pistol slip from his fingers as his right arm and shoulder pulled up instinctively to cover his face.

When the awful bellow subsided, Jack peered over his arm and watched as the glowing eyes began to move left and around the meat case to the corridor that connected the store with the stockroom in back. He could hear the minute clicking sounds of its claws on the linoleum floor. It was moving from behind the barrier. It was coming for him.

That finally broke the spell. No thinking involved, Jack

turned on his heels and attempted a mad dash for the door. However, within the first two steps, his loafers slipped on the debris littering the floor, and his feet went out from under him.

At the same time, the creature reached the open space of the corridor, and in the fraction of a second, it crouched and sprang. Muscular legs propelled the creature across the darkness of the store toward the human trying to escape. Its shoulders and arms reached wide and outward, front claws spread, like some deranged linebacker making a spectacular flying tackle.

The creature flew through the air and would have bent the old man right in half from the impact. But Jack's luck held for at least a few more moments. His torso flattened out horizontally just before slamming his back against the floor.

The monster missed its target by mere inches, its arms closing together over thin air where the man should have been. Surprised just a bit from its miscalculation, the creature had just enough time to look forward and see the heavy metal store shelf before the collision. It slammed headfirst into the shelf, toppling it into the adjoining aisle and bursting open bags of flour and sugar which poofed everywhere to form a cloud that obscured the back of the store.

The air in Jack's lungs exited in a hurry, and he gasped for breath. His entire body ached and his mind was reeling. But despite having the breath knocked out of him, he knew he had to get up, he had to get out right now. He couldn't wait for the pain to leave; he couldn't wait for his lungs to refill. He had to escape before the thing attacked again.

Head spinning, the old man rolled his way onto his stomach and scrambled to all fours. Something powdery was falling all around him, clouding his vision. His senses tried to tell him it was snowing, but he knew better than that. His entire focus was on getting out of the store. His feet kept slipping, but his hands pulled him forward again and again.

His eyes now adjusted to the darkness, Jack could see the doorway, only twenty feet away now, appearing as a deep bluish-violet against the pitch black of the store around him. Somewhere far behind him, his flashlight was buried beneath a mass of shelving and fur. He continued his scuttle, feet continuing to slip on the cans and candies, hands being cut and torn from the shards of glass scattered across the floor.

The creature was stunned from the impact with the shelves, but it recovered relatively quickly. It rolled off of the demolished pile of metal, and as it tried to rise, its legs and arms slipped outward, its torso slamming into the linoleum. It shook its head violently, trying to clear the dizziness. Finally, it regained its senses and turned toward the man who was scrambling for the front of the building. However, the white powder that was still suspended in the air clogged its nostrils. The more it breathed in, the more it became congested, until something had to give. On all fours like a huge wolf, the creature cocked its head sideways and began sneezing violently. Its head convulsed, blinking its now bloodshot eyes in a vain attempt to clear the fine, dust-like particles from its vision.

Jack heard the strange snorts and sneezes behind him, but they only helped to spur him on faster. Ten feet. Five feet. He passed the sill and his hands felt the rough texture of concrete. It was surprisingly bright out here compared to the cave-like interior of the store. And he could hear the june bugs buzzing as they gathered in the street. His focus remained straight ahead. All rational thought had fled his mind long ago. He forgot the safety of his house next door as quickly as he'd forgotten the .38 pistol that made him feel so macho not ten minutes ago. His feet finally finding purchase on the doorstep, he propelled himself up like a sprinter fifty years younger. He might not have the speed of a high school athlete, but he was moving pretty well for a man his age.

Without looking back, or looking in any other direction for that matter, Jack bolted across the street, chest heaving and lungs burning, toward the ball field and the Dredge beyond. His shoes squished several june bugs on the way past. He had no idea where he was running, only that he was heading as far away from the creature as his tired legs could muster.

As Jack was running past the outfield fence and into the tall grasses of the Dredge, a huge dark shape emerged from the Mercantile's gaping entrance behind him. Though on all fours, the creature was still more than four feet tall at the shoulder. It inhaled deeply in the clear night air, tongue hanging out as it panted, finally shaking loose the accursed powder that had disoriented it so badly.

Once its senses had returned to working order, the creature had no problem picking up the scent of the man who'd escaped. There was no hurry now. The creature had fed, and fed well. It could take its time tracking down the human. Sauntering across the street, claws clicking on the pavement, its glowing yellow eyes narrowed to a squint, the creature paused, raising its head to the starry firmament, letting loose a long, deeply harrowing bellow that awakened every person and every animal, for miles around.

Its business at the Mercantile finished, the creature turned its attention to the scent leading into the wilderness. And there were other noises to check out all around the town. It could hear people leaving the relative safety of their homes and entering into its domain.

Prey was a-plenty this evening.

Friday

John and Wayne

Midnight came as Thursday slipped into Friday in the silent woods surrounding Sigma. A light breeze stirred the upper branches of the ancient oaks and maples, their leaves whispering a "shhhh" like an old librarian chastising a group of elementary school kids.

In the depths of the night, neither John Hailey nor Wayne Eastman could see the structural damage done to Jane Whitman's little stone cottage. They couldn't notice the cracked foundation walls that were slowly slipping under the weight of the upper level of the house. Several of the large rocks had already fallen in, creating tunnels into the basement big enough for raccoons to squeeze through. Not that the critters wanted anything to do with that death trap; unlike the humans, the animal population could easily smell the odor of the beast that had until recently occupied the residence.

John and Wayne had tried the front door, but found it tightly locked. Peering through the windows didn't help either. The only thing visible in the pitch blackness of the home's interior was the red and white checkered curtains right next to the glass of those windows. The two men did think it odd that the front stoop seemed uneven, but hey, a lot of things in Sigma were uneven. If the old woman's front steps were sinking into the ground, so be it. Their main concern here was finding John's boy.

Between sobs, Wayne's daughter had mentioned Mrs. Whitman's house, so of course, here they were. With no apparent way in through the front, they strolled around back, each carrying his firearm, both tips skyward.

The crunching of june bugs beneath their boots added to the singing of the crickets in the yard. Someplace in the distance, an owl hooted its lonely song in the night. Despite the warmth of the evening air, both men shivered as they rounded the corner of the house.

The backdoor was open, the screen door slowly swaying in the breeze. John pulled it open and stared, his jaw having dropped wide open, at the scene unfolding before him through the beam of the flashlight. What he and Wayne saw was nearly impossible to comprehend.

About eight feet in from the back door, the floor just disappeared. As John shined the light around the house, it was quickly apparent that the interior of the home had collapsed within itself. A gigantic hole had opened up where the floor should have been, and this chasm enveloped much of the main level of the house. John gasped as his flashlight shined all the way across the first floor to the front door, from where, only minutes before, they had been trying to see inside. The interior walls, the cabinets, and all the furnishings were now taking up residence in the basement.

The main beam running along the middle of the house had collapsed and taken almost the entire the floor down with it. The wall between the kitchen and the living room had also given way, and it was now suspended about four feet above the basement floor, hanging from the attic by a few flimsy-looking two-by-fours. The men could almost hear the framing nails straining under the immense weight as they worked themselves out of the wood a tiny bit at a time.

The ceiling above was sagging down with the house's main dividing wall, while the roof threatened to collapse at any moment.

There was no time to call for help. No one would get here in time anyway. This whole house of cards could go tumbling down at any time.

John took one look around the mess with his flashlight and knew he had to go down there. He called Scott's name several times, listening carefully for any response. But it was silent as a grave. If his son was indeed among that mess, he'd have to drop down there and find him.

He flashed the beam of light around the open basement. Already there was an inch or so of water covering the floor, undoubtedly from a busted pipe somewhere. A layer of small debris floated on its surface. There was food spilled everywhere. The piles of junk below were intermingled with busted boards and broken pieces of flooring and furniture, and all were coated with soggy nuggets of cat food. Among the old newspapers and magazines, the kitchen counters, splashed with the contents of various cans of food, lay below in splintered piles right next to the dented and obliterated appliances. The fridge lay on its side, doors open against the floor, a gallon of milk slowly seeping into the rising pond. Everything was covered in a layer of dust and splinters. The distinct aroma of canned tuna wafted up to the men's nostrils.

And every so often, a loud creak would echo through the house. There obviously wasn't much time to work with here.

"Help me down," John commanded, slipping his body over the ledge. The sharp edge of the broken sub floor pinched against his stomach. Wayne grasped his hands and helped John to dangle above the rubble below.

He reached the basement floor, and then nearly hit the deck as he slipped on a wet, slimy board. He caught his balance by flailing his arms, but his flashlight went flying off into the corner. Its beam shined up on an old, rusty Schwinn bicycle, which had been crushed by the collapsed partition wall. Its riding days were very much over.

John looked up at the floor above and eyed the nine-foot distance. "I'll need you to find something to haul me up with," he said to his partner. "There's no way I can climb up."

"There's some rope in my truck," Wayne answered. "I'll go get it." His footsteps creaked on the loose boards as he carefully slipped to the back door.

John, on the other hand, made his way through the mess below and over to the corner to retrieve his flashlight. He passed the small door to the root cellar, and wrinkled his nose at the stench pouring forth from inside. *Old lady must have something rotten in there*, he thought.

Suddenly, part of the foundation slipped and the upper part of the house began to sway. More boards and rubble rained down upon the man in the basement for nearly ten seconds. The sound was tremendous: the snapping of thick, rough-sawn boards as if they were toothpicks; the jingle of glass shattering; the squeal of long framing nails pulling free. He held his arms up over his head for protection as dust and debris fell everywhere, plopping into the pool of water that was already soaking into his boots. When the dust finally cleared, John was amazed the whole thing hadn't fallen in yet.

"Not much time here," he muttered to himself. "Gotta go, gotta go."

By the time he'd picked up the flashlight, its beam was already flickering. *Cheap plastic,* he thought, *must have let the water in. Now's it's useless.* A few seconds later, it nearly went out, giving John only a tiny, faint glow with which to combat the pitch black of the basement. He tried calling for Scott again, but as before, the only sounds were the popping and snapping of the house as it continued to settle. A few seconds later, his eyes adjusted to the little bit of light, and he started searching around the various piles as best as he could.

The creak of boards above signaled the return of his partner.

"Here," John hollered from below, raising his left hand above his head in the darkness, "hand me your flashlight. Mine's dying out."

His attention still drawn down to the pile of rubble beneath the collapsed beam, John absently raised his right arm back up to the main floor. His fingers opened and closed, expecting Wayne to slip the flashlight into his palm.

But it wasn't the smooth aluminum of Wayne's Maglite handle he felt in his grip.

Instead, his hand naturally closed upon a coarse, hairy forearm. Clawed fingers instantly seized his wrist, sinking deeply into the skin.

Surprised, John whirled, cranking his head and neck upward to see what had grasped him. Even in the very dim light of his flashlight, he could see something horrible standing on the floor above him. As his eyes widened in fear and shock, he tried to yank his captured arm back, but it was far too late. John heaved with all his might, and even grabbed the hairy arm with his other hand in an attempt to pull free. By this time, both legs were off the ground, his entire body weight was pulling downward. He shook like a fish on a line, but there was no escape.

As he was hauled up to the first floor of the house, John saw Wayne, or what remained of him, slumped against the backdoor jamb. The man's Maglite was on the linoleum, the beam of light shining right toward his limp body. John's eyes looked away instantly, refusing to see the mess of limbs and clothing covered in a black pool that could only be blood.

The creature continued to pull him upward as he struggled. As John's torso rose above the broken chasm of what had been the kitchen floor, the creature swung its other hand down upon his shoulder. Claws sunk deeply into the flesh, and John let out his own snarl of pain. The man made one last attempt to break free, by letting go of the creature's arm and grabbing the floor with his left hand, while swinging his legs and feet up to sandwich the ceiling below. Sharp splinters bit into his skin, and his thighs and knees burned from the friction against the floor joists. But then his motion upward suddenly stopped, at least momentarily.

The creature's face leaned downward, staring right at the man. Its glowing yellow eyes narrowed to slits, locked with John's. The creature's long muzzle, like that of a dog or wolf, peeled back its lips and revealed long, curving fangs. Its nose wrinkled up and from the depths of its throat, it issued an evil snarl. Its face was only inches from John's, and he could smell the putrid stench of rotten meat on its breath.

Just then the floor finally gave way.

The eyes of both man and beast dropped to the floor joists as the audible cracking began. All along the walls of the house, the foundation had crumbled enough for the floor to drop an inch, then another, in a jerking fashion that caused the creature to slip and fall prone on the linoleum. John, of course, also began to slide downward, his left hand slipping yet grasping for purchase, and his feet kicking into the open air.

A puff of dust rose from below, obscuring everything in the house; everything, that is, except the face of the demon, which still held him in its iron grip. Their eyes locked one last time, and John saw its muzzle and face change. Rather than snarling at him, it almost seemed to be smiling. It wasn't exactly growling at him anymore, though it was making some sort of noise that John couldn't identify at first.

And then, he felt himself being released. John fell, looking up into the darkness, wondering what that creature was, wondering what it was doing here. Being crushed by the fall might actually be better than what the creature was going to do to him.

The creature nimbly kicked its feet and leapt to the back door in one smooth, fluid motion. It stepped outside just as the outer walls collapsed inward, the roof tumbling down upon everything below.

The windows all shattered, the tinkle of glass adding its own light melody to the chorus.

John's last thoughts as the rest of the house came toppling down upon him were that the monster was laughing at him, actually laughing at him, as he had been dropped.

And then, all was darkness, pierced with splintering creaks and the thunderous crashing of ton after ton of stones and heavy wood.

Nancy

She only had to go back this one last time.

She knew she should have taken everything with her this afternoon. She should have made sure she had everything. But at work this evening, she remembered the photo of her late father. It was still hanging in the hallway. Nancy Butler didn't have any other photos of her father anywhere, and it was of great sentimental value. It wasn't even that great of a picture, just her father leaning against his old '54 Ford. But it was the only photo of him left, the only one in the world. It was irreplaceable. She and her father had been very close, and his death when she was only twelve had been devastating to her.

Who knows what Rick might do to it when he found out she was leaving him. She couldn't take the risk that she'd get it back in a divorce settlement. She didn't want to go back, but she had to. She just had to have that photo.

The evergreen trees, mostly lowland cedars, and the swampy underbrush on Lodi Road passed by her in a blur. Every few seconds a dark brown telephone pole careened by on the left side. At least Lodi Road had a paved surface. It was still rather bumpy, with road patches dating back decades (only Doc Custer could remember the last time it was newly paved). And with no worry about police way out here, she could really push the speedometer.

She slowed to a stop at Sigma Corners. The town was quiet and deserted, as usual. Ingrained in her from her days in driver's training, she unthinkingly looked left and right, even though she knew there would be no traffic. Since she started this night shift months ago, there hadn't been a single vehicle seen here in town as she drove through. Sure, there were a few lights on in the houses, but she was sure that was due to the awful howling. Folks just weren't sleeping. She'd had it lucky. She could sleep all day and still be rested for work, and everything else she'd been up to lately.

Nancy's mind was anywhere but on the road, however. She really didn't want to stay another night, but knew she had to chance it. She was already practicing the story that she'd tell Rick on the off chance that he was awake. It wasn't likely, but you never knew. Especially if that wild howling had started up again, he might not be snoring. *Yet another reason to leave him,* she thought. If worse came to worse, she'd tough it out one more night. The photo of her father was that important.

Turning south, she was ready to hammer down the accelerator when a dark shape emerged on her right side from the darkness between Horner's Bar and the dirt parking lot. At first Nancy's mind couldn't register what it was. It was shaped like a man standing upright on two legs with a body, shoulders, and two arms. But it didn't stand quite like a man. It was slumped over, the arms hanging down nearly to its knees. And the closer she came to it, the more she realized that its head didn't look right either. And it was so dark, covered in some sort of thick clothing that stood out in the night's warmth.

Her headlights finally caught a part of it that wasn't covered in darkness. Glistening white fangs showed from its elongated snout, and its eyes glowed a sinister yellow. And it wasn't wearing heavy clothing—that was some sort of thick, shaggy fur.

Nancy's eyes widened in fear and shock, as she realized she wasn't looking at a person. She was looking at some sort of creature!

Her foot had naturally come off the gas pedal, and she hadn't realized that her car was slowing down. Her head turned to the side as she stared out the passenger window in disbelief, her Chevy pulling right up alongside the creature, which was stalking its way toward her too. It bent down and looked right into the window at her. Her car was ever so slowly creeping near it.

The monster curled up its lips and growled at her through the open window. Its fangs were bared. This close, she could see that they were more of a faded yellow than a dirty white. Its eyes glowered at her malevolently. She smelled its putrid breath wafting into the car and finally lost it. Her blaring, hysterical screams echoed through the car and out into the dark night.

The creature lunged at her, managing to reach one long, hairy arm in through the passenger window. The clawed hand opened and closed, snapping the air as it reached for her. It then gave a full fledged roar this time, and her screams were drowned out.

Nearly out of control herself, she punched the accelerator and the Chevy jerked forward. Her body snapped back as well, her head slamming against the headrest.

The arm withdrew immediately, but the clawed hand caught on the edge of the window's opening. A loud thump on the roof told her that it had swung itself up right onto her little car!

Nancy veered wildly along the road, swerving back and forth as she tried to lose the unwanted passenger. The little Chevy picked up speed, kicking up gravel and hitting the bumps of the dirt road. However, the creature held tight.

She never thought of braking. Such a quick stop would have certainly sent the creature flying. But she was far too hysterical for such a rational thought. The only thing running through her mind was that she had to shake the creature loose, to get him off of her car. And to make matters worse, she was beating up herself mentally. If only she'd taken that photo earlier in the week. If only she hadn't had to come back here. If only she'd been a few minutes earlier, she'd have never encountered this horrible demon.

The air conditioning was out in the little Chevy, and

she'd kept the windows open to get some sort of relief from the intense heat, even late at night. Now the open windows were a liability. Her concentration split between navigating the many potholes and chatter bumps of the road and trying to shake loose the creature on the roof, she didn't notice the clawed fingers that were reaching in through the driver's window. Slowly, the fur-covered appendages inched their way along the ceiling, claws digging into the fabric as they neared the burnt-red tresses of her hair. Another inch or two and the clawed hand could grab her.

At that instant, several things happened, nearly simultaneously. The creature's finger touched her hair just above the temple. Nancy screamed and jerked her head away to the right as she looked toward the open driver's window and the clawed arm. At the same time, her hands counterbalanced her weight shift and swung the wheel hard to the left. As she did so, the tires of her little Chevy hit a series of chatter bumps that ended in a washed out section near the edge of the road. The car left the ground in grand fashion, spurred on by Nancy's intense acceleration and the ramp-like embankment on the side of the road.

The creature looked up as the car swung violently. It yanked its arm back out through the window and drew its legs up under itself. Just as the car was sent airborne, it leapt straight up into the air. The creature landed hard, rolling to a stop a few yards away.

The Chevy, on the other hand, soared through the air. Nancy, still screaming, raised her hands and forearms up to cover her face from the incoming impact.

The phone poles way out in Sigma were relics. They'd been put up decades earlier, when the lines had originally been run. It wasn't even that long ago when everyone in the township had still been on a party line. The poles had been due to be replaced years ago, but since such areas out in the "boonies" were of little concern, they were neglected.

It didn't take much force to snap the ancient pole in two. Nancy's car easily did the trick.

The Chevy hit the phone pole dead on, about four feet above the ground. The pole, once a proud white pine, had since dried out completely. It gave only a little fight before toppling over. The Chevy's grill and bumper wrapped themselves around the pole with a tremendous force, pushing the radiator and engine up almost all the way to the dashboard.

Nancy was wearing her seatbelt, but that wasn't enough to save her. First her forehead slammed against the top of the steering wheel, breaking her nose and jaw as the car horn went off. Then her body was smashed backward as the crumpled metal pinned her against the seat. She died almost instantly from the impact.

The Dogman took a few moments before stirring. But eventually, it did make its way slowly to all fours. It shook off the impact, its head taking a bit of time to clear itself. But within minutes, it had staggered off into the woods south of the Dredge. The creature could suffer the best that mankind could throw at it and yet still survive. It could live through crashes and impacts of every sort. It wasn't a werewolf, and therefore couldn't be taken down by silver bullets, or by bullets of any sort for that matter. It had survived the ravages of fire and ice, of great storms and even time eternal. It had seen the rise and fall of many native civilizations, and it had even aided the destruction of cultures. Its roots traced back to the blackest of supernatural magic. It wasn't any kind of animal native to our world. And it was a far cry from its once human origins.

Beyond the destruction of Nancy Butler and her car, the

crash had other disastrous consequences. The phone lines, stretched to the max, had snapped like fishing line when the phone pole toppled.

Less than three hours later, the sun would rise, bathing the sky in luminescent violet and indigo before the glistening rays of yellow and white clawed their way over the trees of the Au Sable. And despite this one last beautiful sunrise before the town's demise, drastic changes were already in motion. All communication with the outside world had been severed. No one in the area could contact each other, let alone anyone else anywhere.

There was no one to call for help, not that anyone would come to their aid anyway. With every local effort going into the set up for the annual Cherry Festival, phone lines into Sigma were hardly a priority, and therefore would be down for several days or even up to a week. With such big doings off in Traverse City, there was little regard for the tiny community in the backwoods of Kalkaska County.

Sigma (IX)

Doc Custer was the first on the scene that morning at the Mercantile. His mind was distracted from the lack of sleep. Though he didn't notice, he was wearing mismatched socks and his pants were held up with both a belt and suspenders. Adding insult to injury, he'd buttoned up his shirt incorrectly—each button was one notch off. His appearance would have been comical under other circumstances. This morning, however, no one paid any notice.

The noises in the night had escalated from the howls and shrieks seemingly commonplace these days to an ominous series of crashing and banging. Doc had just reached the little sidewalk leading to the entryway when he stopped in his tracks. Suddenly, his head was swimming in the early morning glow. His knees buckled, and he nearly fell over. As it was, he had to swing his arms just to keep his balance. He could hardly believe what his eyes were showing him.

First of all, the entire door was missing. It wasn't lying around anywhere; it wasn't dangling at the hinges. It was simply gone! The door jamb was smashed, splinters of wood scattered across the doorstep, the cracked walkway, and the flowerbeds beneath the store's front windows.

Doc moved in a little closer so he could get a peek into the store. Though it was daylight outside, the lights were still off inside. That didn't stop him from getting a good look at the mess inside. He raised a wrinkly hand to cover his mouth as he took a deep breath. He never thought it possible for the otherwise immaculately clean store to be in such a state of disorder. Then he called out for his friend. "Jack! Jack! Are you in there?"

The only answer was the creaking of crickets somewhere in the darkness. The open doorway was an open invitation to the bugs and other little critters to help themselves to take their fill from the Mercantile's spilled foods. Doc thought about going into the building but decided against it. Looking down at the scattered white flour on the floor, he saw two sets of tracks. One appeared to be made by a man's shoes. The other was some kind of animal. And though he was no expert, even old Doc could discern the size was much larger than anything that he knew normally prowled around northwest Michigan.

Instead of going in, he walked quickly over to Jack's house, and then stopped again as he saw his friend's front door still open, the screen door lightly wriggling against its spring.

A spasm shook his entire body. This wasn't right. None of this was right.

The old timer scuttled back to his own house a block away. Intending to call for help, he picked up the phone. But there was no dial tone. There was no noise at all. Doc clicked the receiver button several times, but to no avail. The phone was dead.

***

During that entire day, the humidity rose throughout northern Michigan as the storm front moved in. The high, blue, cloudless skies previously reaching over the land for many weeks were now home to puffy, grayish-white pillows that steadily piled up as if in anticipating a great slumber party of the gods. Even the air, the breeze, felt different. After nearly two months without rain, folks could feel the moisture all around them.

Change was in the air, and it would be here soon.

However, the oppressive heat remained. Only now, instead of a dry heat, the land was smothered in a muggy blanket of oppression. Folks all around the north were sweating profusely even if they weren't doing anything nearly resembling physical labor.

Thirty miles away, the beaches along Grand Traverse Bay were packed with tourists and locals trying to beat the heat. Cherry Festival would begin in a few days, and of course Traverse City was booming as always right before the Fourth of July. The vast resources of all the surrounding counties, including public services, utilities, and most importantly manpower, were focused on the Cherry Capitol as preparations for this year's festival were completed.

Of course, those in charge of organization were hoping that the incoming storm would run its course and be out of the Great Lakes region by the first day of Cherry Fest. To those in air-conditioned offices, the stifling heat and dryness of the past two months was of little concern. They wanted the heat and the beautiful weather that enticed, called to, and absolutely pulled the tourists away from the concrete jungles of downstate cities for a brief stay, a weekend get-away, or a minor vacation in the north.

The summer visitors meant cold, hard cash to the local economy. The more, the better. And great weather always brought more tourists. The two went hand in hand.

Cherry Fest was a time for the tourists to play, and for the locals to work. And for those farther away from the big lake, such as the folks out in the vastly unpopulated center of Kalkaska County, the big summer festival might as well not have even existed.

Most of the summer folk and the tourists visiting the lake didn't even know Sigma existed. Most never left the thoroughfare of the main highways and the vacation towns en route. It was probably for the best that all of the focus that week was on Traverse City. It gave the backwoods community the uninterrupted time and space to take matters into their own hands.

In Sigma, there would be no festival, no celebration, no good times, especially if they couldn't gain control over their own summer visitor.

Brian and Bonnie (II)

The old, rusty station wagon slowly backed down the dirt driveway as Brian emerged from between the line of maple trees along the road. At least he'd get to say one last goodbye before Bonnie left.

Her mother had a lost, vacant look on her face, and yet there was a sparkle in her eyes. For the first time since being married, Tanya was truly free. In some ways that was even scarier. As a battered wife, at least she knew exactly what to expect on a daily basis, even if it was horrible. Her life was nothing else if not consistent. She had become used to John's violence, the trauma; she was more or less numb to it all after thirteen years.

But now, she wasn't sure how she'd deal with it all. She wasn't certain that she could find a new line of work. She wasn't certain where they were going to end up, only that they were going to head as far south as possible. Maybe they'd end up at her sister's in Elkhart, Indiana. It was quite a ways to the state border, but who knows? Life was full of uncertainties at the moment.

She certainly wasn't sure how her daughter was going to react to everything. It couldn't be easy for a child to lose her father, even if he was abusive. It couldn't be easy to suddenly pack up and leave like a thief in the night. It couldn't be easy to leave everything behind.

However, the one thing she did know for certain was that she wasn't going to spend one more night in this accursed town. She and Bonnie were getting out of there well before nightfall. When John hadn't returned by three that afternoon, Tanya made the decision. As far as she was concerned, he got whatever bad end was coming to him. The two of them packed quickly, literally throwing their bare necessities into the station wagon.

Bonnie poked her small head out the passenger window and looked back. Her freckled face tried its best at a parting smile, but it seemed very sad. She raised her hand in a final goodbye toward Brian before her fingers curled back down against the palm of her hand.

Brian waved, knowing it was likely the last time that he'd ever see her. Bonnie's mother was never coming back to Sigma, that was for sure. At least Bonnie was going to be safely away from here. His heart ached, not because of any romantic feelings he had for her, but because of the friendship they had finally kindled. They'd shared a horrific, terrifying experience and survived. And, even though Stevie saved the day, Brian had acted in a most heroic fashion. He'd certainly won the admiration of the girl whom thought the most of in the world (maybe even more so than his own mother). He'd wanted for so long to be able to talk to her, to spend time with her. But he'd never found the courage to do so. And now, they'd had only one day, one afternoon really, to be friends, before she would exit his life forever.

The station wagon swung north on C-571 and Bonnie's' mother never even looked back. A little cloud of dust rose from the dry dirt of their driveway, obscuring the vehicle as it headed toward the highway and the interstate twenty miles beyond.

Sadly, Brian kept his hand raised in a final farewell. Though he couldn't see her, Bonnie's face peered out of the glass of the large rear window. A solitary tear coursed its way down her cheek, and then she was gone.

Horner's

Every able-bodied person who could carry a gun, let alone fire one, started showing up in the parking lot outside Horner's an hour or two before dusk. Of course, that meant almost everyone in the area had gathered here, except those few who had already skipped town or those who stayed home behind locked doors, taking care of their children. But then again, nearly everyone in the area could fit inside Horner's Bar and still drink comfortably without rubbing shoulders.

There was still about an hour of true daylight left. The world of shadows wouldn't take hold until well after half past nine. The assembled posse, under the direction of Joe Randall, wanted to be stationed in the woods and the Dredge well before nightfall.

Joe was already in the parking lot explaining his directives to the onlookers. A large county map was unfolded and spread out on the hood of his Chevy one-ton pickup. Fingers that were not holding large weapons were pointing toward the various topographical lines.

His orders were specific to each of the captains. "George, your crew starts at the top of the Dredge. Set up a skirmish line from Tarran's farm. Move south at eleven o'clock."

George Schmidt nodded, his fleshy jowls bobbing up and down. He and twenty of his neighbors, along with Steve Tarran would be holding the northern edge of the assault. Steve's farm occupied eighty acres, half on each side of Carroll Road. Forty acres of hay were harvested at the northern extreme of the Dredge each year.

The leader next turned to Mark Willins, the skinny, dark-complexioned man on his left. "Mark, you've got Mecum Road, both sides. Meet Steve in the middle, then double back if you don't see anything. Got it?"

Mark gave a curt nod.

Joe made his way around to all of the captains, pointing to their destinations. The others gathered in the parking lot who were not going into the Dredge were heading out into the many square miles of forest that surrounded Sigma. In turn, they signaled their agreement to the plan.

"Does everyone have lights?" asked Joe a bit tentatively. "There's no moonlight tonight. Obviously, we want to see what we're aiming for."

Heads nodded all around the assembly.

"Then get your crews together. Make sure everyone knows the plans," Joe said gravely to them. They knew how important it was. "We can't afford any screw ups tonight."

***

Thirty feet away, Lloyd Horner stepped out of the bar, having ushered the last couple of Friday-night rounders outside. He left the interior lights on in anticipation of returning quickly. If they finished up business soon, he could rake in a fortune afterward. He might even keep the bar open all night if the mob was in a celebratory mood. If they could put a stop to this crazy business, hell, he might even dance on the bar.

Some of the folks who showed up here early this evening still needed a little liquid courage, despite the considerable amount of testosterone permeating the parking lot. Those who had come out were keyed up, ready for adventure. Standing in small groups, rifles pointed skyward and stocks planted on hips, they joked and laughed. At the very least, they were psyched to head into the woods and shoot something, especially since hunting season was still nearly five months away. Folks in Sigma weren't especially fond of poaching, but they did like to hunt, and any excuse to partake in the hunt was absolutely pounced upon.

"Lloyd," called one of a group of armed men sitting in the back of a pickup parked at the curb out front. He was wearing a camouflage t-shirt and fatigues. This neighbor was also passing a bottle of some clear liquor among the group, and from the slight slurring of his voice, he and his companions were already halfway in the bag. "Why you leavin the lights on?"

The old timer locked the front door, then turned to the street, hands shoved down into the pockets of his jeans. He gave them a sly grin. "Hopefully, this whole thing won't take long. Hopefully we'll all be back here toasting our success very soon."

This was met with cheers from the pickup, and one of the fellows in the truck bed even fired off a round into the air. This was, of course, met with even more cheering from the adjacent parking lot, and not a few other gunshots in chorus.

The men expected a successful night. Though each might have had some nervousness deep in his stomach, the power of the posse, that old mob mentality, took over. Lloyd in particular was looking for a bit of retaliation for his missing friend, Jack Cooper. The discovery of the destroyed Mercantile hit the old timers the hardest. They were their own gang, if it could be called that. Certainly the many hours spent passing the time together qualified them as close friends.

All day he had kicked himself for not acting in some fashion the night before. If he hadn't turned yellow and hid in his upstairs apartment, perhaps his friend wouldn't be among the missing today. He wanted the opportunity to make up for his cowardice.

The face he put on this evening hid the fear he felt deep inside. But he couldn't show that to anybody. And his false bravado was meant to keep himself going, too. Lloyd knew what it was that they were out hunting. He'd seen it through the window of the bar. It wasn't like anything he'd ever seen before, and it wasn't really anything he wanted to see again unless it was laid out on the hood of someone's pickup.

The bar tender and the final customers turned the corner of the bar and saw the fully assembled throng in the gravel parking lot. Joe Randall was standing in the back of his pickup addressing the gathered men.

"Remember boys," Joe bellowed out to the crowd, "this is as much a search and rescue as it is a hunting party. We're still looking for Jack Cooper, Wayne Eastman, John Hailey and his kid, and who knows who else from around here that might be missing. Or some evidence of them at the least. We don't know where they are yet, but we are hoping for the best."

A moment of sobriety filtered through the crowd as everyone nodded silently. At least four members of their community were missing and probably in even worse condition than they could imagine.

"And remember, folks," Joe called out, "there's a lot of us out there. Be sure you know what you're shooting at. And stay out of the line of fire. We don't need any unnecessary casualties."

He sighed and looked around, gathering his own courage. "Then let's move out. Good luck and happy hunting!"

Eric (V)

Eric had never been so unsure of a decision in his life. There was no way he could stop the sheer mass of people from heading into the woods. Even if he were to call for backup right now, they'd never get the manpower here in time to stop this group. By the time they arrived, these local yahoos would be fully entrenched in the wilderness. Plus, there weren't enough conservation officers (or regular county officers for that matter—they were busy in Traverse City keeping an eye on the early birds the weekend before Cherry Fest) to make a dent in this group.

And considering the strained relationship he had with the Warden, Eric wasn't sure he wanted to chance a call for help anyway. He was pretty sure that his boss wouldn't want to be bothered on a Friday night, and certainly not by his least favorite officer. And he didn't know if the Warden would believe the situation he was seeing out here anyway.

Of course, things would have to be even worse. Murphy's law. On top of everything, the phones were out, too. Could the night get even worse? *Don't even ask*, he told himself. *You know it can get worse really quick.*

He was on his way home and had stopped in South Boardman for gas when he caught wind of the happenings in Sigma. Thanks to a tip-off by the station attendant, he had returned quickly to the little town just in time to see the trucks dispersing in all directions.

Seeing several vehicles pass him, beds filled with raucous men holding rifles in one hand and beers in the other, Eric's first thought was to stop and arrest them. There were obviously multiple violations occurring here. But then the enormity of the situation hit home. Sure, one truck might stop for him. He might even make an arrest or give out a few citations. But that would be just the tip of the iceberg.

And what if the driver didn't want to stop? What if the hunters turned hostile? Would they shoot a DNR officer? A few seconds of thought easily persuaded him that they just might.

This community, as he'd come to realize this week, had its own laws. It had its own solutions to problems. And they were not used to interference from the outside.

There was little, if anything, he could do to stop these men. On his way in, Eric thought that he might be able to talk some sense into them. Maybe there would only be a handful of folks. But seeing this great mob head out into the woods, he now saw how powerless he truly was.

There was no way he was going to get in the middle of it all. He valued his life too highly. Sure, he'd seen some very unusual things this week, some things he couldn't explain. And he'd had some nightmares of his own, his imagination obviously making strange connections among the bits evidence he'd seen. Despite the traces of evidence he'd seen and failed to document, he did believe there was some creature running amok in the woods. Roaming a woods full of armed rednecks was a dangerous career move in the daylight, let alone at night. If he weren't mistaken for their quarry, or accidentally caught in the crossfire, he might be the victim of friendly fire. And if that creature was capable of the damage he'd seen, he didn't want to be anywhere near it in the dark.

As he turned the corner onto C-571, Eric saw the last few pickups still in Horner's parking lot, the last of the men preparing to head out. He swung his work truck up in front, blocking the drive. If they were going to leave, at least they'd have to drive over the curb to get out.

He'd almost leapt out of his truck in an effort to stop the lead vehicle. Eric's arms and hands waved out in front of his body like an old fashioned traffic cop. He hoped the pickup would stop for him.

Luckily, it did.

Moving around to the driver's side window, Eric tried his best to be calm and collected, to act like he was in charge. It was obviously a ruse that the driver wasn't falling for.

"Sir, what's going on here tonight?" he asked the driver.

Joe Randall's beefy arm was on the window's edge. He locked eyes with the DNR officer. Eric would never forget the seriousness of the man's visage, the steel gray of his eyes, the tight set of his mouth and jaw.

"We've got our own business to attend to here," Joe answered. The engine of his pickup rattled, eager to get underway. "It doesn't concern you or the DNR."

Eric tried his best to persuade the big man. "Sir, what you're doing isn't just against the law, it's dangerous to everyone. Look how many guys are out here, in the dark, loaded for bear, and itchin' for something to shoot. This is madness!"

"Son," Joe, leaning his head out the window, said slowly and powerfully, "this is a community matter. Our community. We do appreciate your concern, but we'll be handling it. I think it's best if you just stay out of the way." He gave the young officer a faint, no-nonsense smile.

From the bed of the pickup came the familiar clicks of shotguns being loaded. No one was pointing a gun at him, not yet anyway, but the threat was suddenly very real.

The lawman took the hint. Eric stepped back, hands up to show he wasn't going to get in the way. Hey, if these folks wanted to go out and shoot each other up, more power to them. He'd tried to stop them. Eric was only one man, after all. Things might have been different with an army of conservation officers.

.Then again, perhaps there was no stopping these folks. They'd do what they wanted anyway.

North Dredge

Steve Tarran's wife had offered hot coffee and small slices of home-baked strawberry rhubarb pie for the men before they set out. It didn't take them long to eat their way through the four pies she'd spent all day baking. The pie was fabulous.

She watched nervously through the kitchen window over the double sink as the men set out across the back yard and through the rickety wooden gate. The sun had set below the tree line to the west and the ethereal shadow land of violet and deep blue had swept over the Dredge. Her wringing hands ground a dishtowel against her apron. She couldn't remember a time in her life when she was more afraid for her husband. This whole thing was so wrong and so awful that it gave her shivers.

The last of the sunlight faded from the world at exactly 10:32 p.m. Big George, his enormous girth pushing out the sides of his faded barn jacket, dispersed his team in a skirmish line with ten yards between each man. They began their slow, steady advance southward through the hay field and then on into the tall grass of the Dredge. Each man carried both a firearm and a powerful flashlight. As planned, they called back and forth to each other, constantly checking in up and down the line. Carroll Road and the farm now well behind them, the line of men moved steadily into the great field.

Big George reached back and swatted a mosquito that had the misfortune to land on his thick, meaty neck. The bugs were abundant on the Dredge, that was for sure, and tonight was no exception. Once they had walked well out into the tall grass, the mosquitoes would be unmerciful. At least the black flies and the no-seeums only made an appearance during the day. They were far more annoying than the mosquitoes.

Somewhere off in the distance, an owl gave a long, drawn-out hoot. It was eerie in the depths of the darkness. Despite the night's warmth, most of the men in the skirmish line shivered.

Jeff (I)

Let those fools scare it up. While they're down there running crazy, stirring things up, he'd wait for the right opportunity.

Jeff Higgs sat patiently, high in the forked branches of an ancient oak on the edge of the Au Sable Forest. From his vantage point at the center of the Dredge, he'd have the best opportunity to take down the beast himself.

He'd barely moved in the two hours since he'd taken up residence in the limbs of the gigantic tree. Even the occasional peeks into his binoculars were painstakingly slow endeavors as his hands methodically raised them to his eyes while his head swiveled from side to side. He'd scanned the Dredge every few minutes, ever careful to maintain his best sense of invisibility.

His high-powered Remington 700, basically a police-issue sniper rifle, was deadly accurate at 800 meters. However, in field tests, Jeff had blown through targets with a fair bit of accuracy at over a kilometer. This souped-up rifle wasn't exactly the kind that most civilians could get their hands on, but he had a few connections that had paid off. Gun collecting was his favorite hobby, and he'd managed to procure a number of models that most folks could only read about in magazines.

His night vision was provided by the most advanced Gen II monocular device available, attached to the telescopic scope of the rifle with a Picatinny rail. With it, even the tiniest light from the stars would be enough to light up the area below in a ghostly green aura. And the flashlight beams of the hunters crossing from the north and south ensured excellent vision. If the creature showed up on the Dredge, it had no place to hide.

Jeff took a deep breath and exhaled slowly. He was wired from the dozen cups of coffee he had poured into his system over the afternoon hours. He could wait all night up here, silent and still, until the creature appeared. If this night was anything like the previous nights week, it was only a matter of time.

South Dredge

10:40 p.m.
Nineteen men crossed the drainage ditch bordering Mecum Road and entered the Dredge from the south. The ditch was bone dry, and their boots crackled the leaves beneath. Like the similar party several miles to the north, the men spread out in a skirmish line covering the entire breadth of the great field. The beams of their flashlights swung and bounced, piercing the darkness and cutting swaths through the tall grasses.

Mark Willins strode down the dead center of the Dredge. Every fifty feet or so, he called to the men on either side of him: Adam Wallace to his right and Phil Barnes on the left. They'd give back the same response—"Clear!"—and then call on to the next man in line.

Normally, plenty of stars could be seen overhead, shining down like sparkling diamonds on a deep velvety backdrop. The night before, only a few curling, wispy clouds very high in the sky interfered with the otherwise clear night. Though few in number, those cirrus clouds were the harbingers of the storm to come.

Tonight however, the stars that had been so prevalent for the past two months were blocked out by the thick, puffed-up clouds steadily changing from a cheerful white to a deep, dismal gray tinged with black and violet as they piled up upon each other. The cloud cover kept the air up here in northern Michigan very warm and humid, and the men on the Dredge were drenched in sweat. Sure, a front was moving in, but it would still be 24 hours (or more) before the weather shift would play a major role in the town's affairs.

There was no moon this night to illuminate the activity on the Dredge, and the first slivers of the great orb wouldn't appear for another two days, even if they could peek through the heavy cloud cover. No, it was going to be a very dark night indeed.

Jeff (II)

11:27 p.m.

The night vision scope provided him with a view of the whole show. It was almost like watching the Lions from the upper deck of the Silverdome as opposed to standing on the sidelines. The perspective changed tremendously when you were twenty feet in the air.

Jeff had no way of contacting either party, and no way to warn them.

Twenty-two lines were being drawn through the thick grass from the north. At the head of each, a single bright light bobbed back and forth. Nineteen furrows were splitting the grass from the south, and again, each was led by a bright light. The dividing lines through the Dredge were heading on a nearly straight course toward each other. About a hundred feet behind each man, the tall grass recovered from the passage, eventually leaning its way to close back over the trail.

But there was one other parting of the grass, one with no light at its head. And it didn't move in anything resembling a straight line like the others. It angled and curved as it steadily made its way through the Dredge.

After several hours of waiting, after an hour of the skirmish lines' advancement, Jeff knew his quarry had finally arrived. The creature was showing itself.

He carefully adjusted the scope, zooming in as far as he could. A few moments later, the adjustments were clearly displayed through his night vision device. The scene from over a mile away was unfolding before his eyes. Whatever was cutting its way through the tall grass of the Dredge was very dark. From this distance, details weren't discernible. But Jeff could tell that it was human-shaped, and considering its head and shoulders were just visible at the tips of the tall grass, it had to be walking on two legs. It appeared to have large, pointed ears. On occasion, he could even see what appeared to be arms or hands reaching out and pushing the grasses out of its path. It was heading its way toward town, though not in any particular hurry.

The line of lights from the south was moving much faster than those from the north, and they were destined to meet a bit past the Dredge's halfway point, which was about on a line from the trailer belonging to the Alexander family.

Jeff calculated in his head that the two groups of lights, based on their approximate speeds, would probably meet in about fifteen minutes. The errant line in the grass would be right between them.

Night on the Dredge (I)

11:34 p.m.

Big George looked right, then left, calling to the men on either side of him. Though he couldn't see them through the tall, thick grasses, the glow of their flashlights easily marked their location in the darkness.

They were closing in on the southern group. A faint glow spanned the Dredge far ahead of them. There was a bit of comfort in that glow; there were humans behind those lights, not some strange, as-of-yet unidentified creature.

Mike Silva returned the call from George's left. "Nothing yet. How's it your way? Anything to report?"

"Nothin'. Keep sharp, the other group's comin' up. Pass the word to keep tips pointed down. We don't need any accidents." George knew all about hunting accidents. When he was a child, his older brother Winston was killed in a gun mishap. They were scaring up rabbits when the gun carried by one of Winston's good friends went off. Unfortunately, the barrel was pointed upward, right at Winston's head. Holding the tip up was a mistake any young teenager could make, one that many kids did make. George's fourteen-year-old brother was dead before his body hit the ground. Only eleven at the time, George watched the whole thing happen before his eyes, and the image had haunted him ever since.

Eventually, the check-in call reached Tom McClusky, who had joined the western end of the line when it passed his farm. Considering all that had happened on his property, there was no way he'd miss the opportunity for some old-fashioned justice. Something was going to pay for the damage done to his place, that was for sure.

"Clear here," he responded. Like the others, he swatted the mosquitoes from his face and neck.

***

11:37 p.m.

From the south, the skirmish line worked steadily forward, heavy work boots stamping down the tall grasses that would eventually rise back up and obscure the path again.

They too could see the flashlight beams of the group coming steadily toward them. It was an alien scene, like something out of a science-fiction movie.

Phil Barnes carried his 12-gauge shotgun in front of his chest. It wasn't the proper way to do so, but he kept his finger right alongside the trigger. His emotions swung in a pendulum between excitement and apprehension. Sure, it was great to be out here in the company of his neighbors and friends, doing his duty to protect the town. Everyone was so pumped up about the hunt that he couldn't help but join in. But there was a fear factor involved too. The thing that they were hunting was responsible for the bone-chilling screams that had kept everyone awake all week. It wasn't the mere calls of a wild animal; it was something else entirely, something huge and powerful and deadly.

This thing had also damaged a number of homes and other property in the area. Pets and livestock were killed or missing all over Sigma. And there were even a few missing folks—people he knew for God's sake. He wasn't close friends with the other three, but Jack Cooper was a great guy. And the way the Mercantile had been destroyed the night before, Phil couldn't see any way that they'd find him alive. Sure, he wanted to stop the creature before it did any more damage. But deep down, he was also frightened to the core of his being. More than once he thought of slipping back and deserting. No one would know. He could just make his way back to his pickup and get away from the entire mess. But each time, he thought of the others out here. Even an old timer like Lloyd Horner was stationed somewhere in the Sigma darkness. If Lloyd could handle being out here, he should be able to do so too.

While Phil was coming to grips with his emotions, Mark Willins was steady and stoic. Unbeknownst to him, he was closing the gap on another living being out on the Dredge. This one carried no flashlight, and it was far from human.

His path was leading him directly into the path of the creature, and an encounter would be imminent within a few minutes.

***

11:40 p.m.

The crosshairs of the scope were directly over the creature's shoulder blades. It was now or never.

It had stopped, obviously listening and sniffing the air for the oncoming hunters. The creature made an excellent target.

Jeff exhaled slowly through his parted lips as he pulled the trigger. The .50-caliber slug flew straight and true, slicing through the warm air.

The creature swung violently to its left from the impact and spun around before collapsing below the rippling tips of the tall grass. The loud report echoed through the Dredge a second later, catching up to the projectile from which it had issued.

"Yes!" Jeff exclaimed through clenched teeth. The shot was right on target. There would be no recovering from that one; it was a direct hit. He'd dropped the creature right on the spot.

Had he been looking through the night vision goggles, he'd have seen the flashlight beams crazily searching in all directions for the origin of the gunshot.

That's the way to do it, he thought. *Those fools down there couldn't have done half as good a job. With the proper weapon in the hands of an expert, the problem is solved.* He could already see the envious faces of the others when they bought him drinks in Horner's. *City boy, indeed. Well, this city boy could show these hicks how to do things right.* A small smirk appeared on his face. *City boy, indeed.*

But a few moments later, Jeff's jaw dropped open in disbelief. It couldn't be. It just wasn't possible.

The dark shape reappeared at the wispy ends of the tall grass. It shook its head from side to side in rapid fashion, shoulders shrugging. A few seconds later, it was darting in all directions, looking for whatever had injured it.

Jeff stared through the scope, unable to believe what he was seeing.

The .50-caliber round should have blown a hole the size of a grapefruit right through the creature. And yet, here it was, up and moving again.

Jeff took aim once again, lining up the crosshairs on the dark mass that was certainly the creature's neck and shoulders. This time it was more difficult because the target was flitting about. But after a few seconds, the hunter again pulled the trigger.

The dark shape was propelled forward this time and disappeared from view. Another perfect shot! He waited patiently, but was disappointed once again as the creature emerged yet again. Jeff exhaled in exasperation. How was it possible? He'd hit it dead on twice; he'd watched the target tumble from the impact.

In his peripheral vision, Jeff could see the lights of the hunters closing in on the creature. He grunted, angry that the locals might steal his thunder. This was supposed to be his kill, not theirs. A few of their flashlight beams were crisscrossing his edge of the forest, searching for the origin of the gunshots. They knew someone was up this way, but didn't know exactly where.

Angry now, he returned the crosshairs to the creature for a third time. *Third time's a charm*, he thought. Jeff's teeth gritted, and he snarled as he pulled the trigger one more time.

The target went down a third time. This time, there was no movement, no rising of a dark shape in the grass. Jeff watched through the scope for a full thirty seconds to confirm it. The tall grasses showed a whitish-yellow in the green aura of the night vision scope. He could see the dark area which indicated the creature's final location, having flattened the brush beneath it.

He'd finally done it!

Jeff pumped his fist in the air. "Yes!" he spouted into the darkness. It was over.

The lines in the grass were moving faster and converging on the creature's location. Within seconds, the hunters would happen upon the carcass.

Still in the crook of the tree, Jeff looked back into the scope to watch the scene unfold below. He wanted to see the reaction of the hunters when they found the creature. He was sure it would be priceless.

***

11:45 p.m.

The flashlight beams met only yards away from the carcass. Mark Willins heard Big George call out to him through the surreal world of the Dredge. Moving through the great field had become like being in a dream or a nightmare. The bouncing flashlights were creating a nearly strobe-like effect from the excitement of their owners. The tall grasses were illuminated off and on, creating a ghostly scene.

"I think it's over here," Big George yelled across the top of the grass.

The cacophony of voices echoed across the Dredge. It was too difficult to identify who hollered out what in the darkness.

"Where?"

"Off to my left—your right, a few yards."

"There were shots, but where'd they come from?"

"Sounded like over there," someone said pointing off at the Au Sable Forest to the east.

"Who shot it?" another voice asked.

"I dunno, but it looks like it's dead. It's not moving anyway," the first voice answered.

"What is it?"

"No idea. We haven't found it yet."

And then all hell broke loose.

***

11:45 p.m.

Though he couldn't hear the conversation, Jeff watched it all happen. And he was powerless to do much of anything about it.

The hunter's lights had moved in, encircling the downed creature. Just as the first man reached the matted grass, the dark shape exploded upward.

Jeff initially lost sight of it because of its speed. It had leapt right out of the view of his night vision scope. He reached one shaking hand up and adjusted the knob quickly, widening the view. And then he swore into the night.

"Arrrrgh!" he hollered, one balled-up fist pounding into the rough bark of the old oak tree. "There's no way..."

But it had happened nonetheless.

The creature still lived. It lived, and now it was not only ticked off, it was cornered. It turned violently on the men closing in on it.

***

11:48 p.m.

Mark Willins had just pushed his way into the flattened grass where the creature had fallen. The tip of his rifle led the way in, followed immediately by the bright beam of his MagLite. He'd beaten Big George to the spot by about ten yards. Mark was just about to get his first glimpse of the creature when the world absolutely exploded in front of him.

A huge, dark shape, blacker than the night, erupted from the grass and leapt straight up nearly a dozen feet into the sky over the Dredge. It was immediately lost in the darkness overhead. Grass and weeds shook and squirmed from the rapid ascent, and a mushroom cloud of dry chaff puffed out in all directions. Mark's gun and flashlight were knocked right out of his hands by the impact. He had no idea if it was the creature's hands, arms, or body that did it. The gun disappeared to the darkness surrounding the roots of the tall grass. The flashlight flipped, end over end, the light beam making crazy, concentric circles in the night, before landing a few yards off. Its light still shined dimly, reflecting the gold and green of the various weeds and grasses.

The attention of the hunters was immediately drawn upward as they tried to locate the creature. In the glow of their beams, they'd seen the wild explosion just ahead of them, and they knew the creature would be coming back down in a moment or two.

Mark stepped backward, surprised, and lost his footing. He landed hard on his rump and stared straight up. The last image his brain provided him was that of a demonic, hairy face illuminated by glowing yellow eyes plummeting down upon him. Its maw opened wide, fangs glimmering in the beams of the hunters' flashlights. Mark tried to scream, but the creature was upon him before he could muster a sound.

Big George was the first to train his .30-30 on the descending beast. However, he wouldn't be able to get a shot off until the creature landed, and by then Mark's gurgling screams were already splitting the otherwise quiet night.

And then the darkness was filled with gunshots as the two sides opened fire.

***

11:50 p.m.

Mike Silva, twenty-three years younger and much faster than Big George, beat the older, heavier man to the spot. Holding his flashlight alongside the barrel of his hunting rifle, he burst in upon the matted grass where the first man had fallen. But before he could move any closer, his feet slipped out from beneath him. The stock of his rifle jabbed into the earth, and his index finger pulled back on the trigger, firing a shot straight up into the dark night sky. A fraction of a second later, his torso landed in a slippery, slimy puddle of blood, which caked the ground and dripped down upon him from the tall grasses. Holding his hands up to his face, he was sure he was dying until, he realized the blood was from someone else.

Bullets suddenly zipped right over his head, followed immediately by the reverberating cracks of the shots. A little dizzy from the fall, the loud reports echoed painfully through his head. He covered his ears with his bloody hands, tucked his body into a fetal position, and lay on the matted grasses, just trying to get his breath back.

***

11:56 p.m.

Gunshots were fired from all over the small area of the Dredge. The loud cracks drowned out the words of the men, and all that could be heard were the unidentifiable shouts.

The dark shape of the creature, growling and hissing, leapt from place to place in the tall grass. It was far too fast for the humans to train their sights upon.

More hunters arrived, their flashlight beams illuminating patches of the area. But their itchy trigger fingers and adrenaline-infused brains bowled over their better judgment. They began opening fire on any shadow, any movement in the grass.

Like others at the fringes of the skirmish lines, Wade Thompson ran forward to get closer to the action. As he came to within a dozen yards of what was becoming the epicenter of the clash, he was blown backward almost ten feet, a bloody crater in his chest from the slugs of both barrels of a 12-gauge shotgun.

Big George was shot in the back as he had knelt down to check Jody MacIntyre's lifeless body for a pulse. He screamed in pain, dropping his light and gun as his hands trying desperately to cover the bloody exit hole in his chest. He toppled forward, blood gurgling through his lips, and he moved no more.

A moment after Phil Barnes had fired his shotgun, inadvertently blowing Wade Thompson away, he was yanked backward and down to the ground by a hairy, clawed hand. His last thoughts, as the long fangs sunk into his neck, were that he should have slipped away when he had the chance.

The Dredge was filled with the cries and screams of men in pain, men dying from gunshot wounds or from the claws and jaws of the beast. Friendly fire easily took twice as many men as the creature did.

The creature moved low, crawling down on all fours. It wasn't looking for a means of escape; it was simply reacting to being cornered. It crept up on the men, one at a time, and dragged them down to its level.

And still the gunshots continued, as the men pulled triggers to aim their sights on anything that moved. It was the bloodlust of battle that had gripped them, and they were fully caught up in it.

***

11:59 p.m.

The target was far too close to the other men for him to get a decent shot off. And it was moving so quickly that Jeff could hardly keep it within the confines of his night vision device. The creature was so fast! And it was agile, too—turning, leaping, and nimbly sidestepping as it slashed its victims. Only a few of the men were able to keep their heads in the bloody arena of the Dredge, but even they just weren't fast enough. Their number was quickly dwindling.

Many of the flashlights lay still on the ground, but a few more were still bobbing as the rest of the men raced in to join the chaos.

Jeff wasn't sure he could watch any more. Through the night vision scope, he'd seen, to his horror, many of these gruesome deaths. His stomach heaved, and he leaned over one large branch, expelling his dinner onto the ground far below.

Out on the Dredge, a thunderous howl split the night air. It was a howl of triumph.

Saturday

Night on the Dredge (II)

It didn't take the other hunters spread throughout the area very long to respond to the shooting on the Dredge. The first three shots by Jeff Higgs alerted everyone to the creature's location. Those who could get to their trucks fast enough left their posts all around Sigma's forests and hightailed it to the town's great meadow. The subsequent volley of gunshots only added to the adrenaline coursing through their systems. Most were wired, itching to get in on the action. They had no idea of the carnage awaiting them.

Vehicles converged on the Dredge from all directions. Many of the truck headlights were simply left on, the high beams bathing the tall grasses at the edge of the field. There were even a few with lights mounted up high on the roll bars. It was an eerie sight. Millions of buzzing insects and tiny particles of dust rose up into the lights as more hunters burst into the melee. It wouldn't take long before the trucks' grills and hoods were covered with bugs of all sorts.

A few of the locals couldn't even stagger their way out of the truck beds, instead passing out on top of miscellaneous tools and old sweatshirts, while crushing empty cardboard cases in the process. These folks were the lucky ones, the ones who would see another day. Those who made their way out into the great field entered an arena as bloody and horrifying as any seen in the great gladiator battles of the ancient world.

To anybody passing the greater Sigma area within a ten-mile radius, the melee of gunshots sounded like a private Fourth of July celebration. Not that there would be anybody way out in the wilderness, anyway. But at least the loud cracks that split the night air drowned out the terrifying, inhuman growls and shrieks of the creature, as well as the far too recognizable screams and cries of the men who would never see the sun rise again.

Just as the last of the loud cracks and bangs from the guns of the first two groups of hunters were finishing, this new cadre of reserves ran right into the darkness of the Dredge. For a few dozen yards, the shadows of their heads and shoulders extended ahead of them, lit from behind by the vehicle headlights. Whether it was the adrenaline or the alcohol (or a combination of the two) pumping through their bodies, this group of backups charged boldly and fearlessly into the unknown. A few didn't even carry their own flashlights, and instead followed on the heels of those who were illuminating the scene ahead. They didn't know what to expect. Most figured they'd arrive just in time to get in on the photos of the successful hunt that was sure to become legendary.

What found them, what was waiting for them, was anything but a press clipping in the making.

There would be no photos in the *Record-Eagle*. There would be no interviews on Channel 9&10.

There would be no escape for any of them.

***

With his left hand, Lloyd Horner squeezed his plastic flashlight against the stock of his old deer-hunting rifle. The light was nervously twittering because of the old man's fearful shaking (and not the early stages of Parkinson's disease, as he reminded himself constantly). He was cut off from the rest of the group, alone, and wishing he'd never come out here in the first place. The false bravado from a few hours earlier had faded completely. Better to be home like his friends Doc Custer and Fred Waffle. Doc just wasn't quite himself after finding Jack Cooper's store so torn up. He'd gone right home and lain in bed the rest of the day. And Fred had a bad heart and could never attempt such an undertaking. They were both fortunate they weren't out here. So far, it was shaping up to be one of the worst nights of Lloyd's life, and he'd had some doozies in the service.

He began to turn toward the direction where most of the shooting was happening, glad to be out of the line of fire, when he saw the monster for the second time in his life.

One moment, his flashlight beam was simply bobbing along through the high grass, and the next it was shining on the monster, who had stepped out of what seemed like nowhere. It was about twenty feet away, and Lloyd's mind went flying back to the night before when he'd seen it, through the dirty windows and across the street, from the safety of the inside of his bar. Now, however, there was nothing between them but northern Michigan air and a few stalks of grass which were slowly bending themselves back upright.

A few more volleys of gunfire erupted a bit to his left. He couldn't figure out what the other guys were shooting at if the monster was way over here with him. And somehow it had doubled back on them all, coming at Lloyd from their eastern side.

But Lloyd didn't have long to wonder about the other hunters. He had his hands more than full here. The creature was bigger than he had pictured it the night before. Its hulking form stood, motionless, staring at him with those hypnotic glowing yellow eyes. But Lloyd was motionless, too, simply powerless to move. And then the creature slowly took a step forward, testing the waters. It took another step, and then another, gaining confidence. Lloyd knew he should try to take a shot, but his hands were shaking too badly. His face changed to a horrible grimace, and he gritted his teeth in despair.

The Dogman was upon him. It reached out one long arm and gripped the barrel of his rifle, the claws of its hand scraping noisily against the cold steel. It ripped the gun right from Lloyd's hands, leaving him holding only the tiny, plastic flashlight that was now shining its beam up into the creature's face.

Lloyd cried out as the Dogman let loose a deafening, deep-toned roar that blew the old man's wispy hair backward. He closed his eyes tightly, expecting the worst.

But then a loud gunshot blasted from behind him, and a bullet whizzed past his right ear, striking the monster on the shoulder. It jumped back, surprised and angered, and Lloyd thought for a moment that the cavalry had arrived to save him.

It wasn't to be. Just after the Dogman let him go, Lloyd's body was rocked backward and he tumbled to the ground, landing a few feet away. His left hand still miraculously held onto the flashlight. His right hand felt around his chest and there it found a hole in his plaid, buffalo-hunter's wool jacket. Lloyd's index finger reached in and he realized that the hole went a lot deeper than just through his clothing. Pulling his finger back out, the flashlight beam revealed it to be covered with deep red blood.

That shot had come from the woods at the eastern end of the Dredge. *Who could be out there shooting at us?* he wondered. He'd totally forgotten about the creature. Lloyd coughed, and a little trickle of blood seeped from his mouth. His last thoughts were of the mysterious shooter, taking out the hunters instead of the prey.

***

Mike Silva began screaming a few moments after regaining his breath. The absolute horror of being covered in someone else's blood obliterated any rational thought. It was this screaming that led to his downfall. Less than a minute later, his flashlight beam illuminated a gigantic shadow that had crept upon him. As he craned his neck back to see the creature looming above him, he saw, on either side of his head, its clawed paws that appeared almost human. Then the monster quickly reached its clawed hands down and Mike knew no more.

***

Steve Tarran was shot three times in the back by friendly fire. He dropped his hunting rifle at his feet, and his hands reached up to inspect the gaping holes that had opened in his chest. He fell to his knees, his bloody hands and fingers held up before his eyes, like a man praying in church. A moment later, he collapsed to the ground.

***

Tom McClusky actually hit the creature once with a fairly well-placed shot. But before he could pull the trigger again, a stray bullet peeled back the skin of his forehead, gouging a deep groove right in his skull. He died painfully several minutes later.

***

Mitchell Emmonds doubled over as the creature's long claws impaled him just above the kidneys. His attention had been completely focused forward, and he'd never even seen the Dogman stealthily creep up below the tall grass. As the darkness closed over him, his last thoughts were only a fleeting wonder about who would milk the cows in the morning.

Joe (III)

In a hurry, Joe Randall veered off of C-571, driving his pickup straight up Mike Silva's dirt-packed driveway, across his backyard, and right into the Dredge. It was night, fortunately, and Mike's kids weren't playing outside or they'd have been diving for cover. As it was, Joe crushed a number of cheap plastic toys and mangled a tricycle beneath the truck's off-road tires.

The big pickup bounded a good twenty yards into the tall grasses of the Dredge before Joe killed the engine. It took out a handful of skinny, shoulder-high red pines just beyond Mike's backyard. Their needles gave the undercarriage a good polishing as he plowed over them. As he swung out of the squeaky driver's side door, another series of gunshots echoed through the night. He wiped the sweat from beneath his camouflage cap with one muscled forearm. He didn't push too high on the cap, however, because he didn't want to disrupt the headlamp attached to a band that crossed behind his ears. Joe had been thinking ahead—the headlamp would give him hands-free light.

Joe was on his own. His wife had fled town the day before, finally unable to cope with the chaos that now surrounded their once quiet life. One day life was peaceful, normal, and sane; the next, everything had been turned upside down. The screams in the night were bad enough, but when their home suffered an attack, she'd really had enough. It had gotten personal for her, and she couldn't take it. She'd tried a number of times to convince her husband that they needed to just get out of town, to get away until it all simply blew over. She begged him to leave, to take a vacation, to find any excuse to just go. It didn't matter where. But he wouldn't budge. And she couldn't see why he was so adamant about staying behind, so determined to gather the troops and kill this creature, whatever it was. As sorry as she was to do it, leaving Joe in a lurch to be sure, she just couldn't stay any longer.

Her husband, on the other hand, wasn't one to just pack up and go at the first sign of trouble. Joe was ticked off enough that his trucking fleet was marred and he'd had to shell out a fairly healthy sum to cover the damage. He wasn't going to just let some *thing* scare him off. He had a business to run, and a home to protect. And there were others in town who needed someone to step up, to take charge. At least four townsfolk had disappeared so far, and those were the ones they knew of. Who knew who else way out in the sticks was unaccounted for? Joe wasn't about to see any more of his neighbors, his friends, simply disappear.

Now entering the chaos of the Dredge, Tough Joe was quite a sight. Sure, his jeans and lightweight flannel shirt, rolled up to his elbows, were the norm. But he now also sported two bandoliers, crossing his chest from shoulder to rib cage. A few inches below, slung low on his hips, were a pair of holsters tied down around his lower thigh with a thin cord to keep them from flapping. Protruding from each holster was an ivory handgrip attached to a vintage Colt Peacemaker revolver. These were the classic cavalry standard, 7-¼ inch long barrels—the ones that won the West. The handguns had been originally collected by Joe's father, a Wild West buff, and then inherited after the old man's death fifteen years ago. Joe always had kept them clean, polished, and in great working order. He even fired them on occasion, usually around the Fourth of July, when he and his wife would put on a huge BBQ for the driving crew.

If that wasn't enough, Joe also carried a double barrel, 12-gauge shotgun on the top of which he'd duck-taped his flashlight. The Remington 870 would be fed from the dozens of cartridges slung across his wide chest, and he was fairly quick at reloading.

Another gunshot, followed by a scream of pain, erupted from the Dredge about a hundred yards in. The big man raced through the grass, the way ahead of him bathed in light from his headlamp and the bobbing light attached to his shotgun. The tall grass parted easily for his big frame as his thick-soled boots smashed down on the hard-packed soil.

Ahead, he could see a few beams of light bouncing wildly in the night. It looked as if some lunatics had gained possession of an airport's searchlights and were wildly swinging them in all directions.

In pretty good shape for a heavy man of 52, Joe thundered his way through the underbrush for a good minute, listening to the growls and shrieks in the darkness, before the tall grass abruptly ended. One second he was pushing his way through, the tips of the grass smacking against his shoulders, and the next he was standing in a matted down clearing.

The first thing that struck him was the enormity of the carnage all around. The flattened grass was stained a deep, dark red from the blood that was seeping its way into the greedy, dry earth. There were a number of bodies lying around the clearing, ripped and torn clothing and skin, and also what appeared to be body parts strewn all over. Weapons littered the ground as well, and a number of flashlights still shined their beams in all directions, criss-crossing each other in awkward patterns. Joe glanced from left to right across the clearing, his jaw opened in disbelief. There was not a single recognizable person in all this mess; he couldn't even tell who anybody was by the clothing they had once worn.

And then he saw it. The creature stood, high and haughty, on its back legs at the far end of the little clearing. Joe had never seen anything like it, not even in his worst nightmares as a child. He had never been much of a movie watcher, so he had never seen the special effects that modern Hollywood used to bring werewolves and other monsters to life.

It must have stood seven feet or more in height, though it did slump a bit, legs bent at the knees, arms dangling at its sides. It had broad shoulders and wide hips. It appeared to be standing on the tips of its feet (or were they paws?). The creature was completely covered in a coarse, dark, matted fur that was wispy at the ends.

A long jaw, like a wolf's muzzle, protruded from the creature's enormous head

Its eyes reflected the light in a golden twinkle from his headlamp. The creature curled the right side of its mouth into a snarl, revealing a row of sharp fangs.

Joe didn't flinch. Deep down in his heart of hearts, the initial shock and fear were replaced by anger. This was the creature that was responsible for the missing people in town. This was the creature responsible for ripping up his truck fleet. This was the creature responsible for running off his wife. Joe gritted his teeth, snarling himself, and stared back at the creature. Very slowly, he raised the barrel of his shotgun as he kept his eyes locked with on those of the creature.

There would be no taking prisoners here tonight.

The monster reached both forearms backward, clawed hands clenched into fists. It puffed its chest out and raised its muzzle to the sky as it bellowed forth a long, deep, growling howl into the night. Its head slowly rotated on its powerful shoulders.

When it finished its war cry, it locked eyes with Joe again. Then it slowly crouched, knees bending to an impossible angle as it gathered its strength for the attack. The creature's knuckles nearly grazed the ground, and it looked to Joe as if it would instead charge from all fours.

Joe waited, shotgun at the ready. There was no use firing from twenty yards away and taking a chance of missing. He'd wait until it was at point-blank range and then he'd pull the trigger.

As these thoughts were coursing through the big man's mind, the Dogman sprang ahead. It moved with lightning speed, the first leap crossing a third of the distance between them in the blink of an eye. Joe couldn't aim; he didn't have the time. It was a good thing that the shotgun was already raised into position. The creature was illuminated by the flashlight taped to the double barrels, the spot of white light creating a bulls-eye on its hairy chest. It landed and sprang again, closing the distance. Half a second and it would have him.

The big man pulled the single trigger, and the left barrel expelled a powerful slug. It flew, straight and true, hitting the Dogman on the upper sternum, just beneath the neck. The blast thundered through the still, dark Sigma night. The creature was in mid-air, arms out and wide, claws spread in its full attack mode when it was slammed backward by the blast. Its balance was lost, and it dropped to all fours, shrieking loudly in pain.

The tip of the shotgun rose as the recoil slammed the weapon into Joe's shoulder. He immediately brought it back down to train onto the target. The Dogman, in the meantime, had risen back onto its back legs and stared at the human. One hand had reached up and was feeling the spot where the slug had entered its body. It staggered for a step, trying to regain its balance. All the while, it was regarding Joe and preparing to strike once more.

Joe pulled the trigger again and the right barrel fired. The second slug slammed into the Dogman's chest, knocking it completely head over heels as it flipped and landed face down only a few feet away. The creature was not ready for the second shot. Its hairy form lay in the matted grasses, seemingly dead.

Joe exhaled a sigh of relief, then wiped the sweat from his forehead and cheeks with his left hand.

And then the impossible happened. The creature moaned, then propped itself up on its elbows, then its hands and knees. Slowly, it rose to its hind legs once again.

Joe stood, rooted to the spot, staring unbelievingly at the creature that just wouldn't die. Two 12-gauge blasts at that close range would have put down even a grizzly bear.

Despite the fact that he was crossed with dozens of shells on the bandoliers, there was no time to reload. Joe dropped the shotgun to the ground, where its landing was cushioned by the matted grass and weeds. He reached for the Colt .45 revolvers, some of the most powerful handguns in the world. They were each loaded with six rounds, and his hands had them out and ready in a flash.

The creature didn't leap and fly at the man this time. It slowly and steadily strode menacingly forward. Claws at the end of each hand opened and closed, clicking against each other. As it walked, the Dogman's shoulders slowly rotated like a pendulum, first one ahead and then the other. Joe had an awful thought that he actually saw the creature's mouth curl up in a horrifying, evil grin as it closed in.

Joe Randall, the only son of John Randall, began to fire the Colts in rapid succession. Each kicked in turn after firing, right then left, right then left, before the big man's hands brought it back to bear on the target only a few feet in front of him. Joe emptied both guns in a matter of a few seconds, twelve rounds all blasting their way into the Dogman's body. It shuttered and shook, its body contorting as every shell tore into its flesh. The last two shells finally did it in, and the creature's knees buckled as it dropped like a sack of dirty laundry to the ground.

Most any other creature would have been finished off by the shotgun slugs alone. Most any other creature that might have survived the first round of shots would have been surely put out of its misery by a dozen .45 shells. There was no way an animal that roamed the Michigan forests could take such a beating and live.

But this was no mere animal.

The big man stood, breathing heavily, not from any exertion on his part but from the adrenaline rushing through his body. His head hurt, his eyes were watering, and his ears were ringing from all of the loud reports of the gunshots. The smoking barrels were pointed down at the ground now, heavy in his tired hands as his arms hung at each side of his body. Joe exhaled a deep breath of relief and closed his eyes for a brief moment trying to clear his head. A few seconds later, he opened them and surveyed the damage.

But as he stared down at the apparently lifeless form crumpled on the matted grass of the Dredge, Joe cocked his head, then shook it to be sure he was really seeing what his eyes showed him.

The creature should have been dead. It sure shouldn't be stirring yet again. And yet, there was movement. Tough Joe had seen enough.

He reached down and unlatched the long hunting knife he'd strapped to his lower leg. Obviously, guns were of no use here anymore. Perhaps the only thing that could stop it would be to cut it up, to slice it into a million pieces. Joe was a long-time hunter, and skinning and dressing a carcass was no big deal. He'd done it dozens of times with this particular hunting knife, too.

If the guns weren't going to work, he'd take care of this monster with the eight-inch blade of his hunting knife.

Now it was Joe's turn to stride forward in confidence. He'd take care of this thing once and for all.

But as he reached the creature and bent down to begin the carving, a powerful arm shot out and the Dogman grasped Joe's left ankle in a vise-like grip. The sharp claws easily pierced the tough leather work boots, and Joe could feel their points enter his lower leg. He stifled a shout through his gritted teeth, his head thrown back as the pain shot up through his nervous system.

And then the Dogman had him. It released his ankle and stood upright. It towered even over the big man, who had recovered himself. Joe swung the knife in a wide circle, meaning to slice the creature across the neck, but the Dogman was too fast for him. It blocked the attack with its forearm, and Joe's knife had to be brought back around for a different approach. Quickly, he stabbed in and scored a hit under the beast's ribcage. He pulled back and thrust again, this time in the belly. The Dogman roared in rage and pain, but it finally managed to grab a hold of Joe's right hand.

Joe reached out with his left arm, grasping a handful of the creature's fur on its right shoulder. The two grappled for a few moments before the sheer power and strength of the Dogman took over. He might be the biggest man in the town, maybe in the whole county, but he was no match for the creature that walks upright in the depths of the woods. Joe just couldn't get his knife in close enough to do any real damage.

The Dogman pinned Joe's arms backward at an impossible angle until the man's shoulders began to make popping noises. Joe's face strained in pain as his shoulders were slowly snapped out of their sockets.

The beast roared in triumph as Joe's knees buckled, his heavy weight sagging down to the ground. Between the cries of sheer agony, Joe saw the creature's long fangs coming ever closer, its elongated maw moving in for the kill.

He knew he'd never see his wife again. His time here was up.

Morning on the Dredge

There was no official count regarding the number of missing men. Over the next few weeks, it would be difficult to discern who was officially missing and who had simply left town without looking back. As the population quickly dwindled in Sigma, these two groups merged into one.

The handful who survived the night awoke in the beds of pickups and the backseats of sedans, heads afire with hangovers, not ready to face the daylight that burned straight through their eye sockets and into their brains. None of these folks could remember exactly who was with them the night before, and whether any had wandered into the Dredge or disappeared in some other direction.

With the phones out, it was impossible to tell for sure.

Not one of those survivors wanted to investigate the Dredge to see what horrifying secrets it held, what stories it would tell from the previous night. If their comrades hadn't returned to the trucks by now, they weren't likely to do so. Those who survived weren't sure they wanted to know what happened.

By mid-morning, the handful of lucky ones managed to right themselves and find ways back home. Those that did packed up their families and left town immediately. It certainly wasn't worth hanging around here any longer.

Almost a dozen trucks and other vehicles were abandoned at the tree line, either in town or on the immediate outskirts, their owners long gone. A few of them still had the keys dangling in the ignition and the headlights slowly dimming from run-down batteries.

Though some of the men lost in the Dredge were single, there were many who should have returned to families the next day at the latest. Girlfriends, wives, and children anxiously waited by the doors and empty driveways for hours. Since the phones were out, there was nobody to call for information, and there was nobody to call for help. Few of the families had a second car that they could use to go find help if they wanted to; most of the folks who lived in Sigma were lucky enough to own one vehicle.

Jeff (III)

He swore again and again. It was a loud, echoing sound in the big open house he had to himself. Jeff had never married, though he'd had many chances. Work, and subsequently play, were more important than the other distractions that families would make. He certainly wouldn't have moved up the ladder as quickly as he'd done if there had been a wife and kids to hold him back. He certainly couldn't have made a million dollars by his thirtieth birthday. He certainly couldn't have bought all of the toys he currently possessed, or built the luxurious home he now lived in. He certainly couldn't have retired, very well off, before the age of forty.

Sure, there were times when he was lonely, when he would have liked someone to come home to. He always kept his options opened, and was always on the look out for a future Mrs. Higgs. But the deterioration of his personality was unlikely to attract many women.

Jeff kept moving from the house to the spacious garage and back, searching for and gathering the right materials for his project. His engineering skills, unused for a number of years, were quickly coming back to him as his design took shape.

His mind kept wandering back to the events of the previous night. Over and over, the scenes from inside the night vision scope kept playing back in his brain like a VCR tape on a weird and horrifying loop. He saw the men, glowing a phosphorescent white in the eerie green background. He saw them take on the beast, and he saw them run from the beast. He saw the creature attack stealthily and swiftly, faster than any animal he'd ever seen or hunted himself. And he'd been on many big game hunts all over North America and even once to Africa.

He even saw many of the men taken down by their comrades' fire. Many were in the wrong place at the wrong moment, and there were far too many wild shots in the dark that had found human targets instead of the creature the hunters were all aiming for.

He saw the shots he'd taken. He saw the direct hits that the beast took.

Jeff wasn't close to any of the townsfolk, and quite honestly he was more upset that his sniper rifle didn't do the trick itself. He should have been the one to put a stop to the creature. Then none of the rest of the night's carnage would have happened. But having watched the death and dismemberment on the Dredge, from his vantage point high in the relative safety of the tall oak, he couldn't help but feel horrible for those men down below. It was terrifying to see anybody ripped limb from limb, let alone folks he actually knew. He might not have liked any of them, but he certainly didn't hate anybody there.

Again and again, he saw himself attempt almost a dozen shots after he had wiped the puke from his lips. However, the creature was just too fast. And though he couldn't confirm it, he was nearly convinced that he was responsible for some of the deaths below. The bullets he'd fired at the monster during the melee had to have hit something or somebody.

He'd never know for sure if his Remington had ended the lives of anybody on the Dredge. But he had the sinking feeling in his stomach that he'd done just that.

Even without any evidence that he may have indeed shot folks in the tall grass, he still blamed himself for much of the carnage. It was his failure that cost those men their lives. The Remington was the best weapon he had in his arsenal, at least at that range; it should have stopped the creature cold. Certainly, the gun would have dropped a moose, an elk, hell, even a polar bear, especially after three shots. The creature had taken those blasts and still it bounced back into action. Jeff had watched in complete disbelief. It should have worked—the Remington should have stopped it dead in its tracks. But it didn't. Jeff had done everything he could, but he still blamed himself.

Well, no longer. This time, he'd have the firepower to do the job. And he'd have backup. He'd been planning carefully since the daylight took over the world and he finally felt safe enough to climb down from his perch.

And he wasn't just going to wait for the creature to appear. This time he'd bait it. He'd draw it into a trap from which there would be no escape.

His hands, gripping a wrench, tightened a lock-washer on his contraption. It was nearly complete. He needed to finish up soon and test it, and then move on to acquiring the other items he'd need for this evening's work. There was still a lot of work to do.

Sigma (X)

The changes in the air masses created high winds that plagued the region that afternoon. They didn't help the temperature, which still clung in the lower 90s. They just blew the hot air around until being outside was nearly intolerable.

To make matters worse, the power went out all over a five-county area. It wasn't that big of a deal in Sigma in the later afternoon, but night would be here soon. And since there was no communication with town, and Cherry Capitol Electric was busy dealing with downed power lines in the immediate Traverse City area, Sigma was once again relegated to the bottom of the list.

Jeff Higgs was only mildly annoyed by the loss of light in his garage. He pushed up the large doors by hand, since the automatic opener had no juice. That let in plenty of daylight to work by. Besides, he was nearly finished. He'd gotten everything he needed from the house anyway, and he was ready to start setting up the trap.

It wasn't unusual for power to be lost out in the sticks. Sometimes it would be out for whole day or even longer. A few years previously, half of Kalkaska County was out for nearly three days in the bitter cold of early December. The electric cooperative tried its best to restore power, but after hours and weekends were trying times. The relatively low population in the hinterlands was just not a priority compared to the bigger towns.

And being that Cherry Fest was set to begin in a few days, the top priority was to restore the power necessary to keep the tourists happy and spending money.

The humidity continued to rise across northern Michigan. The front had fully moved in, now settling itself over the tip of the Mitt and bringing forth a wave of nearly overwhelming muggy heat that enveloped the region. The few folks walking outside developed sweat stains on their t-shirts within minutes.

With no power, no phones, and not much prospect of the husbands and fathers returning, the few who could get away loaded their vehicles and drove off fast. More than one did stopped in Kalkaska, but the local police were busily dealing with the rapid influx of tourists and their usual crazy antics. Besides, they told the families, it took 24 hours before someone was officially "missing", and even then it was more probable that the men-folk were holed up at somebody's huntin' cabin, pounding back beers and listening to the Tigers on the radio.

Though the sun couldn't be seen behind the thickening cloud cover, the light was quickly fading from the world. The few folks who still stayed behind battened themselves down, waiting for whatever the night would bring. Doors and windows were locked. With no power, candles and kerosene lamps were lit. Many families huddled together in the hallways or windowless rooms. Things had steadily declined over the week. Who knew how bad this night would become?

Unseen to the residents, the sun had set. There was only about a half hour of daylight left in the world. The graying clouds continued to darken, both from the approaching night and from the impending storm.

Sigma's last day was coming to a close.

Stevie

He knew it was time to go to town.

He didn't know why, just that it was time. There was an inexplicable call. A feeling.

The call came to him strongly this past Thursday when, after work, he'd nearly pulled into the driveway of his Grandpa's mobile home before that feeling almost wiped him off his bike. He barely kept his balance and barely stopped himself from skidding though the gravel. He had been called back to town. He needed to be back there, and as quickly as possible.

Stevie had no idea why he got these feelings. But it was good that he did.

That day, he'd pedaled his way back to Sigma Corners as fast as he could and then, nearly out of breath, he turned right instead of left toward the Mercantile, the way he usually went. He was passing the winding driveway of the crazy old cat lady when he felt that pull again. It was like some invisible hand was actually tugging him in that direction. His hands turned themselves and his bike came to a rest by her mailbox. He could see the faded white numbers 2274 on the black box. The little stone house could barely be discerned through the thick brush and skinny little red pines that grew up all over the line of trees at the road's edge. Stevie had never been up there, but he was sure that was going to change very quickly. Again, that unseen hand took over, plucking him off his bike and pushing him forward. And luckily it had. As he came close to the house, a crashing sound emanated from the basement. That was followed by the awful roaring they'd all been hearing at night. But this was the daytime! Stevie had paused, frightened badly and fighting against that force that was pushing him closer to the house. He didn't want to see, he didn't want to be there. He wanted to run, to get away from that horrible sound.

But he couldn't resist. That feeling brought him closer and closer, until he was actually on his hands and knees looking into the dust-covered casement window. And there, he'd seen a face looking back. He was startled, thinking it would be the monster. However, it turned out to be Brian of all people. Stevie had nearly laughed out loud. What was his friend doing down there? It was an awful place to be playing, especially with that awful sound so near.

Brian's shouting through the glass answered that question quickly. He needed out and fast. Well, Stevie could do that. He'd kicked in the glass and pulled not only Brian to safety but the girl Bonnie, too. Then, again following his feelings, he'd grasped their hands and practically dragged them down the driveway, past his sprawled bike, across the road, and into the Dredge. It was a good thing Stevie had an excellent sense of direction or they'd have been lost in the tall grass. But his bearings were accurate, and just under ten minutes later, they'd traversed over a mile until reaching Brian's fort. They had made remarkable time, considering that the two younger kids were not athletic at all. It was just pure adrenaline that had kept them going. That and Stevie tugging on their arms the whole way.

On Friday, the feeling told him to stay at home. He didn't know why, just that he didn't need to be in town. It told him to stay away from work. He told his grandpa he was sick, and asked him to call Mr. Cooper and let him know. His grandpa tried to call, but the phone wasn't working. Somehow, Stevie knew the phone being out was connected to all of this, too. It just confirmed that he should stay home that day. He pretended to be ill, hiding out in his room all day.

Of course, Stevie would overhear Mrs. Roads telling his grandpa about the mess at the Mercantile when she delivered the mail. His hearing was excellent, even through the window screen and across thirty feet of badly dried-up lawn. The store had been torn to shreds. Stevie gasped. He could picture each shelf in the store, shelves which he meticulously arranged and dusted daily. It was his pride and joy. His mind could identify and remember the exact location of each can and bottle, every box of nails and screws, the playing cards, the mousetraps, the flyswatters, and everything else, down to the individual packets of aspirin. His heart sank as he thought of putting it all back up again.

But perhaps the worst of all was that Mr. Cooper was missing. The only sign of him was a set of shoe prints in the spilled flour that covered the entire floor of the Mercantile.

He could still recall what Mrs. Roads had said quietly to his grandpa.

"And, there were other tracks there too. They looked like wolf prints, only five times as big, so I've heard. Annie Wallace told me, and you know she lives almost right across the street. She was there a-lookin' in before the Sheriff's patrol came in. She said she seen 'em, bigger than her husband's hand, so she tells me. And you know Allen's a big feller, so he is."

And now, Stevie had that feeling again. Sure, he was frightened. It was almost dark and he was pedaling into town. It would most certainly be dark when he had to pedal back. His grandpa wouldn't notice; he went to sleep early these days, well before the sun went down. He wasn't worried about the howling at night, since he could take out his hearing aids and be totally deaf to the world. There was very little for the old man to do at night. He didn't watch TV, and preferred to be outside most all day. When it came time to go inside, he'd just go to bed.

That call, that unseen hand, pushed the boy toward Sigma Corners. There was something he needed to do in town. Stevie didn't know what it was just yet. He just knew he needed to be there. His course of action would be revealed upon his arrival, as it had before.

Brian

While Brian was still out playing in his fort, his parents had left for the Cherry Speedway in Fife Lake. Hot laps began at 6 o'clock, followed by the time trials at 6:15, and then the races at 7:15. Brian, Sr., almost never missed a race; it was one of the only true sporting events he truly loved. Brian's mom just enjoyed a night out, even if it involved drunkenly cheering on cars that boringly went around and around the track. And it was nice having a speedway so close. Brian's dad could slam back a few beers before leaving, sip on one or two on the way there, and then enjoy a few at the race. And since it was all back-roads to get to Sigma, even his wife could down a few of her own and still drive home, taking her time without worrying about being stopped by any cops. Brian, Sr., would more than likely be passed out in the passenger's side by then.

And best of all, the races went on power or not. The racetrack had its own massive generators to light up the track and the concessions. Besides, most of the action would be finishing up by true nightfall anyway. The only hindrance was the post-race celebration. Brian's parents would have to drive in closer to Traverse City (where the power had been quickly restored) to find a bar serving beer and pizza.

Brian was left home alone, in the advancing darkness.

He made himself a peanut butter and jelly sandwich and grabbed the bag of Doritos. It wasn't the first time he'd been left home alone—it happened a lot on Saturday nights, actually. However, he couldn't remember being left home alone with no power.

The daylight was fading fast.

Considering all of the week's events, Brian was scared to be home alone. But he fully believed that he was safe in his house. The sounds of the Dogman (for so he'd fully come to believe that's what the creature was) in the night were always outside, usually a ways out on the Dredge. And though Brian had faced the monster, in a way, that had occurred in a dark, dungeon-like basement below a deserted house. If ever there was a haunted lair for the Dogman to inhabit, it would be the old cat lady's house.

Neither Brian nor Stevie had told a soul about the encounter two days earlier. For one, it had affected them severely. For another, they didn't believe anybody would believe them anyway. Even that nice DNR officer was unlikely to take them seriously. Sure, he'd listened intently a few days ago when Stevie shared the legend of the Dogman. But he could have just been nodding his head politely, thinking that they were a couple of foolish kids.

There were no lights in the Alexander home, so Brian dug through the cupboard drawers until he found several flashlights. He then moved his dad's recliner to the middle wall of the living room. There were no windows on that wall, so his back was covered. He certainly didn't want to look back and see something watching him from behind.

The sandwich and chips lay on the recliner's arm, and a can of cola rested on a folding tray table next to the recliner. Brian was wishing he could put part of the Star Wars trilogy in the VCR when he heard a scratch at the living room window. He didn't want to acknowledge it; in fact, he fancied that he really didn't hear it. But he couldn't convince himself—he knew he'd heard it plain as day. Then it came again. It was fairly soft at first, but then it became a bit louder. The boy didn't want to look that way, certain of what he'd see. Images flooded his brain, scenes from the basement encounter raced back to the forefront. His heart immediately began thumping. His feet felt far too heavy to move, even if he had someplace to run and escape to.

Brian noticed he'd stopped breathing in an attempt to be silent. *Doesn't matter, it's already seen you*, he thought.

The scratch this time was replaced by a tapping on the glass. Brian was sure that it was the Dogman's claws.

He gulped loudly and clenched his fists, taking in a deep breath. Then he forced himself to look out the window. His head and shoulders slowly turned away from the dark TV screen.

There was something looking in through the glass, but it wasn't the Dogman. Even in the fading light, Brian could recognize the face of his friend, Stevie. The older boy peered in the window, his chin just high enough to rest on the ledge. He'd been tapping on the glass to get Brian's attention.

Brian exhaled deeply and dramatically, stomping over to his friend's visage in the dusty glass. The window was shut tightly and even the little latch was locked. "What're you doin' here? It's late, and I'm not supposed to have any friends over," he said loudly so Stevie could hear him.

But before Stevie could respond, another visitor arrived at Brian's home. Like Stevie, this visitor was unannounced.

A pair of headlights suddenly lit up Brian's home, brightly shining through the front windows. Both Brian and Stevie swung their heads in that direction.

"Are your parents home?" asked Stevie tentatively, his voice muffled through the glass. He knew to avoid Brian, Sr., whenever possible, even without his friend's negative stories this past week.

"I don't think that's them. It looks like a pickup, see, the headlights are up higher than my dad's car," Brian answered.

Stevie stared at the lights. In his slow, calm voice, he said through the window glass, "Yeah, you're right, it is a truck. So who would be here?"

Brian only shook his head. He had no idea.

The headlights kept blaring into the windows, but the vehicle had stopped in the driveway. There was a long pause as the two boys looked apprehensively at the vehicle. There were never any visitors on Saturday night. This whole thing was highly unusual.

A squeak made Stevie jump, and Brian jumped from his friend's reaction. The truck's windshield wipers had just come on, smearing the ugly splats of bugs with the first of the light, misty precipitation that had begun to fall on the little town. The darkening clouds were finally letting their bounty loose upon the land.

Jeff (IV)

From deep in the darkness of the third-base dugout, Jeff peered through his night vision monocle, which was now attached to the most powerful weapon he owned. Sure, the Tommy Gun might not have the raw stopping power of his Remington. However, it made up for it by utilizing a 100-round drum magazine that could be emptied in a matter of seconds, thanks to a few special modifications. Hugo Goeller, a close friend and gun smith back in Muskegon, took the basic Thompson M1A1 and converted it from a semi-automatic to a fully automatic weapon. It cost Jeff dearly, and of course, it was highly illegal to even possess.

Jeff only fired it a few times each year, usually when he needed to take out some aggressions. In a deep gully behind his newly built log home, he'd set up a target range. The Tommy Gun's .45-caliber bullets made short work of every target he'd set it against. Just squeezing the trigger one time could quickly send a burst of three to five bullets screaming at anything unlucky enough to be in the line of fire. Holding down the trigger, the operator could literally saw a piece of plywood in half in mere seconds.

He'd learned from those sessions that the gun had a propensity to kick hard and rise naturally when a long burst was squeezed out. Jeff practiced keeping the pressure down with his off-hand so the full automatic wouldn't cause him to shoot wildly.

After last night, he knew what he was up against. He'd seen the creature in action. And he wasn't going to take any chances. Every shot was vital. Every shot had to count.

He knew that individual shells didn't stop the creature; he'd seen that first hand, both with his own shots and then with those of the hunters on the Dredge. If there was any chance to kill it, it would have to be cut right in half. Jeff had watched as Joe Randall attempted to cleave the creature in two with his hunting knife. But Jeff wasn't planning on getting that close. He thought the full automatic would do just the trick, and from a fairly safe distance at that.

Though it was still about a half hour before full darkness, it was still very difficult to see with any clarity. The heavy cloud cover above merged with a bank of light fog at ground level to obscure anything more than fifty yards away. A light mist had been hanging about in the air for the last hour or so. It didn't feel like rain, not quite yet, and it wasn't quite a drizzle. But the mist covered everything, slowly soaking its way into the dry soil, the nearly burned-up grass, and the dehydrated cedar posts that marked the ball field's perimeter. The cracked wood of the three-seat bleachers next to each dugout greedily absorbed the water. There would be no puddles in the dirt at home plate; the ground easily sucked down every drop.

There was little noise in the Sigma night. The crickets had stopped, and the cooler, wet weather had driven the other bugs into hiding. Somewhere in the distance, a lone vehicle could be heard traveling on C-571, but it too was quickly silenced.

Jeff could easily see the pig carcass lying atop the pitcher's mound of the little beer-league ball field. He'd cut it up himself right there a few hours earlier, letting the scent fully disperse throughout the entire area. And he could just barely see the outfield fence that separated the ball field from the wilderness of the Dredge beyond. He was relatively well-protected by the cinderblock wall at his side and back and the chain-link fence at the front of the dugout. And he'd created a makeshift hunting blind by weaving dry grasses through the holes in the fence to give him cover. Jeff was completely covered from most every direction, and only a small opening allowed him to poke the Tommy Gun's barrel and scope through. He didn't think the fence was enough to stop the creature if it really wanted at him, but he hoped his arsenal would do the trick. At least it couldn't sneak up and attack him from behind.

His eyes caught movement in the fog at the far end of right field where the fence following the foul line cornered to begin its graceful arc across center. It was the right time of night. It had to be the creature. Now he'd just have to wait for it to take the bait.

Indeed, as he'd believed, a large dark shadow hopped over the six-foot fence easily and gracefully, landing lightly on its two back legs. Even through the night vision scope, it was as difficult to see as it had been the night before. Its fur was very dark black, and it kept its arms in tight to its body. The distinguishing features included the pointed, dog-like ears and, of course, the glowing yellow eyes. As it turned its head one way and then the next, Jeff could see the creature's muzzle and the sharp fangs just visible beneath its curled lips. Slightly hunched over, it made its way cautiously toward the infield.

Jeff held his breath. His heart was pounding and sweat poured down his forehead and cheeks. It was his first look at the Dogman up close and personal as it began to fill up the entire scope. It was huge! He could see the muscles rippling beneath the hairy skin, the rhythmic opening and closing of the clawed fingers, and the hypnotic pendulum-like swinging of its head as it searched the area for intruders.

The creature stalked forward in the mist, arms hanging low, its knuckles nearly dragging on the burnt grass of the ball field. Its nose sniffed the air, and it gave a brief, low grunt. Jeff held perfectly still, not even blinking. The Dogman came right up to the carcass, still sniffing the air and the meat upon the ground.

Its eyes darted in all directions as if looking for the trap that was surely here. *It's very intelligent,* Jeff thought. *Not just wary, but actually working through the situation. It's trying to figure out why the meat is just lying there. It's searching for the rest of the story.*

After nearly two full minutes of speculation, the Dogman cautiously dropped down to all fours. Jeff was amazed that in this position it could so closely resemble a gigantic wolf, and yet when it stood up on its back legs, it maintained the humanoid features. The two body positions seemed mutually exclusive from another, and yet the Dogman easily swapped between two legs and four.

The Dogman began to feast, ripping great chunks of flesh from the pig carcass. Sitting upon its back legs and knees, it held the pig down with both of its spread front claws, while its head reached down for bite after bite. It would raise its muzzle to the sky and shake its head violently, spraying bloody juices that joined the drizzle now falling from the ever-darkening clouds. Every so often, it would issue a low, rumbling growl as if to warn off anybody that might be lurking nearby.

A few minutes of gorging itself quickly passed, and yet it still wanted more. Greedily, it sank its jaws into the carcass. Jeff knew it was time to act. The creature was perfectly aligned in the night vision scope. It was now or never.

Jeff inched his index finger to the trigger. He double-checked the sight. He gripped the stock tightly, knowing it would surely rise upwards upon firing. He took a quiet, deep breath, and exhaled, pulling the trigger at the very end.

Fire erupted from the camouflaged dugout. The bullets raced to their target, bursting into the Dogman's skin at chest level. The first burst was only to startle the creature into standing up and creating a better target. This part of the plan worked perfectly.

The Dogman heard the gunshots well after the bullets ripped into its body. Completely unaware, its eyes sprang open wide and its jaws gaped, fangs bared in a bloody grimace. It was knocked backward but regained its balance on its hind legs as it took two steps backward.

It was just the opening that Jeff needed. He squeezed off a long burst, tugging downward with his left hand on the stock to keep the Tommy Gun on target. The stream of bullets tore a wide gash in the creature's midsection. Deep red blood spurted in all directions, bathing the grass between first base and the edge of the pitcher's mound. The Dogman screamed loudly with great shrills of pain as it was again pummeled backward.

Another long burst echoed its blasts through the town.

Jeff was ready to have at it again, but the Dogman was too fast. It might have been ambushed, but it had the skill to escape. Instantly springing from its powerful back legs, the creature leapt to the top of the first base dugout, just hitting the ground once on the way there. It crouched and stared back at the Jeff's blind, still unable to see the hunter or the weapon camouflaged within.

Retraining the sight on the Dogman again, Jeff opened fire and this time he emptied the entire drum. He knew he needed to deal it a heavy blow before it slipped down behind the first base dugout and out of sight. The .45-caliber shells rocked the creature, opening new fissures in its skin from right to left. It shrieked again, a horrible sound that pierced the night which by now had completely overtaken the world.

Jeff tugged the drum from the Thompson, while pulling the barrel back in from the fence. He then quickly raised the scope to his eye as he slipped around the entrance. The Dogman was reeling atop the dugout, its clawed hands moving around the various deep wounds on its torso. It continued to scream, and folks miles away could hear it, even inside their homes.

Jeff had already clicked his second 100-round drum into place and took aim at the creature as he stepped forward onto the wet grass of the infield. He was feeling very sure of himself as he pulled the trigger again, sending another long burst into the night.

However, he lost his balance from the kickback of this burst. In the safety of the dugout, he could keep tight, constant pressure on the stock and his feet and legs were locked in against the dry cement floor. Now Jeff was on slick grass. His left hand tried its trick at holding down the barrel, but he over-shifted his weight, accelerating his downfall. The powerful kick from the full automatic caused him to slip, and the hunter suddenly found himself falling. He watched as his legs and feet amazingly moved up parallel to his waist. Jeff's finger still held down the trigger, and the bullets continued to shoot up into the black sky. After a very long second, Jeff's back hit the ground, instantly soaking the many-pocketed hunting vest and the lightweight backpack he wore. He winced as he felt the clinking of metallic cylinders from inside the backpack dig into his back, but bigger things occupied his mind at the moment. The Thompson continued to fire until the entire drum was empty.

The Dogman had lucked out this time. It turned its attention to the human down below, and its eyes narrowed to slits. It gritted its teeth, its lips curled up, and its nose pinched as it hissed at the man lying on his back. The Dogman's front hands dropped to its sides, paws forward and claws wide, curled and ready for action. It would finish him now.

But Jeff hadn't made this date unprepared. He sat up, shaking off the tumble. Immediately, he pulled the night vision scope to his eye and located the beast, which was now moving to the edge of the dugout. His hands flew, ripping out the spent drum and reaching down to his backup. Tucked into the waistband of his trousers were several extra clips, ducked taped together so one was upright and one was upside down. That way Jeff could pull the clip out, flip it over, and re-insert it with very little down time. It was an old military trick Hugo the gunsmith had taught him, and it really came in handy just now.

Just as the Dogman was crouching to drop down to ground level, Jeff sent a quick burst of bullets its way. Surprised, the Dogman sprang backward and slipped off the plywood roof of the first base dugout.

It was exactly what Jeff didn't want to happen—he'd lost sight of the creature. That made it that much more dangerous. He hopped to his feet and strode in rapid fashion, curving across the ball field, all the time searching through the scope for any sign of his quarry. There wasn't time to check the contents of his backpack—he just hoped the items stored there were still in fair shape and would work when the time came.

And then he saw the creature through the backstop. It was limping its way toward the main street and the town proper. Keeping it in the sight, Jeff moved as fast as he dared across the wet grass and then out through the opening at the end of the first base dugout. He'd certainly dealt it a near-lethal set of blows, and the creature was reeling.

Jeff sent yet another burst in its direction. From this distance, most of the bullets missed the target, but the Dogman did turn to face its pursuer. Again, the hunter was provided with a perfect target. Jeff's next volley sent a few shots straight home, drilling holes into the creature's stomach. The impact, combined with the previous direct hits, took the starch out of the creature. It stumbled backward into the street in front of Joe Randall's home, tried to regain its balance, failed, and dropped to the ground.

The hunter had seen this act the night before. He didn't want to give the creature the opportunity to heal itself and stand back up again.

Hustling his way toward the Dogman, Jeff popped out the long, narrow clip and flipped it, clicking its companion into place. And sure enough, the creature began to raise itself once more. Jeff wasn't surprised or amazed this time—he'd fully expected it. Somehow that monster could heal itself with supernatural speed. He was twenty-five yards away when it regained its footing and began to limp forward again.

Suddenly, the creature was bathed in bright, golden light. A set of headlights had illuminated the street, coming from a vehicle heading south into town. The Dogman turned instinctively in that direction, trying to use this as a distraction, and bent its knees to spring to safety.

But Jeff wasn't going to let it get away. His index finger squeezed the Thompson's heavy trigger and letting loose a line of fire that began a bit to the left of the creature before coming back on target. The Dogman hit the deck again, and most of Jeff's bullets slammed into Joe Randall's house, destroying the shutters and blowing holes in the front door big enough to pass golf balls through. He continued to stride forward, feeling deep in his heart that the end was near. It was time. There would be no escape.

In Town

Eric Martin watched as the hunter opened fire again. Most of the bullets slammed into the cinderblock house on the opposite side of the shadowy beast. Cement chips flew in all directions and a set of rusty iron pipes sticking out of the ground was sliced right in half. Eric could hardly believe his eyes. There was indeed a monster in this town, and it was just thirty yards dead ahead, shining in his work truck's headlights. The creature turned and stared directly at the oncoming truck, fangs bared in a menacing look of rage. The creature was slightly crouched as if to attack. Eric gaped as the automatic weapon spat fire from its barrel again, the hunter's bullets finally finding their mark. Turning his head to follow the shots, he saw the creature drop and roll onto its side.

At first, the young conservation officer didn't recognize the hunter. He could have been any of the crazy inhabitants of this town. And then it hit him—it had to be Jeff Higgs. Nobody else had such an arsenal of weapons. He'd even showed them off to Eric a few days ago. Eric had been searching diligently for clues of the mysterious creature's whereabouts and had found his way onto Jeff's property. They'd had a very interesting discussion about the evidence Eric had found, and each had shared his own hypothesis. Jeff was eccentric, Eric thought, but otherwise one of the few in the town with a level head and a rational mind.

Now, however, Eric wasn't sure how rational the man was being.

"Stay here!" he ordered the two younger passengers, putting the truck into park. Neither Brian nor Stevie said anything. They just pressed themselves back into the bench seat as far as they could and shook their heads to acknowledge the order. At first, they were very happy to have the company of the DNR officer when he showed up at Brian's home. They'd felt a great deal of safety riding along with him. But now both were scared beyond belief, seeing firsthand the horrible monster that had finally escaped their imaginations and materialized on the broken and bumpy street only a stone's throw in front of them.

Brian had not gotten a really good look at the Dogman in the basement below Mrs. Whitman's house. Now he had a front-row seat as the monster was illuminated in the bright headlights.

Eric slammed the driver's door shut and marched around the front of the truck, keeping to the side of the headlights so that his field of vision was unimpeded. He cautiously approached the hunter, who didn't seem to notice him yet, even though the truck was providing the only means of light on the street. Eric knew he had to take control of the situation right away. It was his job to protect both the man and the animal, whatever it was. He might not be able to stop a whole mob of hunters, but he could stop this one.

"Hey!" he hollered at the hunter. "Jeff! Hold it right there!"

Jeff never took his eyes off the Dogman. "Stay where you are, officer. I've got this situation under control."

Eric didn't see how anything here was under control. He unbuckled the strap on his service pistol. "Jeff, I'm ordering you to stop where you are. Put down your weapon."

But Jeff was ignoring the conservation officer. The hunter did carefully lay the automatic weapon down on the wet asphalt. He'd worry about cleaning the gun later. Right now, he had to take advantage of the time given to him. Luckily, the truck's headlights allowed him to adequately watch the creature while he made a few adjustments. It was a good thing, too, because the Dogman began to stir, rolling a bit on the pavement and beginning to raise itself up yet again on its hands and knees.

Jeff reached back over his shoulder, pulling something long and narrow from the backpack. It was still connected to the sack by a coiling tube of some kind. With his left hand, he reached back and rummaged into the pack, finally locating the knob at the top of the metallic cylinder. He gave it a few twists, and a hiss seeped from the end of the long tube he'd previously produced.

A simple lighter emerged in Jeff's left hand. The little flame danced in the drizzle. Eric watched incredulously as the hunter moved the lighter to the hissing tube.

Instantly a tongue of flame shot out six feet from the makeshift flamethrower Jeff had fashioned that afternoon. Eric bounced between his anger at being ignored and being truly impressed by the man's ingenuity.

"Jeff!" Eric called one more time in his best authoritative voice. "Stop whatever you're doing and step back. You don't know how dangerous that is!"

"Officer," Jeff answered, moving forward toward the creature that had now risen to one knee, "I suggest you step back. I'm gonna cook this thing, once and for all."

A quick turn on the little knob doubled the length of the flame as it cut through the night. Jeff moved in for the kill.

***

Brian's sleeve was tugged to the right, and his head flopped against his shoulder. Stevie was pulling him across the seat. "What? Hey! What're you doing?" Brian asked, puzzled.

Stevie had pressed himself against the faded, cracked dashboard in an attempt to trade spots with the younger boy. He paused a moment, his face lost in shadow. "We need to get out of here," the older boy answered in his slow, calm way.

Brian stared, dumbfounded at his friend. "Why do we need to leave?"

"We just need to go. It's not safe here." That feeling had once again crept upon Stevie, who by now knew to trust it. Something bad was going to happen very soon, right here. They needed to get away.

"What do you mean?" Brian squeaked, his voice rising to a high pitch. He was terrified to leave the relative safety of the truck. He pointed past Stevie to where Eric was confronting Jeff Higgs. "I'm not getting out! He said so."

"We're not getting' out."

"Then how're we gonna get away?" Brian asked, very confused.

Stevie couldn't explain it to his friend, so he just kept pushing his way over to the driver's seat.

Then Brian understood what his friend was doing. His eyes widened and his jaw dropped open. "You don't know how to drive, do you?"

The older boy, having settled himself behind the steering wheel, turned to his younger friend and smiled. "Nope, I don't. But I've watched my grandpa drive a lot."

Brian groaned and rolled his eyes.

***

The Dogman reached its feet, standing up on its two hind legs in a most human-like fashion. It stayed nearly doubled over, clawed hands feeling the wounds on its abdomen. The creature still moved slowly, seemingly unaware of the bright stream of flame arching toward it.

Jeff closed the distance, shooting flames well out ahead of him. The heat licked the asphalt, sending the drizzle evaporating back into the thick atmosphere that pressed down like a weight on the town.

Finally, the flames reached the feet of the creature, singeing the hair. The Dogman screeched in pain, nimbly leaping backward a few feet. It landed right next to Joe Randall's simple home.

Jeff pursued it across the street. The Dogman was now cornered, pinned against the house. The hunter smirked, his face lit a bright red in the hot glow of the flamethrower.

***

Out of the corner of his eyes, Eric saw the monster rise to its feet, and he forgot all about Jeff. It was incredible! His mind simply couldn't accept what his eyes were showing him. The creature should have been dead, its lifeblood seeping into the ground with the light rain that had replaced the drizzle. Eric had seen Jeff blast it with a dozen or more bullets, all direct hits. He'd seen it crumple and fall.

In a scene out of a horror movie, the monster regained its former strength. It was the stuff nightmares were made of. Eric could hardly believe it was real in the first place; this supernatural recovery made it simply unbelievable.

The stream of fire shot from the tip of the flamethrower, and the creature sprang back in an attempt to escape. But Jeff was relentless. He kept on the attack.

Eric's eyes were drawn to another slight movement a few feet away at the house's corner. The air just above the rusty, iron pipes was shimmering, wiggling. It reminded the officer of the heat waves you'd see, dancing over hot pavement in the summer.

Eric finally recognized the pipes for what they were and realized where they went.

***

The old DNR truck roared to life after a few coughs and sputters. Apparently, Stevie knew how to start a car.

Brian put his left arm up on the top of the bench seat and looked out the back window. When the truck lurched forward, he swung his head back to stare at Stevie. He wasn't expecting to be heading this way. "Where are you going? If we're getting away, we're goin' the wrong direction. Shouldn't we be backing up?"

Stevie calmly pointed to the windshield with both index fingers and replied, "We need to get him first."

The light rain was beading up on the windshield, blurring the scene ahead of them. Stevie didn't know how to operate the wipers. Instead, he cranked the handle, rolling down the driver's side window so he could stick his head outside.

"We're not getting closer to that thing, are we?" Brian squeaked again, panicking because of the open window.

Shrugging his shoulders, Stevie just said, matter-of-factly, "We got to save him."

"Save who from what?" the younger boy asked.

But Stevie couldn't put his thoughts into words quickly enough to convince his friend of the urgency of this action. That feeling was strong again, and the older boy was being pulled along a course by this unseen force. He couldn't describe it to Brian, but he had to be here, just in this very spot. And after the Big Bang happened, he would have to act very quickly. That much he knew as well.

The truck crept forward very slowly, unbeknownst to the three in the headlights, as Stevie kept one foot on the gas and one on the brake. Every few feet the truck jerked as his right foot pressed down too hard.

When they were just yards away from Eric, the hunter,

and the monster, Stevie pushed both feet down hard on the brake, completely stopping the truck.

To add to Brian's confusion, Stevie suddenly pushed his right hand and forearm on Brian's head, holding him down against the bench seat in a gesture of protection.

Brian thought his friend had lost it. "What are you doin' now? Hey, stop it!" Brian hissed. "That hurts!"

Stevie only shushed his friend. "We got to be quiet," he whispered. "It's about to happen."

Brian was completely confused by this time. "What's about to happen?" he asked in a whisper.

But Stevie was dead quiet. A second later, as the deafening roar blew past both sides of the pickup, Stevie laid his body down and hugged his friend, nearly crushing him against the cushioned seat.

***

Eric's eyes flashed widely open and he instinctively took a few steps backward.

"Jeff, no!" the officer screamed into the night, but it was far too late.

There would be no stopping him. Eric did the only thing he could think of—he jumped in the opposite direction.

The Dogman looked back at the hunter bearing down on it and the glow of the flaming stream that sliced through the raindrops. The creature gave the hunter one last malevolent grin, its lips curled back, as if it knew what was going to happen next. When the arching flame had just about reached the Dogman, the creature leapt straight up, its powerful leg muscles propelling it a dozen feet in the air. It landed for the briefest moment on the roof of Joe Randall's house and then sprang again into the darkness beyond.

Jeff swept the arching flame through the dark night from left to right, just barely missing his target. However, as the flame naturally continued on, the escaping gas from the severed iron pipes at the building's corner caught fire. These were the original vent pipes for the gas tanks buried beneath Joe Randall's front yard. The gas station might have been closed up and refinished into Tough Joe's house, but the tanks had never been removed. It definitely wouldn't have passed an EPA inspection. Now, these pipes were a direct channel to the foot of gasoline at the bottom of the tanks that had never been emptied.

The gas created a flaming torch at the tip of each pipe that lasted for a few seconds before the flames were sucked down into the dark depths.

And then the underground gas tanks, buried and untouched for decades, exploded in a maelstrom of fiery fury. Despite being buried several feet beneath the hard packed soil, the tanks' superheated interiors expanded in all directions in a fraction of a second. Rocks and chunks of concrete sidewalk flew in all directions, embedding themselves into cars, trees, and buildings.

The force of the explosion opened a crater in Joe Randall's front yard more than fifteen feet across. Like an opening to Hell itself, gigantic flames licked the blackness of the night like long, pointed tongues. The fire was so bright that it couldn't be looked at directly. Dark, acrid smoke bellowed forth, covering the town in a thick cloud.

As his feet reached the ground after his initial jump, Eric Martin was thrown further back a good twenty feet from the blast. As he soared through the night, head first, feet and hands up in the air, he thought he was dying. His time was up; waiter—check please. The skin on his face and hands was itching from the intense heat. The wind had been knocked out of him, and his lungs burned as he desperately gasped to refill them.

He hit the asphalt hard enough to dislocate his shoulder and break both collar bones. He suffered an immediate concussion from the jarring impact. But luckily, he landed just a few feet from the driver's side door of his trusty old pickup. The truck body and heavy-duty off-road tires shielded him from the waves of intense heat that immediately followed.

Jeff Higgs wasn't so lucky. He was incinerated instantly.

Houses up to a half mile away shook from the rumbling explosion. Trailers rocked on their frames. Every window in Joe Randall's house blew inward in a shower of glass dust, though most of it melted in mid-air from the massive heat.

The fireball rose over a hundred feet in the air. Small trees, shrubs, and all of the grass within a fifty-foot radius of the tanks were vaporized instantly from the intense heat. Moments later, the Randall's house had become an inferno fueled by the gas vapors continually leeching upward from the burning pit of Hades in the front yard.

**

Stevie did act fast. In fact, it all happened before Brian realized it.

The explosion blew in the windshield of the DNR truck, spraying glass fragments all over the two boys. Brian screamed, though it was more from the surprise and not from any true pain. His face was pressed against the cloth seat and was thus well-protected from the thick little shards that were cascading over him.

Just after the blast, Stevie pushed open the driver's door and reached outside. His eyes were squinted because of the intense heat, and he had to act almost blindly. But he could see the injured man lying right outside. He resorted to using brute strength. He was almost the same age as Officer Eric, and just about the same size. But Stevie was very strong, and of course, the adrenaline was flowing madly throughout his body. He grabbed the officer's bicep with both hands and yanked back and upward. Eric popped right off the ground and into the DNR truck's cab.

Brian cried out again, this time from the unbearable heat. The three of them were sweating profusely, and their bare skin prickled as the superheated air attempted to suffocate them. The paint on the front of the truck was blackened and peeling from the blast. Already, the metal was beginning to glow from the fire raging all around them. They only had a few more seconds before they were cooked alive.

Eric's feet still protruded from the open door as Stevie popped the gear shift lever to reverse and floored the gas pedal. The trusty old pickup flew backward away from the inferno that was now engulfing the entire town.

Stevie chanced one last glance back at the disappearing town. In the glow of the great fire, he could see a dark shape, a human-like shadow against the brightness. It was quite a ways off, but Stevie thought (or maybe imagined) that there was a pair of glowing eyes staring back at him. A moment later, the already fading shadow dropped down to all fours and bounded away into a section of the forest that had yet to catch on fire.

Amazingly, he kept the truck on the road, though he couldn't see much of anything. Stevie didn't slow down until the blaze and the creature were well away, off in the distance.

EPILOGUE

The pavement of C-571 became a huge griddle, melting the tires and frying the bodies of the few parked vehicles nearby before they too joined the inferno.

Above, the leaves and branches of the gigantic maples surrounding Joe's house were cremated in the flames. Within a minute, the great old trees were aflame, passing the fire along in the light breeze. Flames jumped between the branches, which nearly touched across the roads, spreading the blaze to every part of the town. Before the night was over, this part of the forest, old enough to have seen the coming of the white settlers, old enough to have seen the first of the logging operations in the north, old enough to have seen the heyday of the town and its slow decline, would be reduced to ashes.

The remains of the mercantile and Jack Cooper's house were next. When the store roof collapsed, thousands of fiery paper products, napkins, rolls of toilet paper, labels from cans, puffed upward into the sky like little lightning bugs before they floated back into the awaiting flames below.

Horner's Bar went up quickly as well, the fire greedily eating its way through the old wood paneling, through the tables and chairs. Glass bottles of alcohol exploded behind the bar, spraying out like little incendiaries.

The fire spread to the remains of Jane Whitman's house, fully erasing all traces of the human remains trapped beneath the rubble.

The dry grass of the Dredge alighted easily, and soon the great field became a sea of golden, orange flames. The remains of the many dead hunters were charred and buried beneath the ash. Tom McClusky's farm was spared, though the paint on the north side of the barn was singed and peeling from the great heat of the burning field.

Mitchell Emmond's farm was not so lucky. The flames roared right into his yard like a burning wave of destruction. The barn, house, and outbuildings were nothing more than a pile of ashes, lost in the roiling, boiling sea of fire.

It only took a few minutes before the Alexander trailer joined the great conflagration. Brian's folks had left the Cherry Speedway and were sharing a pitcher and a pizza at Rocky's Roadhouse in Traverse City. They wouldn't know about their destroyed home until after closing time when the huge fire had been reduced to hissing smoke in the downpour of rain. Brian's dad would later actually burn his hands severely while digging through the rubble that was once their trailer looking for any clues about their son's whereabouts. Of course, they assumed the worst until Stevie's grandpa brought him back early the next morning.

On the Dredge, the great fire raced up and engulfed Brian's little homemade fort. The last vestiges of the boy's youth and innocence burned up as the old, weathered boards went up in a bright white light. He'd never be the same little boy again after this week. Few would be.

Sigma (XI)

No one was able to call for help because all of the phone lines were down. Even if someone was able to find help in Kalkaska, it would have been far too late. There weren't enough fire departments in the area anyway to make a dent in the great inferno. Unlike the states out west, Michigan wasn't used to dealing with great forest fires. It would take an act of God to stop it all.

But really, there were few folks left to even notice the town take its last breaths. As Lloyd Horner thought nearly a week ago, Sigma had been dying. This night saw it finally expire, though it went out in one last blaze of glory, or at least a blaze anyway.

Anybody in the immediate area simply grabbed whatever items they could, leapt into their cars, and drove away as fast as possible. Folks went in all directions, many without a thought as to where they were going.

The smoky haze was lost in the dark cloud cover blanketing the north. Sigma was so far out in the wilderness that no one in the county even noticed the fire until after nothing could be done about it.

***

Deep, dark clouds fully covered the Lower Peninsula. They'd been forming, building, piling upon each other in a towering mountain stretching now from western Ontario back west to Wisconsin. Michigan, the epicenter, was beginning to be pummeled by the now-breaking storm. Such great storms, fueled by streams of warm, moist, southern air riding the jet stream from the Caribbean and slamming into the massive wall of cold air sinking down from Canada, were most common in the late fall, winter, and early spring. In the winter, such storms could drop a foot of snow or more very quickly, especially once they cleared Lake Michigan. But on occasion, these perfect storms hit right in the middle of the summer months.

Just before midnight, the first of the heavy raindrops began to fall upon the north lands. The storm had started a few hours ago as a light mist coming off Lake Michigan, but before long, these large teardrops of rain pelted the once dry, arid earth. The evening's drizzle only made the ground act like a sponge, greedy to absorb more.

The individual, sporadic droplets increased in number and intensity until a steady downpour rained upon the land. The storm moved its way across the Lower Peninsula like the hand of a long-lost lover: casually, carefully, in no great hurry. The front had picked up a tremendous amount of moisture from the great lake and the resulting storm clouds took their time now that they were full, moving slowly as they distributed the moisture back down to earth.

It took the pounding of the raindrops, a heavy sheet of precipitation continuing for several hours, as well as the next day's steady downpour of lighter rain to fully extinguish the conflagration in Sigma.

By the time the last of the flames had died out, hissing and sputtering their way into oblivion, the main part of the town had been completely leveled.

Joe Randall's cinderblock home was a pile of rubble. The fleet of trucks out back existed only as burned out hulks of twisted metal. The gaping hole between the street and the house still poured forth smoke like the rim of an awakening volcano. The soil all around was blackened, the watery streams of runoff slowly dragging the burned particles away into the street or down to the depths of the crater.

No buildings in the town proper had made it through. Even the cinderblock dugouts of the ball field were superheated until they burst and crumbled. The chain-link fence and backstop curled and warped their way to the ground.

Tree trunks thick enough to survive the initial onslaught were burned up ten or twelve feet high. The survivors would keep those blackened scars the rest of their years. No bark would grow again on those areas, though it would later come back in normally above and below.

The grass and low underbrush was completely singed to a flat black color, and the ground was splotchy where the sandy soil showed through. The smell of campfire lingered in the air. But it wasn't a pleasant smell, nor did it conjure up pleasant memories of camping trips long past. It was an acrid, overpowering odor.

It really was a wonder that the only rain of the early summer had come at just the right time to keep the fire from spreading beyond the borders of Sigma. Considering the extreme drought in the area, and the fact that no one could call for help before it spread out of control, such a forest fire could have truly wrecked havoc throughout all of northern Michigan. The two-day downpour completely doused the fires. It was as if Sigma was sacrificed so that the rest of the north could be spared.

The great fire only made for a small article somewhere in latter section of the Traverse City *Record-Eagle*. There wasn't even a picture to go with the little story. No one could be reached for comment, and no one had any idea how it started or how long it had burned. There was only the damage to look at, and though it was bad, at least the heavy rain had stopped its progress. Folks in the surrounding areas and communities were glad for that.

***

Sigma disappeared into the warm summer air of 1987, swept away with the rain of the last, and only, June storm of that year. All traces of the little town were now gone. Only the charred remains of buildings, the blackened trunks of trees, and a large amount of unrecognizable rubble were left.

No one really seemed to notice. It was the kind of tiny community that could vanish without anyone seeing the difference. The folks who survived the week of terror found that they really wanted to try living someplace else anyway. Few ever spoke of that terrible week or its fiery ending.

A handful of people whose homes were spared the great flames did stay, however. They were the true diehards, those with no place else to go. Their houses and trailers, mostly a ways out from Sigma proper, were far enough from the great inferno to be affected. These few folks comprised the only legacy of what Sigma had been, and what had truly happened there.

But nearly all the rest moved on. Some relocated in nearby towns and some even left the state completely. Some of the survivors packed up everything and left without ever looking back. Most were very pleased that they got out while the getting was still good.

And some folks just disappeared with the town, like ghosts in the early morning mist on the Dredge. No one came looking for them or their remains.

There were no more sightings of the creature that summer in Sigma. No one knew why it came. No one knew why it stayed for a week. No one knew why it finally left. All that folks knew was that the howling in the night had ended. Many did stay awake out of habit, listening and waiting for the awful noise to start again. But the night remained quiet.

***

Eric Martin awoke the following morning in the Grand Traverse Regional Hospital. He couldn't recall how he'd gotten there. He wanted to shake his head to clear the cloudiness and blurriness, but it hurt too badly to move it much at all. His head felt like he'd taken several beatings from Al Capone's baseball bat, just like in that *Untouchables* movie he'd recently seen.

Arms tied down tightly to his chest, Eric had to wait for the nurse to come in and give him the information he requested. An old man and two boys had brought him in, she said, saying he'd had a bad accident.

Lucky for him, most of the events of the previous night had been lost from his memory. He would never have any recollection of seeing the creature. However, Eric would have terrible, haunting nightmares periodically throughout the rest of his life.

Brian Alexander would also have nightmares, though they did finally stop around the time he graduated from high school. His family had left Sigma and relocated to the outskirts of Cadillac. It would be a long time before he ran into Stevie again, and he never did see the DNR officer once more.

Stevie was the only one of the three survivors who remembered the entire encounter vividly. He was also the only one who returned to Sigma. It was difficult for him to ride his bike down those familiar roads and yet not see the town he knew so well. It had all disappeared—the houses, the buildings, and the people were all gone. There were so many details of the last days of Sigma that he didn't know, that he didn't want to know. He'd seen and lived through plenty.

***

Now Sigma stands a ghost town. Gone is the Mercantile, Horner's Bar, and the little barbershop. Gone are all traces of the logging operations that first brought folks to this wilderness community. Gone is the little ball field where the Lovett boys routinely cranked out home-runs over the dilapidated fence in left-center. Gone is the old gas station turned home and business of Joe Randall.

330 souls had vanished from the area.

Over the years, a few folks have returned to repopulate the remnants of the town. A few houses and trailers mark the once proud stop on the timber trail where loggers would send the mightiest trees to the mills and factories in the south. A handful of people still live where the Dogman once prowled the night.

No one could explain why the creature chose to haunt the little town of Sigma. And of course, anybody who did share the stories was routinely laughed at and ridiculed until the sightings and encounters were reduced to mere legend. And then the legend faded from memory and was forgotten.

But it would not be the last time that the Dogman would be sighted in northern Michigan. For somewhere in the north woods darkness, a creature continues to walk upright. And the best advice you might ever get is this: *don't go out at night.*

ABOUT THE AUTHOR

With an English degree from Michigan State University and a master's in educational leadership from Central Michigan University, Frank Holes, Jr. teaches literature, writing, and mythology at the middle school level and was recently named a regional Teacher of the Year. He lives in Northern Michigan with his wife Michele, son James, and daughter Sarah.

Frank's first novel, *Year of the Dogman*, took the Great Lakes region by storm, and his new children's series, *The Longquist Adventures*, written for upper elementary students on up, blends ancient mythology with classical stories in a modern retelling. Many adults familiar with mythology and folklore will enjoy the themes and adaptations of these well-known and well-loved stories.

See all of Frank's novels on his website:

http://www.mythmichigan.com

ABOUT THE COVER ARTIST:

Craig Tollenaar was born in Petoskey, Michigan, was raised in Indian River, Michigan, and currently lives in southwest Michigan with his wife Traci, daughter Isobel, and a peculiarly skinny dog named Ruby. He earned a Bachelor of Arts from Alma College and has been working as a creative artist of some sort for some time.

He spends a lot of his day with any type of instrument that makes a mark on a page. He enjoys living in the Midwest (and its meteorological uncertainties) and an occasional good time. Craig's impressive artwork can also be seen on the cover of the novel, *Year of the Dogman*, and on the cover and interior pictures in *The Longquist Adventures: Western Odyssey*.

Stop by sometime and visit Craig's webpage:

http://www.cjtcreative.com.

Made in the USA
Charleston, SC
16 September 2010